Fay Sampson was born in Devonport but grew up in the fishing and farming village of Lympstone. She had her first children's novel published in 1975 and since then has had a further sixteen published, as well as two educational books and the first book in this sequence of novels, *Wise Woman's Telling*. She has taught adult education classes in writing and visits schools as 'writer in education'. She lives in a sixteenth-century thatched cottage in Tedburn St Mary, is married and has two children.

*Also by Fay Sampson*

Wise Woman's Telling

*Children's novels*

# White Nun's Telling

## Book Two
## in the sequence
## Daughter of Tintagel

Fay Sampson

**HEADLINE**

ISBN 0 7472 3297 0

Typeset in 10/11 pt Mallard
by Colset Private Limited, Singapore

Printed and bound in Great Britain by
Collins, Glasgow

HEADLINE BOOK PUBLISHING PLC
Headline House
79 Great Titchfield Street
London W1P 7FN

To Kate

# Author's Note

In physics, Dark Matter forms an unseen world that is the inverse of the matter we observe. The two were created to exist in equal proportions. Together they hold the universe in balance. But when they come into contact, the result is mutual destruction. Morgan's story is the Dark Matter of Britain.

The name Tintagel, formerly believed to be Norman, may be much older and Cornish. If so, it should be pronounced with a hard g. One possible meaning is 'the strong place where the two currents meet'.

The Tintagel of legend is a fortress, the birthplace of Arthur and the seat of King Mark of Cornwall. The archaeologists who excavated it believed that in Arthurian times it was in fact a Celtic monastery. Others have challenged this. The headland was certainly occupied in the fifth century, but as yet there is no conclusive evidence of its function.

The Western Sea

The Sisters

The Convent
of the
White Nuns

Tintagel
Haven

Barras
Nose

Tintagel
Island

The
Mother's Hole

The grave
of Gorlois

To Padstow

To Dimilioc

Bossiney Haven

The Oak Forest

The Great Oak

Pasture

Bossiney

Pasture

Waterfall

Nectan's Hut

Peter McClure 1989

# Chapter One

I hate Morgan. She corrupted me. You will think when you read those words that there is penitence, because I have acknowledged my sin. There is not. Morgan showed me an unholy joy. She has fed a poison into my blood that I am powerless to cleanse. It offered me the means of power, but now it has power over me. I cannot give it up. I do not want to. So I am damned.

Once I loved Morgan. At least, I think that is what women mean by love. I had little to compare it with. For a time I was willingly enslaved by her, though I had been set as her warder. Now I think I have no will. I have lost everything – ambition, hope. I hate her for that.

It was not fair to set me, low-born as I was, to watch a princess.

I was always proud. Yet I suffered as with a physical pain because I had so little to be proud of. I was not a slave or a bondwoman, and I carried my head high past those who were. Yet I despised what I was.

My parents were farmers. I came from the red lands of mid-Devon, near the holy forest, Great Nymet. From a sheltered farm among apple trees. Strange that when I think of it now it is always springtime there. The waves of blossom foaming round the thatch, nesting songbirds darting in and out of bushes. The blood comes hot in my cheeks when I remember Maytime, and a pulse starts to beat. I knew so little then.

May Eve always disturbed me. I knew that people

drank too much. That boys reeled, tugging at girls, into the grass – the lush, green, wet grass of May – that they came home in the morning, wild and dirtied, singing and dancing behind a garlanded pole propped on a cart. It frightened me. The great horns of the oxen poking out of the wreaths of silver and flowers. That thing on the cart, like a great lance, thrusting fearfully. When it was set up I danced around it with the others, stiffly, resentfully, hating the sweaty feel of boys' hands round mine. On the night before May Day I hid my head under the bed-covers.

Yet when I lived there it was not the blossom-time that filled my mind. It was the mud. The slick, red, Devon mud that covered the roads, the yard, the house, weighing down boots and skirts and soul. The weeping sky. The sodden wool around my shoulders. The stench of cows and pigs. The fetid breath of animals and men crowded together in one too-small dirty house. No privacy.

My parents were not ungentle with me, though they thought me strange. Between teasing and scolding they tried to push me in the way of red-faced boys likely to inherit a good farm. They could not understand that I should prefer to be alone.

I chose the quiet of the evening, not the morning loud with bird-song and the sweaty bustle of the day's work already beginning. I would leave the paths, where I might meet curious homecomers, and seek solitude among bramble bushes and whispering elms. I disdained to huddle and shiver against the chill of the wind. I lifted my face, unsmiling, to be cleansed of the soil of my labour. I did not spare my aching body. I forced my feet into an unvarying rhythm, up hill and down. There was no joy in my walking, only the need for distance and quiet. Even then, with the animals bedded and the food cooked and eaten, I could not afford to be idle. My hands must always be spinning or knitting as I walked.

I did not heed my mother's chiding. I did not understand her warnings. Indeed I often doubted that she was my mother. She, round and slow and comfortable. I, tall, bony, furiously sharp of mind. Sometimes I dreamed I was a king's daughter, hidden with rustics in time of great danger, waiting to discover her rightful inheritance.

So I went from the house into the grey evening pastures and never even turned my head to answer her.

I did not dream it would be the daughter of a king who would wreck my inheritance.

I say I had no joy, but I knew peace. When I had passed beyond the reek of the chimney-smoke and the lowing of cattle was too distant to be heard, I felt that other life drop from me like a wet cloak. I was myself at last. Alone with myself, as I would always wish to be.

The day had been wet, but the rain-clouds were breaking. There was a streak of yellow sky at the head of the coombe. The sun had gone down and the evening star was bright behind me. I picked my way through the filthy bog of the cows' hooves and began to climb, lifting my skirts clear of thistles and thorns. There was no sound but my own breathing. No company but a hare bounding across my path. I would climb to the top of the ridge that enclosed our narrow, smothering coombe. I was subtly driven to extend the boundaries of my world. Even then it was no satisfaction to stand on the highest point, for I only saw the land that lay beyond, that was still not mine.

Yet it must be done. Our valleys are steep. I clambered up slopes, round boulders, through bushes, seeking open ground.

My first warning was a shower of earth from overhead. Then a frightened bellowing and a man's curse.

I have never been quick to move. It seems as though there is a great gulf between my mind and my body. I

3

stood paralysed by fear, struggling to comprehend what was happening. Dirt pelted me. Then, after the first moments in which I should have run, danger appeared more threateningly. A young red milch-cow was slithering and roaring her way down the slope above me. Her eyes rolled wildly and beneath the mud her hooves were as sharp as axe-blades. Behind her leaped a man, brandishing a stick, his face black with anger. I saw in a glance now what it was. Why else should the two of them be out on the hills after suppertime where only I, Luned, and the hare walked? The cow had wandered out of her keeper's sight and gone astray on the hills at nightfall. And the man had lost his supper and wearied his legs to find her before darkness swallowed them both. Even now she would not go gently home, and the two of them battled against each other in mistrust and haste.

I was in their way. Suddenly understanding my danger I scrabbled aside across the hill. The cow took fright and leapt the opposite way, like a hare, skidding splay-legged on the steep incline. The man yelled louder.

'Don't you break your leg now, you black-eyed fool! Not after all the trouble you've caused me.'

Then he saw me.

'You meddling little varmint! 'twas you startled her.'

It was anger first, backed by the unchecked rush of his body downhill towards me. I knew physical terror. I had feared the cow. That was a sensible fear, born of her weight and motion, her position above me, and the damage her hooves and body might do if I stopped their onrush. From the man I feared all that and more. A personal vindictiveness in his eyes, as if I and not the cow were now to blame. I was the butt of his lost time and effort. I the witness of his masculine ineptitude.

I knew the man. Tewdar of Blacklake, with a wife and seven thin-faced children. And he knew me, starting suddenly in the grey twilight out of the red dazzle of his anger, just as I was turning to run another way.

'Luned, Kevern's daughter! You're a long way from home, maidy.'

I did not turn back to him but stayed, still poised on one foot to run. When I met anyone walking, far less startlingly than this, it was always my first instinct to step aside and avoid them, not to be noticed, not to exchange pleasantries. Even if the other was a near neighbour, or a cousin. I do not say friend. There were none I called such. But what should I say to an angry man, alone and unexpected at nightfall? For once I wished myself back home in the firelight, and my mother opposite with a pile of mending on her knee.

Tewdar was breathing heavily. A smile was beginning to spread across his face. It frightened me more than his shouts, though I could not tell why. I moved before he did. It was not a conscious decision. I ran, like the hare, to escape that smile. The smile pursued me. It was in his voice as he chased me down the hill. Wheedling. Eager. Urgent.

'Luned. Little Luned. Have 'ee lost 'es sweetheart? Wait. I won't hurt 'ee.'

The shout of a man running to catch a cow now, not to drive on.

I ran. Clutching my skirt. Praying I would not stumble. There was mist gathering in the pasture. I dived towards it like a kingfisher into the stream.

There was silence behind me. My own feet thudding on grass. My breath sobbing with haste. Terror returned. Had he outwitted me? Was he ahead, not behind?

I must have stopped and turned, because I saw him. Close above me. And he knew that I saw him. He pulled up too, and the smile spread to a grin. A man's confidence in his overpowering sex. Before my young gaze, he dropped his breeches and displayed his member, pale in the twilight but all too fleshly and real. Hard, stiff, menacing. Like the fresh-cut May-pole of my nightmares.

Do not mistake me. It was not the first time I had seen a man's penis. How could I help it, living as we did? That sign was all around me in the things of power. In wood and stone and leather. On the White Mare's Teaser. In the May Day dances and the Midwinter foolery. Fearful, grotesque. I had seen the little pricks of my younger brothers. Men pissing against the wall or in the bushes. A glimpse of my father half-naked before I hid my face in the blankets. But never before like this. Never aimed deliberately at me. At Luned, at my very self.

I don't know what he expected in his arrogance. That I would falter and blush and pretend to run again, only to own myself beaten, like the cow, now bellowing disconsolately for company on the hill above us.

I have always thought it an ugly thing. That dangling appendage that seems scarcely part of the rest, leading an existence almost separate from the man. I blessed the neatness of women's bodies. Our parts were decently hidden from view. I did not understand then how women's sex is at the core of our being. So I saw that threatening penis, and noticed that his breeches were hooked around his knees. I ran in earnest.

He was angrier then. It would have gone ill with me if he had caught me. By that time it would have been no fumbling, mumbling roll in the grass. I had denied his power.

But I was young and strong-willed. Unweakened by illness or age or deformity. The few moments it took him to snatch up his breeches was enough for me. Pride lent me wings. I flew across the last fields and into the house, like a mouse cheating the hawk. But pride had been humbled. I did not walk in the dusk after that. I was not truly free before I became a nun.

My body was whole, but my mind was violated. I had seen what I wished I had not. Ever afterwards that sight was seared on my imagination. I could never be rid of it. I was soiled, disgusted, shamed. It seemed to me there was a demon in every man I met that might leap out of its cover at me.

You may think this is why I became a nun. It is not. I did not go to Tintagel fleeing what I feared. I went eagerly seeking a higher good. When you know what I worship now you will not believe that. But I set it down as the truth. I thought only of what I was gaining, nothing of my loss. I was too ignorant for it to be otherwise. No dog-eyed boy had made my heart beat faster. I despised babies. How should I miss what I had never wanted?

In my mind there was a vast distance between that bared phallus on the hillside and the marriage-bed. I made no connexion.

Morgan knew more of the ways of men than I did when she was half my age.

She was eight years old when Uther Pendragon killed her father. That same night he came to the convent of Tintagel and entered her mother.

# Chapter Two

Morgan's father was not yet dead when I was baptised. A Christian came to our village, swinging down the road from the east: Ruman. A fleece-white tunic over a whiter gown. Strong sandals on his feet. A stout staff. Simple, you understand, but not poor. Good-quality stuff, made with care. This was no ragged vagrant tramping the roads till the bottom fell out of his shoes. He did not carry himself like a beggar either. He was young and tall, and his head was shaved strangely. The front bared to the crown, and the brown hair at the back growing free and curling. I had only seen slaves with their heads shaved. But this was no slave. It was a strange conjunction.

We had not long to wait. He set up his staff at the cross-ways of our village, and bound another stick across it. He took from the leather satchel on his back a box-wood lyre and began to play, and then to sing.

If we had been curious at first we were more so now. Few can resist a minstrel with a new song. There at broad noon, in the middle of the working day, he drew us round him. The children came first. Not shy, as they were of any overseeing noble, or frightened by a beggar in his dirt and deformity. He smiled at them and they squatted round his feet. The women followed next, wiping their hands on their aprons. The men paused at the doorways of workshops and the edges of fields. They wanted to show their neighbours they had important work that could not be left. But they strolled closer too before the song was finished.

I was like the men, I resisted. My mind was hungrier than the others could know for the sound of new things, for the world beyond the ridge of the coombe, but my pride would not let it be seen. I waited, tying weights to the loom, my back to the sunshine and the man in white singing beside his cross. Only when I seemed the last one left in the shadows did I creep slowly to the back of the crowd.

The song was almost over. He sang now of a golden city on a mountain top. Of a king and his bride. Of rewards and rejoicing. He sang for me. It was the dream of my girlhood. Of a crown, of treasure, of rank, of homecoming. Of right restored.

I did not hear what must come before.

And then he talked to us. I did not know the word for 'preaching' then. To me, it seemed like hard words and difficult thoughts. Yet all the time Ruman smiled on us, like a young mother with her first baby. As though he loved us, though we were all of us strangers to him. I could not understand it. That a man should wear the badge of a slave yet carry himself as sure and easy as the greatest lord who rode in Devon.

I wanted to listen. Never have I wanted to hear a man so much. But every sentence he spoke sent my mind racing away down new roads. By the time I had caught it and brought it back to the present he had jumped ahead of me and was telling new wonders. I was dazzled. He told of a wide and marvellous world beyond Britain. He spoke of priests and emperors, of Pharisees and fishing-boats, of dangerous voyages, of desert roads, of cities and armies, of wandering shepherds and a pilgrim cross. How could we understand this? We who never moved from where we were, watching the seasons circle round us monotonously.

He called us to leave our old ways and travel with him on the new. To cut down the dark groves and to build a city of light. There were many who growled with fear and anger that first day. And others who gazed at him with a hungry hope. But more and more his roaming eyes came back to me, as though for once I wore my soul in my face.

I sought him out. Snatching hot loaves from the oven and racing off before my mother could catch me with another task. I knew that Cadwal and his wife had taken him to share bread with them, but they told me he had gone out again, down to the river. To pray, they said. I could not make any sense of that. How could a man worship alone? I do not mean the words we murmured at every turn of life, as we crossed the threshold, as we put fire to wood, as we set milk to separate, as we lay down to sleep. You would not go apart to say those. They were bound into the thread of living. But a true meeting with the gods was done with awe and preparation. All my life I had known and feared holy places. How could I not, living so close to the Great Nymet? It was unthinkable to go there alone, without the protection of priests and priestesses. Without the drums and dancing. Without the tribe bringing gifts and prostrating themselves. Without the proper sacrifices.

I did not know that prayer which is thus sacred and set apart could also be solitary.

I heard him before I saw him. He was chanting indeed. But in a low, rapid murmur, as though he talked to himself alone. I parted the hazel stems and watched. He sat cross-legged on the grass beside the stream. Not near the ford or the stepping-stones, but round a bend out of sight of the path, where the water ran swift and deep. The sort of place I might have been drawn to myself, though not to pray. The sound of the nearest waterfall sang beneath the babble of his voice.

There was something in his lap. I felt an instant chill. This must be his thing of power. Something more secret and dangerous than the cross of sticks he had made while he preached to us. Something I should not be seeing. Something I must see.

My steps were light and the grass was soft. I saw two stacks of sheets, like kerchieves of linen, yet stiffer than cloth. Joined at one edge so that they could open like so many doors. Patterned in black. Row after row of signs that I knew at once to be powerful magic. You who read this account will laugh that I had never seen a book before. Stranger yet was that I knew in that first moment of seeing the power of the pen, and hungered after it.

He had a feather in his hand, the white plume of a swan. And he was tracing the signs from left to right, line after line, and chanting rapidly aloud at every mark. I did not heed the meaning. It was the act itself which astonished me. I did not know the word for reading.

'Come closer. Sit down. Look and listen.'

Ruman did not turn his head, but there was laughter in his voice. I obeyed.

'So,' he said, seeing my face now, 'you followed me.' And he meant more than my walk through the hazel bushes. I nodded. I did not need to ask. The hunger was in my eyes for him to see.

'Can you read?'

I shook my head, storing the word away like a jewel.

'What is your name?'

'Luned.'

He took a twig and scored some marks in the soft earth between us. He pointed to the first. 'L. For Luned.' And so I understood the signs had sounds. I looked at his L. Two strokes. Straight and plain, like myself. I made the same and raised my eyes to meet his. They were not difficult, these symbols of power. I could master them.

There were several in the village that offered him house-room. He refused them all, with that smile of his. He wove himself a green-roofed hut there among the hazels by the brook where I had found him, with only the fox to guard him and the blackbird's chatter for company. I understood that. Few others did.

He would not stay long. Devon was wide, he said, and the darkness deep. I felt that darkness too, with the forest shadowing us round. The past faith of kings and courts had become a rustic, secret thing. There were not many Druids left. The Romans killed some and stripped others of their power. They overlooked the women. An older growth had sprouted like nettles in a neglected field. I feared those long before I sided with the Church. It would have appalled me if I had seen my future then.

The Christian, Ruman, dazzled me. I begged him to teach me all he knew. He smiled and told me of a village Exeter way where anyone who followed his Christ was welcome. A fortress of work and worship and learning. The wonder of it was that they would take anyone who asked. The sons and daughters of chiefs, nobles, craft-workers – yes, and farmers. Young and old. Even a slave might learn to write Latin. They demanded no payment but work. I could not think why they would not ask gold from the nobility.

There were others I knew who went. Whole families of new Christians. The pious seeking a home safe from old temptations. Some of the highborn sent their sons and daughters to learn, nursing dreams of a lost Roman empire.

But it was not for me. It is pain for me even now to write it. My parents refused. Morgan was bitter because Uther Pendragon sent her to such a school. My bitterness was because schooling was denied me. I was the eldest. I was wanted about the house. I was a girl. I could not be spared. And my parents believed they loved me.

I humbled myself to beg, to weep even. It did no good. All they said was that it was time I was thinking of getting a husband. I was nearly fourteen.

I saw my situation then with horror. All my life I had lived with this dream, that I was someone else. Not Luned, Kevern's daughter. Someone greater, wealthier, more powerful. Free. I had only to wait and my heritage would be revealed.

So I had never simpered and nudged and flashed my eyes at boys, in the way of those other girls. I hardly noticed them. What had they to do with me? I do not condemn them. It was not the young men of my village I turned from personally, it was the lives of the women. I saw the running bowels of their babies, the greasy steam of bacon and cabbage, the skirts thigh-high in mud, the nights of fleas and snores, the same stale gossip year after year. I could not believe this was all life had to offer me.

I saw Ruman as my saviour. I had not realised how close the danger was. I had not allowed myself to imagine marrying.

If I had been humbler-born yet it would have been easier. I could have bedded with whom I would, or not at all; lived where I would, alone if I dared. I would be fourteen soon and no man's property.

But I had not the licence of absolute poverty. My parents owned land. Not much, just enough to imprison me. They would want to see me handfast, before witnesses, bargains made, my future contracted. I was trapped between the freedom of wealth and the carelessness of those who have nothing.

When I understood that I fled to Ruman. Running in the afternoon, when I should have been repairing the hurdles round the pig-pen, and never mind who stared after me.

I thought I would find him alone. There was a path through the hazels now where there had been none before. I must have come crashing along it like a stray heifer.

I pulled up short. There was a man with Ruman on the bank of the river. No common man. A warrior. I do not often start and blush but I did then, suddenly conscious of who and what I was. A young and rustic girl. Alone in a wood.

Warrior-bands sometimes rode past us to the Nymet to ask for victory. They were beings from another world than ours. Noisy, gorgeous. A caste apart. I had never come upon a soldier so close, alone, on foot. And he was all that I had heard of them. Hard, male, vigorously young and well-fed. Sporting his weapons of steel like Tewdar's fleshly one. A menace to my femaleness.

His horse was tethered to a hawthorn tree. Well-groomed. Dapple-grey. With a neck like a bent bow.

Ruman saw me, but the stranger did not. He knelt before the saint with a jingle of chains and a creak of leather.

'Duke Gorlois has summoned the war-hosts of Dumnonia. Ambrosius's brother is raising the red dragon again. We'll make Woden's army lick their own blood from the British soil they came to conquer. So bless me, father, that I may kill many Saxons for you.'

'And for that killing you want me to feed you with your Saviour's blood?'

The man's head flew up then, as though Ruman had challenged him.

'Fair's fair! That's what the Druids and your Church both teach us. Glory for the hero dead or alive. The Isles of the Blest or Heavenly Paradise if we fall. It's all one to me. But you both say I must cleanse my soul before I dirty my sword.'

'Pagan against pagan! The red dragon and the white.

Who will cleanse my soul if I give the holy flesh of Christ for that?'

'Uther Pendragon is a Christian king, and Gorlois fights under the sign of Christ. If our lifeblood's not good enough payment for you, take that! It should pay for a curse or two against Britain's enemies!'

He tossed a gold ring at Ruman. The saint stood like stone. The ring rolled away to the edge of the brook.

'My curses joined to Emrys Merlyn's? The lamb of God yoked with the serpent?'

'What's wrong with that? You're both men of power, aren't you? I offer my blood and my sword for Britain. You holy men must fight with prayers and curses. Get on with your work, man, and leave mine to me.'

He knelt and bent his head. It was not shame but Ruman's look that drove me back down the path out of earshot of his confession.

The soldier mumbled his sins and Ruman spoke forgiveness to him. I watched the soldier take the morsel of bread and the holy cup, wiping his long moustache with the back of his hand. Everything about him alarmed me. The lusty way he drank the wine. The leap of his body as he rose from his knees. The sudden neigh of his mare as she pawed the turf with wicked hooves.

He turned then and saw me. I was right to be alarmed. His eyes scanned me slowly from head to toe, undressing me.

'Come here, Luned!'

Only Ruman's voice gave me the courage to run past the warrior to sanctuary. I hated both that man and my own weak self for the fire in my cheeks.

Ruman raised his palm.

'In the name of the Father, and the Son, and the Holy Lifegiver, go in peace. And keep Britain safe.'

'Safe! Duke Gorlois wouldn't thank you for a prayer

like that! There's no honour to be got in safety, and no gold either. Or women!'

He laughed at me then, and flung himself into the saddle and galloped away.

Ruman forced a smile to his troubled face.

'Don't look so frightened, child. He is right. The Church needs his kind as well as mine. These are dangerous times.'

Then the smile slipped.

'I sometimes think the Kingdom of God here is as brittle as a film of ice over a running river. But you, Luned? You love Christ truly, don't you? You won't turn back to the Druids when I've gone?'

'Never!' I told him vehemently. And then, 'Who is this Gorlois? Is he our king in Dumnonia now?'

'Chief warlord of Devon and Cornwall. No king. He takes the Roman name of Duke. A mighty man of war under the Pendragon. Pray for him, Luned. Rome has left us in his hands.'

I knew nothing of Saxons. I feared Duke Gorlois and his warriors far more. No one warned me Gorlois had a daughter more dangerous than himself.

# Chapter Three

Ruman bent and picked the ring from the brookside. His arm flexed as though he would have hurled it over the water. I must have gasped. He turned and smiled as if in apology.

'You are right. It could put bread into the bellies of the poor.'

And he knotted it into the sleeve of his gown.

'So. Why have you come in such haste? I am not leaving till tomorrow.'

It was like a blow in the face.

'Tomorrow! You are not going away from us so soon? You cannot! You will come back, won't you?'

He shook his head. 'I have told you from the beginning, I am a pilgrim for Christ. I must sow his seed in many fields. Three days from now is Pentecost. I am going back to my village of Christ to keep the festival. Then I must travel on.'

'But what will we do without you? Who will be our priest?'

'Someone will come to offer the bread and wine for you at feast times, as often as may be. I may return myself sometimes. The labourers are few. You must strengthen each other.'

'I cannot bear it here alone!'

'Alone? With eyes like yours? Not for long, I think.'

'That is what I mean!'

I poured out my soul to him then. I did not think he was

attending. His eyes kept slipping away down the path that the warrior had ridden. His hand played with the jewel weighing down his sleeve.

'You're not listening to me! What shall I do? I cannot bear to be married to one of those clods. I cannot bear to live my mother's life. Help me!'

'I hear you, child.'

'I am not a child. I am fourteen tomorrow.'

His eyebrows rose then with something of his old smile.

'Fourteen? And a free woman?'

'Yes.'

'Then why are you crying? You do not need your parents' blessing. The law of Britain makes you mistress of your own fate. You can walk over that threshold tomorrow and take the road to the west, and no one can forbid you. How brave are you, Luned? Will you travel that road with me?'

I was not brave. I was afraid and unready. The thought of leaving home, village, familiar people, appalled me, though I had never loved them. I wanted a home to come back to. I wanted glory, not adventure. But I was desperate. What else could I do? What other means of escape did I have? I was more than Luned of Lower Orchard. I must be more. That was the dream that Ruman held before me.

I wanted to leave with him then, just as I was, without a word of farewell. I feared to tell my father.

Ruman came home with me. It was a bitter parting. I do not suppose my parents have ever understood. They argued that they loved me. I have not seen them since.

We set out next morning. Once it was done I felt inexpressibly happy. The kingdom of God beckoned me. I had only to climb the path to achieve it.

It was no golden citadel. A bank of earth around it with a wattle fence, clusters of thatch, smoke, animals. It looked much like the village I had left.

As we neared the gate a handbell was rung for noon. At once everyone stopped working. Men, women, children stood straight and still and burst into singing. The psalm rose from a hundred throats. Ruman was chanting beside me. Haltingly, I tried to join in. On and on, the melody rose to heaven. I found myself lifted up on waves of song.

The psalm ended. Work began again.

Ruman watched my face. 'A chain of praise. By day and night. In this and every house of God. Throughout this land. Across the world. The song that never dies.'

The world. It was beyond my imagining then. Even the thought of Britain was too big for me. And that was only the beginning. The rest was infinite. Choirs of angels singing round the throne of God into eternity. And I was being offered a part in that choir. The gate of heaven was opening for me.

The reality was different. I slept with a family: Jenna and her husband and their three children. I helped with the cooking. I hoed the fields. I shared their life.

Apart from the psalms, heaven on earth was very like the home I had left. The same dung-spattered beasts to be tended, the same teething babies squalling in the night, the same mouths to be fed. Only the praise was different.

I watched a woman gathering the little children round her and teaching them their letters. I felt a stab of envy. Even they knew more than I did. At last, as I stirred the porridge beside Jenna, I cried out, 'Where is the school where they teach Latin and Greek and rhetoric and geometry? Where is the library?'

Words I had heard Ruman speak, that I did not even know the meaning of.

Jenna laughed. 'Oh, that! We had some holy men and women that had got book-learning in the monasteries of Gaul and Egypt. But it seems we were too homely here for them. Some of them have gone off to be hermits in the woods and caves. Then there were some scholar-women that went further west, to live as virgins under the rule of Bryvyth in some fortress by the Cornish sea. A place they call Tintagel. But that's not for the likes of you and me. They're mostly noble-born. You won't need to bother with that. Brokan was asking me yesterday if I thought you were good with baking and babies.'

Brokan, a freckled boy with wet lips. Next time I stepped outside I felt that every young man in the village was looking me over consideringly. Ruman had tricked me. I began to despair.

It was Crida who saved me. A short, square woman, with a firm step and a quick mind. She came marching down the road from the east. She was no fool. She travelled with a champion to fight off bandits and carry her across fords, and had a band of nuns with her, and a pair of monks. They had tales to tell of Saxon invasion, of churches burned, of priests and virgins as well as layfolk hacked to death, of the Pendragon battling for the cross and Britain. We hung on her words as if she had been a minstrel from the king's court. But it was not her tales of the wars in the east that filled my dreams.

I had plucked up the courage to go to her hut. I told her of my hopes and their betrayal. I would learn nothing here. I begged her to take me with her on her travels.

She looked me up and down with a short laugh.

'What gifts have you got to offer? Do you know your Bible? Can you read and write? Paint or embroider the marvels of God? Preach the word of Christ before commoners and chieftains?'

'All that is what I *want* to learn! It is why I came!'

'And not to be the handmaid of any earthly lord! You would rather be Mary of Bethany, learning alongside the men, than Martha in the kitchen or the mother of your Saviour and a carpenter's wife? You blush too easily, girl. There's nothing to be ashamed of in having a mind. You are right. You must not stay here. You are not the woman to be a drudge even to a Christian man. Go to Tintagel, to the women's fortress. There are others there like you. I will give you a letter to the abbess. She is a tough shepherdess, is Bryvyth, and needs to be. Heed her well. Take her for your chief, your druid, under Christ. If you obey her, she may help you enter the kingdom you've dreamed of.'

'I will! I will!'

She laid cool hands on my forehead.

'Be warned, Luned. It will not be as easy as you think. We carry our earthly bodies with us on the pilgrim road. Do you know how I spent the night before last? Emptying a bucket for Gwaynten. She had sickness at one end and diarrhoea at the other. It was her monthly time too. Puke, blood and shit all night. It nearly killed her.'

I almost vomited myself.

'You see? And you wanted to travel with me? You haven't started to learn what it means. Copy Bryvyth. She has the finest mind in Dumnonia and the constitution of a fishwife. Remember, it was Martha the housewife who took our Lord into the stinking tomb of Lazarus to raise the dead. They left Mary the scholar behind on her knees in tears.'

I did not heed that warning.

'I will do anything she says, bear any hardship, if they will only teach me.'

'Why, Luned? Why do you truly want to go to Tintagel so much?'

I looked up at her, startled. Was it not obvious why I should want it? To feel my mind expand like a flower in the sun. To drink in all the wealth of knowledge and enlightenment. To achieve greatness. Had she not wanted this herself? Then I saw the hope earnest in her face as she gazed at me, and I knew what she wanted me to say.

'To serve Christ my Saviour. For the glory of God and the spread of his kingdom on earth.'

And in the moment of saying that, I believed it was true.

I came to Tintagel to deny the flesh, seeking a splendour of the soul.

# Chapter Four

I did not know until I came to Tintagel that I would be afraid of the sea. I had never seen it before.

Crida took me across Devon with her band of nuns. At the banks of the Tamar she left me with a group of pilgrims. She made her champion carry me across the river. I would rather have waded through the cold pluck of the water than have his hot, hairy arms about me, than to cling to his back and see the lice crawling in his hair.

But I was near my goal. Where Bryvyth ruled like a bishop over her nuns. Where women could rise to the highest of men's work. Where I should be free at last of churning butter and brewing ale and washing dirty linen. I saw that to move beyond the sphere that men allow to women it was necessary to separate myself from the world of men.

So I crossed the Tamar determined to become one of Bryvyth's nuns. Of my own free will, not sent by my parents. I was a child of fourteen. I would have said I was a woman, the law declared it thus, but I was more innocent than I knew. Many a slave-child knows more than I knew then. I thought I knew what I was giving up. The child's games of making a home, the girl's scrying to see whom she will marry. That was no sacrifice at all to me. I wanted more from life than that.

For all that my mind was set on the kingdom of God, I will not pretend that I did not give the world a second look. I came from a poor farming place where we might not see anyone greater than a blacksmith between one festival and another, and my eyes had been opened on this journey. Pride kept me silent, yet I could hardly hold back the gasps of wonder at what I was daily learning of the world. We had passed many forts on the road to the west, crag-built, dominating the spurs and tors. We had stepped off the road for chariots of fine, jewelled ladies. I had lowered my eyes when armoured nobles came riding by, grizzled men too old now for the Pendragon's hosting. I had met merchant-trains, craftsmen, minstrels. All around me I saw wealth, skill, power.

I had thought in my sleepy valley that the world stayed the same from year to year. But I was wrong. Everywhere I looked there was evidence of trading, fighting, travelling. The world was changing all the time.

But even as I set eyes on the halls of power I had dreamed of, I was already leaving them behind. I was changing too. Our ways were parting. I looked at the noblewomen in their gold and tartan and I did not feel inferior. I had vowed myself to God. I felt pride stiffen my back. Could they read and write? Had they studied astronomy and the Greek philosophers? With Bryvyth, Crida had promised, I would do all this and more.

I saw a dazzle in the sky before we reached the coast. It seemed to me like a sign, the light of the New Jerusalem changing the air above it. Heaven on earth. The aura of knowledge, beauty, truth. When we came over the ridge and I saw the shining plain of the sea, I did not know what it was. I had said little to my companions on the journey. I am not one to gossip. But my face spoke more than I wished it to. They chuckled at my wonder.

'That's Bossiney down there.' One of them pointed to a wide, thatch-filled round in cattle pastures. A great hall stood out above the rest. 'Duke Gorlois's dun. There'll be nobody there now, though. He's away with the warhost, fighting Saxons with Uther Pendragon.'

Nobody there. Only his wife Ygerne. His three daughters. As though the women of that family were nothing.

Even so I started. I had heard that name: Gorlois, Duke of Cornwall. Ruman had said he held our fate in his hands.

So I came closer to Bossiney's walls with a calculating look. The fence on the bank was freshly-repaired. The watchman was ageing but alert, the women servants in good clean gowns. It spoke of wealth and order. I felt no envy. An alien camp, so close to Tintagel and so other than it. A man's place. A warrior's home. Power of a sort to be reckoned with, but no rival to what I dreamed of.

It astonishes me now that I could have walked past those walls and not felt who was within.

My eyes were already seeking ahead. I was afraid to ask, but I knew I must sight it soon. The end of my pilgrimage.

I began to hear the sea, more rhythmic than the sound of wind in the trees. I began to hear the grating of shingle. I felt the push of the breeze against my face. I started at the scream and swoop of the gulls. I was afraid of the wild noisiness of this coast, disturbed by experiences I did not understand.

We dipped into a rocky cleft and crossed a stream.

I do not know what I expected. A golden-walled city. A river of crystal. A temple glowing with all the jewels of the rainbow. I was very young, you must understand, ignorant, unlettered still. I had seen a vision.

But not of this. The site was stronger than Ruman's village of saints, more forbidding. A black-sided headland, with a glimpse of the sea swilling at its foot between narrow cliffs. We began to climb. A huge earth bank and ditch above us. A porter's lodge. Beyond, a sense of windy space. Tintagel. A grey-green island hung between sea and sky. Its steep sides scattered with lime-washed cells, clinging to the slopes like the nests of the gulls that flashed above them. And even as the gate-keeper came towards us I saw the path I must tread still to reach my goal.

Nothing had prepared me for that bridge of stone. No one had warned me. Or if they had, they had used words that held no meaning for me until then, coming as I did from that sheltered coombe folded among the gentle hills of Devon.

Even now it comes back to me in nightmares. At home I could not climb the damson tree beside the house without vertigo. Now I must walk a path scarce two strides wide, while dizzyingly far below me the sea, like a heaving devil, waited for me. Black rocks below the foam on one side. Sunless shingle lapped by cold green water on the other. Even without that drop the hugeness of the sea would have dismayed me. Its endless movement. The oncoming herd of breakers, each one a separate beast menacing me.

This time the pilgrims roared with laughter when they saw my face. I was not the first to be appalled by it. No doubt they remembered their own fear. How could Tintagel's convent look so small, so quiet, at the end of such a road as this?

Yet this was the path I had chosen. I could not turn back. I followed the nun who summoned me across the bridge. It was a fitting passage. It is hard indeed to enter that holy city by the narrow way.

I do not remember which nun it was who led me. I only remember the agony, the giddiness, the terror of con-sciousness, the terror of losing consciousness. I never wholly conquered it.

I still fear the sea. Year after year I lay awake, listening to the breakers beating against the cliffs, till I thought the rocks would shatter and we would all go crashing into a cold hell.

So it is not surprising that I loved Bryvyth from the moment that I first saw her. She was a stronghold of a woman, a sure buttress of rock against which the waves of the world and the dark gods would beat and not gain entrance. She had a keener mind than I had ever seen in a woman, and the muscles of an ox.

She made me kneel at her feet. I must have been a pitiful figure, trembling with physical fear and the tension of shyness. She bade me tell her why I had come.

I am not a fluent talker. I find it difficult to bring the deep thoughts of my heart to my lips. Even in daily conversation I sit silent. I hear the other women voicing observations that would never have occurred to me to be worth the effort of words. When I am challenged to say what I think I pick a phrase here and there. It never tells the whole.

She watched me shrewdly while I stammered out some fragments of my hopes. I felt myself pale and then redden under that gaze. When I had done she still looked at me, as I often saw her later staring consideringly at a sickly cow. Then she laid her hands on my head and spoke.

'Welcome, Luned. You have walked a long road from Devon, following your star. But not as far I have travelled. I journeyed from Cymru to Erin, seeking for knowledge, like you. They consecrated me a virgin first, and then made me a scholar. When I had learned all that they could teach me, I set sail with a handful of sisters in a little boat, on a pilgrimage for God. His winds washed us to this cove. There was nothing living here then. Nothing earthly, at least. The Romans had come and gone. They left what was here before them, some caves in the rock, and a black reputation.

'I preached Christ to Gorlois and he gave me this island. I think he fears it. He has the ways of a wild barbarian yet, but his soul is struggling for the light. We

drove out the Dark Son and his Mother from here with
the might of prayer. Now we wrestle for Gorlois himself,
and his family.

'With my bare hands I raised my own cell, as you will
do. Next we dug a garden. Saints should live by the
sweat of their own backs. Then stone by stone and soul
by soul we built this abbey. The oratory first, to praise
God. A library for our books, to bear witness to his glory.
Then a schoolroom to bring more lambs to his flock. The
name of Tintagel is spreading beyond the coasts of
Cornwall. They have heard of us as far as Jerusalem.'

She must have seen the flame in my eyes. She chuckled
deep in her throat and hugged me.

'Is this what you want, Luned? Is this the hard road
you choose to tread?'

'Yes!'

'Glory be! Then I can use a girl with strong muscles
like yours. There are too many here that were not bred
to lift anything heavier than an embroidery needle, and I
need to free all that are old and wise for scribes and
teachers. You'd be as welcome to my heart as the first
apples of harvest if I could put you to work tomorrow
with the cows and the kale.

'What do you say, girl? Will take on my yoke?'

Cows and kale. Did she read my face? Had I escaped
being housewife to a monk to become a drudge for other
nuns?

I was too proud to change my mind. I could not trudge
back across the length of Dumnonia and admit to my
family that I had made a mistake.

I will never forget the bitterness of that first winter. I
did the work of slaves. Cleaning the byres that the cows
had fouled. Hoeing the endless rows of muddy kale. And
the weather was like nothing I had ever known before.
Rain driving into the pail as I milked the cows, the everlasting gales hurling the sea into my face when I stepped

outside the door of my cell, the icy mud, the broken chilblains on my feet. And always the sea, churning away below me, so that my stomach was tight with fear as I fought my way up the paths to the top of the cliff.

I do not write this so that you should pity me. I made my choice freely. I set it down so that you shall know how great the price I paid for the pearl that Morgan robbed me of.

# Chapter Five

It seems impossible now that I should not remember the first time I saw Morgan. I remember the pride of that first Sabbath morning as a full-vowed nun, singing psalms as I strode with Bryvyth's virgins across the causeway on our way to Nectan's church. Bryvyth was a great warrior-woman for Christ. She was not one to shelter in her fortress. All summer she rode the country in her chariot and sent her nuns trudging the lanes two by two. On feast days and Sabbaths we celebrated the Offering with Nectan's congregation. I must have worshipped with Morgan every Sunday after I had made my final act of obedience.

Well I remember Gorlois and his warriors, home from war, gorgeously jewelled and cloaked. It was hard for me not to blush and shrink with fear from them. I was glad to keep my eyes down. But Ygerne his wife I looked at with contempt. I, Luned, plain-faced as I was, despised the duchess for her beauty. I did not imagine she could be wise as well as fair. I saw their two tall daughters, the white gold and the red. Elaine pleased me, grave and stately. Margawse disturbed me, tossing her fiery hair and flaunting the curves of her body. Will you believe me when I say I did not notice there was a smaller sister?

I had no interest in children. Ambition rose in me as I watched Bryvyth hold the chalice to the lips of Gorlois's warriors. Power was in our hands.

33

But all that was later. It was a year before I completed my vows. All that time I was shut up in Tintagel, safe behind its bank and causeway. Nectan visited us. I took the bread and wine in our oratory with the school-children.

It did not grieve me. I saw enough of the world even on our island. Old Padarn, who once helped to dig that mighty ditch and now served as porter. Nectan, a saint more gaunt and joyless than Ruman, coming to feed us the sacrament. A stream of pilgrims, honoured guests at Bryvyth's table. A glimpse of traders at the gate or on the rocky wharf below our convent. I kept well clear of them, and left that business to those to whom it was appointed.

On Sabbath Eve I sweated the dirt of my labour away in a bath of steam and heard Bryvyth speak absolution for my sins. Next morning, after milking, I donned a fresh gown and discovered again the sense of cleanliness, dignity, worth, of a day without work. For once I could give myself to the full glory of worship without the feel of a hoe clasped between my palms. I learned the beauty of that day.

The rest was more painful. In the midst of drudgery I had tantalising glimpses of glory. What others called work, to me seemed a foretaste of Paradise. That first week I hurried along the path to the work I had to do, to be out of the wind and the giddying pull of the sea waiting for me at every turn of the cliff. Yet there was one doorway before which I found my steps slowing.

It was the library. My stare probed the open doorway, the shelves stacked with scrolls and books, the opened leaves gleaming palely on the desks. The murmur of words, rhythmic as the waves on the beach. Cigfa and Eira, our two most famous scribes, worked in the best places in the sunny porch, sheltered from the wind. They sat on either side of the doorway, white-gowned, like two guarding angels.

Cigfa, herself nobly-born, looked up suddenly and saw me staring. She said to me, 'Be off to your own work, sister. A calf died to make this one sheet of vellum. We do not want it spattered with cow-dung again.'

I walked on without a word, hot-faced. I, who at home had thought myself superior to the other girls, was here the lowest of creatures.

On the other side of the path I had to pass the school-room. I did not linger there. I was afraid to meet the curious stares of the children, so much younger than I was, and so much more wise. Some of them, I had heard, were princes and princesses. Others were farmer's children like myself. I could have envied them. If I had been sent to Tintagel as a child I might not have needed to become a nun. Yet I would not waste time in regret. I had chosen a higher path now. Bryvyth was my star, my lighthouse. I would be like her. I would never marry a man. I would never simper and feign and pretend to know less than I did to flatter a husband's vanity. I vowed that one day I would know as much as any man, yes, and more than most.

Yet that winter was dark and long and empty of joy.

Looking back, I see that I could have used the time differently. I could have begged my sister nuns to teach me what they knew. I could have scratched my letters in the earth with the hoe and chanted the alphabet among the rows of beans. But I was too proud to ask. I have always found it difficult to beg a favour. I could not risk the humiliation of being refused. Bryvyth might have forbidden anyone to teach me. Was it only their own scholars' jealousy that had made Cigfa and Eira chase me from the library door?

So I did the physical labour of a farm-slave. I hated the work. It seemed to me an abuse of the soul. But I was strong and skilled. I did it better than anyone else around me. I was always careful of that. It was a matter of pride and calculation. I wanted Bryvyth to praise me. I strove to earn the right to do what I wanted.

Spring came at last. The sea fell quiet and the sun was warm on my face. Bluebells spread themselves across the slopes. Those nuns that had lighter tasks than mine came each one to the door of her hut and sat on the grass to work as they would do all summer. The classes from the school spread out of doors, chattering like finches, the little children of both sexes, the adolescent girls. I watched the groups going from nun to nun, under the hawk-eye of Rathtyen, singing to the harp, embroidering, chanting Latin, reading the stories of the Bible. It frightened me. They knew so much more than I did. Time was passing.

The porch of the library was open to the sun. In the evening light the nuns would be tidying away their wax tablets, and Cigfa and Eira would be wrapping the precious skins on which the Holy Word blossomed in paint and ink. I watched how lovingly they laid them in the satchels hanging from beams, safe from the teeth of hungry mice. I am not one to gossip on doorsteps. I would not linger to be rebuked again. But I nursed my dream. One day these hands that washed the stinking udders of the cows would lift those books and mark those leaves. It would be mine to lay on the page the glory of the Gospels.

In my brief hours of leisure I sat at the door of my cell looking across the cove to the cliffs of Bossiney. Sometimes I caught the flash of colour and the sparkle of metal. Then the young men would be riding or running in games of war outside the dun. They belonged to another world, a world I had not tasted and believed I never would.

I took my vows. Another winter came and went, and another summer. I served two years hard labour before Bryvyth called me to her. She took my hands in hers. My nails were broken and my palms calloused and lined

with dirt. But they were no harder than her own. She
was stronger than any of us. Where the work was
heaviest she would be at the side of the nun who did it,
singing in a joyful shout against the wind. She had
milked the cows with me when there was ice on the
bucket. She had a body as hard as any man's, and a
keener mind.

'Luned,' she said, 'you have a brave soul. For two
years the breath of God has blown hard on you, and your
spirit has not been stunted by it like the hawthorn or
been uprooted before it like the proud oak. God will
not wrestle with his beloved beyond daybreak. It's time
for a change, girl. I shall not take you away from your
sisters, the cows. They could still teach you a fine lesson
in humility and service, if you didn't think yourself too
clever to listen to them. But I fancy it won't grieve you
too much if I tell you to leave the hoeing of beans to
newcomers.

'These hands will soon heal. When the morning's
work is done, wash them well and eat, and go to Eira in
the library. How would you like to learn to read and
write?'

The laughter in her eyes mocked me.

'Oh!' I cried. 'If you only knew!'

'Child, child!' she said. 'Maybe I know more than
you'd like me to. And don't think I am doing it to please
you. A farmer has many animals. Some are good for
wool, others for milk or pulling wagons. An abbess must
be a canny farmer. She must set each beast to the work
she is fitted for, to the greater glory of God. If I please
you today, then praise Christ for it. And if I take it away
from you tomorrow and give it to others, then praise him
all the louder.'

'I will,' I said, though I had no idea then what she
meant.

It was like entering Paradise. The first tasks that Eira

gave me were child's play after the hard and heavy work of the farm. The nuns showed me how to mix ink. Just the plain lamp-black, not the glowing colours Eira and Cigfa used for their title-pages. I learned to smooth wax tablets on slats of wood. I sharpened quills. I learned to read.

It came to me so easily; it was as though the alphabet had been asleep in my mind all these years. Soon I was reading from the Scriptures. And learning numbers too on the bead frame. It did not take me long to see that before long I would be quicker at this than my teachers.

But the first blow to my pride came when I tried to scratch my words in the sand. I found a chain of letters was not as simple for my hand to manage as the plain, bold strokes of that L so long ago. The stick wavered and straggled like a bird with a broken wing. It was bitter to me to think that even the youngest child in the school could write a fairer hand than I, but I would not be beaten. Hour after hour I worked at it, even at night, scratching the letters upon the floor of my cell by the gleam of moonlight. In time I became perfect.

I worked hard that next winter, safe indoors, once the cows were milked, in a world of books. Across the path gusts of laughter broke from the school. Few of the nuns who taught there could hold the girls for long in silent obedience. Only Rathtyen, our greatest scholar, who taught Latin. Even I was afraid of her. On our side, in the library, there was a murmuring like bees as each nun mouthed aloud the words she was copying. They complained of the cold, but to me it was like the warmth of heaven.

In the doorway, in the best of the light, Eira and Cigfa wrote their Gospels and Psalters. When it was time to illuminate the capitals, Cigfa tended to fruiting vines and palm trees. Eira favoured furred and scaly creatures. Their vision seemed small to me. I, what would I do when my turn came? Each scribe was free to use her own fancy for the greater glory of God. Should I paint the towers of the golden city? The archangel Michael's sword? The thrones of the saints in heaven? What is the highest to which the spirit can aspire?

That summer Cigfa led me along the seashore. In all my time at Tintagel I never wanted to set foot outside the convent bank. I had not Bryvyth's courage. Other nuns fished from the rocks and even splashed and paddled in the cove. I did not like the sea. I was not playful.

But now, as the year turned to the sun, Cigfa and I went across the bridge, searching out the colours for our inks and paints. When the psalm-singing came to us on the wind our voices would rise to join them from a distant wood of green holly. Or we might be scrambling over the rocks gathering lichen. Or on the brink of the waves looking for the skeletons of fish. I learned not to shrink back from the body of a dead gull, but to plunder it for its feathers. I gathered the autumn berries not for food but for their colours. In the mornings the mud clogged my feet as I herded the cows from milking. But when I walked on the beach in the afternoon I was testing the sand for the fineness of its grain and the sharpness of its texture.

Along the beach we passed many cave mouths. Black, dripping caverns, where the sun never penetrated. I was afraid to enter them, dreading always that the sea would rise and trap me. But one cave was stranger than all the rest. It was shunned by all of us. A narrow cleft, under the heart of the convent. A passage not dark like the others. At the far end I glimpsed another sky, another sea. But for all its light it held a horrid fascination I could not explain. I watched the tide rise towards it, until the wash from that other sea came flooding through the tunnel to meet the lapping waves of Tintagel Haven. As I saw each foaming collision I felt as though a wild ocean beyond was coming in to overwhelm us. The other nuns whispered about that cave behind their hands. I did not want to know its secret.

One day we wandered a little further, round one more headland. An old woman was sitting propped against the cliff, dozing. A black-haired child, with her skirt kilted above her knees, was scrambling over the rocks searching the pools, like us. For what? They both looked up, startled, at our approach. The woman hauled herself to her feet, making signs I had wanted to forget with her hands, and muttering hoarsely. Cigfa drew me back by the sleeve till the rocks hid us and we saw Tintagel behind us. The child had just stood on the rock with her legs apart like a boy, laughing soundlessly as we fled.

I am not bold. If I sighted strangers I always turned away at once and carried my search elsewhere. But Cigfa seemed more agitated than I was.

'Gorlois's youngest daughter, Morgan ... and her nurse,' she told me.

'There are three daughters?' I asked. 'I did not know.'

She looked at me curiously. 'You must have seen her at worship every week.'

'I never noticed her.'

But Morgan was there next Sunday. Her little face was grave, her lips ignoring the words that others sang. Her heart was in her eyes as she gazed at her father.

# Chapter Six

The coming of Uther Pendragon shook the convent. It was like one of those great cliff-falls whose crash loosens foundations and leaves the landscape altered.

We were not innocents. You may think we were cut off from the world's affairs, there in the far south-west of Britain, near the Land's End. But we stood on the highway of the sea. Ships put into our haven, or others along the coast, bringing news from Wales and Ireland, from Gaul and Carthage, from Rome and Constantinople and Holy Jerusalem itself. Bryvyth was shepherdess to a large flock in Cornwall and had the ear of great and low. On the ledges of Tintagel we were part of the mighty commonwealth of the Church.

So we knew of great wars in the east and the north of Britain. How Gorlois had rescued the Pendragon and his army from death and destruction, taken Hengist's son captive and saved the city of York. We heard of Uther's crown-feast in London, and the lust he conceived for Gorlois's lady, Ygerne. Of the family's flight to Cornwall and Uther's command to return. So there it stood. King Uther for his honour must lead a warhost to fetch Ygerne back. Gorlois for his honour must defy him.

It meant war between Britons, here on the quiet cliffs of Cornwall. We looked at each other in alarm but Bryvyth's eyes sparkled and the colour was high in her cheeks. She related to us all this news of Gorlois, half-scolding and half-chuckling, like a mother telling tales about her hot-headed son, hiding her fear behind pride. She was nobly-born. Fighting was in her blood.

When the message came that she was summoned to Bossiney, we were at our prayers. Her head went up like a horse's that hears the hunter's horn. Fast we sang our litanies and psalms. Short was our blessing that day.

'The man has seen sense at last! I could have told him. He must send his wife and daughters here to Tintagel. Where else can love and faith and honour find sanctuary but on this holy island? Gorlois, poor lad, must fight the enemy outside the gates. And may God defend the right. But if he falls and the angels carry him up to glory, then Uther Pendragon shall still not have his wife. It is Bryvyth Crook-Staff herself who will bar the bridge. Even the high king of Britain shall not pass that way.'

The light of battle was in her eyes already, and her nostrils were flaring. I knew in that moment how she saw herself: a warrior-champion, standing alone on that neck of rock, defying the king of the Britons with her staff.

She bade us make ready the guesthouse for Gorlois's womenfolk. The place was always clean and decent. Pilgrims and travellers were many. We lodged them better than a common inn. But Bryvyth would have fresh beds laid, the blankets changed, the curtains beaten, fresh rushes on the floor, good meat butchered. She left us busy.

She took Rathtyen and Cigfa with her. We watched their three white figures dwindling over the cliffs to Bossiney.

She came back with a face like thunder.

'Godless man! Does he think I will give Tintagel over to the sword? Shall warriors yell for blood where the angels have sung? Damn him! May the devil take him before he steals what is ours for a fort!'

'It was Gorlois gave us Tintagel to use for a convent,' said Rathtyen drily.

'And who gave it to Gorlois but the God of Cornwall?'

She swept us into the chapel and we prayed. For a curse on the ungodly, for the safety of Tintagel, for Britain whole and Christian. Power was in her voice and a holy anger, the pain of her gift rejected. She made us wrestle all night, prostrate, against the forces of evil. I leave you to judge how far those prayers were answered.

We heard that Gorlois and his household had ridden out to Dimiliock. Silence fell over the cliffs. We waited, like the rest of Cornwall, for what would break it. I sat in the sunshine among the sea-pinks and bluebells looking across the cliff-tops towards Bossiney. There was no stir of movement, no smoke ascending. It had always given me a shiver of unease to catch a distant sight of Gorlois's young warriors, to hear on a sudden gust of wind a shout or the clash of arms. Power tangible. Now the absence of men sent a chill through me. Tintagel felt suddenly vulnerable.

Then there was smoke in Bossiney, in plenty. A great brown wall of it in the sky, shot through with flames. We all ran out of doors to see it. It was all we saw. Tintagel does not stand high. The mainland cliffs walled us round so that we could glimpse little of what passed inland.

We gathered in fear and apprehension. Bryvyth came late to join us from the top of the island. Tears had furrowed the dust of labour on her cheeks like the tracks of snails. Long and silent she stared across the cove towards Bossiney. I wondered that she should grieve so for an abandoned fort. She had damned it heartily enough when it was tenanted, and everyone in it.

She drove us back into the chapel and we prayed again, more urgently than before. For our good Duke Gorlois and his family, for the overthrow of tyrants, for the peace of Cornwall and the Cornish.

They came like ghosts out of the thinning smoke. I think we feared them more than the Pendragon's army. Five women, three old warriors, and a child. Bryvyth's face was white as she watched the womenfolk cross the bridge, weary and grimed but proud. She said no word to us, but the question was in all our hearts. Where is their warband? Where is Gorlois?

I could eat little that evening, though Bryvyth feasted her strange guests royally. I watched those two women duelling each for her honour, while Gorlois at Dimiliock battled for his life. Bryvyth, lavish in hospitality, brilliant in conversation and telling of tales. The duchess courteous and affable, as though she were not the target of a great king's lust, the cause of war, her husband's deathwrit.

I did not envy her, great lady though she was, and beautiful. It was better to be like Bryvyth. I scarcely looked at her daughters. I seem to remember that Elaine was pale and nervous, Margawse hot-cheeked with excitement. When I glanced at Morgan her face was white and her eyes hooded.

I woke in the night. My cell was perched on a sheltering ledge below the oratory. From overhead I heard our warrior-abbess weeping and groaning as though her heart would break. I was drawn to help her. But when I stepped out on to the path a thick moon-silver mist baffled my eyes. Even the sea was silent, misleading me. I waited for my eyes to become accustomed to the tricking light. They did not. One step outside my door and I was lost. I knew the peril of that cliff-path to the chapel. I did not go to Bryvyth.

And yet I prayed, there in my cell. Not for Gorlois or his lady, still less for their daughters, but that this troublesome family might leave us quickly, and I and Tintagel be left to prosper in peace.

I did not know then what we battled with.

I rose early to milk the cows before morning prayers. The sea-fog crept clammily between the walls of our cells. The treacherous silver had darkened to grey. I moved cautiously. Every building loomed like an unfamiliar shadow. I cannot say how I missed my way, but I found myself not at the byre but before the guesthouse.

Then I heard a most shocking sound. Men's laughter. Low, but triumphant. Three unfamiliar figures were coming out of the guesthouse. I met the jingle of mail and weapons in the place of unarmed women. I tried to scream out, but I could not.

I did not learn who they were until the morning. Bryvyth believed it had been Gorlois and his friends. Not otherwise would she have allowed them entrance. It was sorcery. Blurred as they were, the faces they turned on me told yet more lies. It was Uther, Merlyn and Ulfin who trespassed on Tintagel that night. Gorlois's enemies, coming from Ygerne's bedchamber.

He knew I was there. He put his seal upon my mouth when I tried to cry out. Merlyn, that wrecked my life along with Morgan's. Merlyn, that tricked and ruined us all. I know my lips have never spoken true since that day.

Dread chilled me so that I had not even the wit to pray. I heard the feet of those false men going across the causeway. I was keener than Bryvyth to know the presence of witchcraft. I feared it more than she did.

The sun vanquished the fog at last. It was a bright May morning. We saw the truth. Uther Pendragon and his whole warhost filled the skyline beyond our ditch. I was quicker to sense that magic had been among us, but Bryvyth was the first to realise just what sin Uther had done. When the herald told her that Gorlois was dead she saw at once that the duke could not have been in Tintagel that night. She knew who had. Her gate had not opened in the dark to admit a faithful husband but an adulterous king.

If she had been red with rage for Gorlois before, it was a white anger that burned in her against Uther now. It was terrible to behold. She bawled Ygerne out of her chamber

and commanded her on to her knees. She drove her in
shame off the holy island of Tintagel. I loved her for that.
I rejoiced that a nun could be more powerful than the
paramour of a king.

There was one short check. A tiny figure standing alone
on that windswept bridge with her hair black and stream-
ing, defiant as I had imagined only a mighty woman like
Bryvyth could be. Yet ridiculous too. A little girl oppose all
the might and magic of the high king of Britain?

Those men had not seen, as I had every Sunday morning, Morgan gazing up at her father as he thundered out
the hymns to Christ. Uther was High King of the Britons,
but Gorlois was Morgan's high king.

Uther had slain Gorlois with his own hand.

The brave gesture ended in bathos and accident. Her
old nurse shuffled forward to fetch her out of harm's way.
The child turned in a fury and the nurse lost her balance.
Before all our eyes the two of them tottered on the brink of
that terrible drop. From the two hosts of men and women
rose a roaring gasp of anguish. Would Morgan hold
Gwennol? Or would Gwennol drag Morgan to her death?
The terrible moment passed. Morgan and Gwennol stood
clasped in each other's embrace.

Ygerne moved swiftly onward. It was then I realised.
She had been the only one of us near enough to have saved
Morgan. Yet she had not moved to catch her. She swept
past her daughter now without turning her head, straight
into the arms of Uther Pendragon, who had killed
Morgan's father.

I often wonder why that holy island held Gwennol and
Morgan safe. Why did Tintagel not hurl those two on to
the rocks that morning, so that the convent and the
Pendragons would have parted company then?

If her brother Arthur should struggle thus on the brink
of disaster, will he be saved?

# Chapter Seven

The nuns of Tintagel lamented at Gorlois's funeral. They did not sing for Uther's marriage to Ygerne.

After the wedding-feast the Pendragon sent costly gifts to the convent. I thought Bryvyth, grim-faced with anger, would refuse them. She did not. She deemed them a small price for honour lost. To me they were riches unheard of. Plate, jewels, silks, wine, enough for a queen's ransom. I know. I helped to count them.

I had been given a new responsibility in the book-room, keeping a fair record of the convent accounts. They were not the great Gospels I had dreamed of, but they were not as dull as you might imagine. Tintagel was no mean place. Ships came into our cove from near and far. In summer they might be crewed by swarthy brown men and even black, grinning and calling up to us in a barbarous tongue. Like the other nuns I kept away from the landing-stage. Bryvyth and Nonna our cellarer did business with them. They brought us wine from Gaul. Red glazed tableware from Italy. Books from Africa. We traded with tin and corn, with fine weaving and embroidery. We had farms that flourished. People gave us generous gifts. Our nuns were skilful craftswomen. It did not matter to me that I wore a coarse white robe and went barefoot in summer. The wealth which came to us was lavished on the beauty of our oratory, on hospitality, on education, on the care of the poor. That was a cause of pride to me. Riches should be used so, not for self-indulgence but to win power and fame. I had chosen well.

We knew when the Pendragon's son was born at Bossiney, on Midwinter's Day. We spoke little of it in Tintagel, and not in Bryvyth's hearing. It was not a cause for rejoicing. But the news at Epiphany shocked even us. On the stormy night before his christening, Merlyn stole the boy away. The two of them had disappeared without a trace.

I bent over my figures on a dark day in January and heard a sudden rush of chattering from the schoolroom. Rathtyen was hurrying away up the path, following a younger nun. It was nothing to me, except that I paused to ease the cramped muscles of my hand. I do not have a quick, flowing style. My letters were still slow and painful if I tried to form them perfectly, as I wished.

Then a sister came to summon me to Bryvyth in the guesthouse. I took it for some business of buying and selling. Nonna the cellarer was growing old. Sometimes her memory wandered in the middle of bargaining. I had been called for several times recently to settle the account and see that we were not cheated.

But these were no traders. There were three men-at-arms lined up on the far side of the causeway. They had been forbidden to cross bearing weapons, yet their warlike presence dominated the place even at that distance. Pendragon's men, for sure, all curling moustaches and heavy fur cloaks. There was a hardihood and swagger about them that would not let them huddle in their wraps and shiver. They moved briskly about in the cold wind, stamping their feet.

I turned into the guesthouse with an uneasy look at them. I lived now in a world of women. I had drawn a barrier in my mind deep as the convent ditch. All men were on the other side of it.

Inside the guest-hall stood Bryvyth, girded with a sack

covered in blood and slime, so that I knew she had been gutting mackerel. Rathtyen was there, and two others. A small old woman, bent, with knotted hands resting on a stick. She had sharp bright eyes that looked everywhere and turned on me with uncomfortable keenness. And there was a girl, thin and straight, with long black hair and a white face. She was dressed in good cloth, but wore no jewels. She carried her head proudly. Even without the tartan and the gold you would know at once that she came from a noble family. My mind connected. The bare-legged urchin combing the pools on the beach; Ygerne's daughter, defying the Pendragon from the causeway; Morgan. What was she doing back here, in the place of her father's betrayal and her mother's shame?

The girl was scowling, staring in front of her at nothing and nobody, out of eyes that burned with green fire.

'Luned,' said Bryvyth, with heavy emphasis, 'this is the Princess Morgan, third daughter of Gorlois, that was Duke of Cornwall, and the Queen Ygerne. Her stepfather, King Uther Pendragon, is sending her to us to be schooled.'

I must have drawn my breath sharply in astonishment. Yet my curiosity centred on Bryvyth, not the child. It was not like her to be angry yet not to lose her temper. We were all accustomed to the lash of her tongue yet she was reining herself in as she spoke those hated names.

I bowed my head to the unsmiling girl, with courtesy but no servility, as the nuns had taught me. But I did not understand what I was doing here. What had this frowning princess to do with me? What did I care that she was stepdaughter now to the king of all the Britons? We had other princesses at school here, from Dumnonia and beyond. My work was in the library, with the convent accounts. Cigfa was glad to find at last a nun with a head for numbers. She could occupy all her daylit hours

with curling script and glowing paints. It was Rathtyen,
beside me, who had charge of the schoolroom. And there
were homelier nuns, who should have been mothers
themselves, to care for the children's bodies. It was not
my business.

Bryvyth turned back to the girl, and her voice startled
me by its hoarse gentleness.

'Morgan, daughter of Gorlois, you are welcome.'

She clasped the girl in her strong embrace. Morgan
did not move. She stood unyielding to the warmth that
encircled her. Bryvyth's arms dropped away and she
turned briskly towards me.

'This is your foster-mother. Her name is Luned. She
will be your soul-friend, closest to you in this family of
God. You will sleep in her cell, and spend your leisure in
her company, and do everything she commands you in
obedience and humility. You will confess your sins to
her, and she will show you the road to Christ. You must
be a loving daughter to her, and she will tend your body
and soul.'

Shocked out of obedience, my voice broke out in
protest.

'But, Bryvyth . . .!'

She must have expected it. She rounded on me
quickly.

'Hold your tongue now, Luned. I'll speak with you
alone.

'Now, child, go with Rathtyen. She will show you how
we live and labour here in Tintagel. In your working
hours you will be subject to her, as to the other teachers.
Profit by it. They have a storehouse of treasures to offer
you.'

The girl's face did not move as she looked at us all. She
held out her hand to the old woman. Unadorned as she
was, she bore herself like a queen. She gripped the
knotted fingers, but her voice was steady.

'Don't cry, Gwennol. My day will come. Remember what you promised me.'

The old woman caught her in a fierce hug, while the tears ran down the furrows of her face.

'That wicked man! After all I've suffered for you. He can take your body away from me, my lover, but I shall still have your soul.'

'My soul is my own, Gwennol. Not yours or anyone else's. Never forget that. I will vow it to whom I choose, and when I please. But I shan't forget what you've taught me.'

Did I fancy Bryvyth's face darkened at that? The old nurse sucked in her breath sharply.

'Hush! I'll wait for you, my chick. You'll see. It won't be for long. The king and your mother will be going away to London soon. They won't want to stay in Cornwall . . . now that Merlyn's stolen our Arthur.'

Three nuns, with eyes cast down, listening to a tale of murder and childbirth and magic.

'Uther Pendragon will never set me free as long as he lives. He knows that if I could strike either him or his son, I'd do it.'

Bryvyth said loudly, 'It's time for you to go, Gwennol Far-Sight. And I'll have no talk of killing here. Tintagel is a holy place.'

Gwennol laughed at that, sudden and bitter. 'Oh, yes! Tintagel's a holy place. It always was, long before your sort took it from us. And always will be, after you're dead and gone.'

Bryvyth tensed. I waited for her to thunder back. The words did not come.

Morgan smiled then, for the first time, wide and brilliant. She did not return her nurse's kisses, but she endured them more patiently than Bryvyth's hug. Then she unclasped Gwennol's hands from her shoulders. Their fingers knotted and fell apart.

The old woman sniffed and handed a bag to me.

'A few clothes,' she said. 'And little enough for a fine young lady like her.'

She hobbled away across the bridge, leaning heavily on her stick.

'Come!' Rathtyen ordered the girl.

As Morgan walked to the door she paused and stared up into my eyes, deep pools of mistrust on either side. We were waiting to learn what sort of bridge there might be between us. She followed Rathtyen down the path to the schoolroom, straight-backed. There was nothing boyish or impetuous in her movements now.

Bryvyth snorted, like a horse relieved of its harness.

'Well, Luned? Here's a pretty pickle!'

'But why me? I don't like children. There are many here that should have gone to the sort of monastery where they could have married and had babies. Why didn't you give her to one of those?'

'I know the ones you mean. It is not easy for them to be the brides of Christ. I meant Tintagel to be the roost of eagles, like you and me, but there are some little hens that have found their way on to its cliffs.

'But look you, Luned, you don't know the whole of it. It is told abroad that Merlyn stole the baby Arthur away. No one says why. Morgan, his half-sister, took him first. They found her here, in Tintagel Haven on that night of storm. Do you see that rock down there, below the tide-line? She was standing on that, with the boy in her arms, and waves dashing all around them. She meant to kill him. The king's firstborn son. She was lucky to keep her life.

'This whelp of Gorlois's is a heavy burden laid on us. Too heavy for most women here. The Pendragon has charged me that I have her watched day and night, that I never allow her to go beyond these cliffs or be the cause of any more harm to him and his family. You know how I have cursed that man. If I could have said no to him, as I have done often before, I would have. I did not sing at his wedding, and I would not have feasted at his son's christening.

'But how could I refuse this? If Morgan is found anywhere outside this island, his orders are that she is to be taken and killed, as he slew Gorlois her father for opposing him. So what choice do I have? Could I say I wouldn't shelter her, and see her die?'

Oh, Bryvyth, if you had known what this would cost you, you might have hardened your heart!

'Pity her, Luned. This is the daughter of sinful parents, and one who has been much hurt, by the look of her. A soul Christ died to save. Nine years old, and come within a finger's breadth of damnation already. Did you mark Gwennol, the nurse? Morgan's soul needs guarding, even more than her poor body. She will need prayer and constant vigilance. We'll save her by love if we can, by whipping if we must. I see a hard battle and a high reward.

'They tell me she's a clever child, and of a wilful, proud spirit. There are only two nuns in Tintagel to match such a temper. Rathtyen is one, but she has her hands full with the care of a whole school. That leaves you, Luned.'

She clasped my shoulders. It was hard to resist such warmth.

'What do you say, girl? Will you fight this battle for us? Your cleverness and strength of will against this proud little princess? It's no easy road I'm setting you on. You're young yourself, and she's a child that's already old in hating. I'm not easy in my mind, for her or us. I'll pray for you both, day and night. You heard the old hag. If you fail, it's the whole of Tintagel that may be prey to evil. I'm thinking you're the best champion our side has.'

She flattered my vanity. Pride tempted me, as she must have known it would. Yet still I recoiled from the task.

'I have my own work in the library. I cannot be spared from that to mind a child.'

Bryvyth nudged me and smiled slyly. 'It occurs to me, mind, you'd need to give up milking the cows. Would that break your heart, now?'

'You know it wouldn't.'

'Well, we couldn't be having you running off and leaving her alone in the early morning, could we? From now on, you'll not be taking your eyes off Morgan till she's safe in the schoolroom. After that, she's Rathtyen's responsibility until work is over.'

'There's Padarn at the gate.'

'And who's to watch the beach? There are more ways in and out of Tintagel than the high road.'

'If she's so clever, she won't run away if she knows she'll be killed.'

Bryvyth raised her eyebrows. 'I'm thinking I've not made myself entirely clear. It's not her mortal life I'm most worried about. It's her eternal soul. Do not forget Gwennol Far-Sight. She and her kind cursed and spat on us when we marched into Tintagel behind the sign of Christ. Watch over Morgan well, Luned. Keep the devil from her, and shield us from harm. And armour your own soul with mighty prayers.'

She looked at me searchingly. Did she not see how brittle a thing my faith was beside hers? Why did she trust me with the task?

She made me kneel at her feet and I felt the warmth of her hands on my head.

'In the name of Saint Michael of the heavenly sword we send this our daughter into the fight for God. May the Father arm her. May Christ go before her. May the flame of the Holy Spirit give her heart courage. And may she lead Gorlois's daughter safe into blessed Paradise at last. Amen.'

'Amen,' I answered.

But I was thinking more of the sharp stone under my knee and the draught from the door cold in the small of my back.

# Chapter Eight

The older girls were coming out of the schoolroom when I went after Morgan. Their heads were turning and they were full of excited chatter. I could not blame them. Fearful things were happening in the world beyond us. Yet only once, at Arthur's conception, had the shock-wave breached Tintagel's bank. The coming of Morgan was an event.

They filled the path, but I stopped and frowned at them till they stepped aside, subduing their noise. I passed them without a smile. What were they to me? And what was I supposed to do with a nine-year-old child?

My cell was almost the last along the lower path, perched under a ledge out of the wind. All I saw from the door was the cold sea and the cliffs of Barras Nose across the cove. Beyond that headland lay Bossiney, and our king and queen. But until now that had meant almost nothing to me, a world apart from mine.

Rathtyen and Morgan were waiting for me at the door of the hut. A space separated them. Neither of them was smiling. Someone had left a pile of clean hay and some woollen coverings.

'I'll leave you with Luned now,' Rathtyen said. 'Attend to her and she will show you how to make your bed.'

The girl stiffened. She became hard as rock. Her mouth a crack in her face. Her eyes cold as slate.

'I am a daughter of the queen of Britain. I do not make my own bed!'

'You'll do what I say. There are girls here that are the true-born daughters of kings, and that doesn't stop them emptying slops. I will have obedience.'

When Rathtyen spoke sharply, nuns that had done no wrong trembled. I felt the knot of fear in my own stomach but Morgan did not move a muscle.

'Pick up that hay!'

'Pick it up yourself.'

No one had ever spoken to Rathtyen like that. Other nuns pleaded and scolded and even slapped the pupils, and still could not get what they wanted. But one grim word from Rathtyen was always enough to quell the bravest heart. I stood frozen, with my arms full of blankets. I looked at Rathtyen to find what would follow, and was shocked by what I saw. She did not know what to do.

'Pick up that hay, or you'll feel the taste of my whip,' she muttered angrily.

'I am the Princess Morgan. You would not dare to lay a finger on me.'

'Princess, is it? Who fathered you? There's no king's blood in you that I've heard about. And no honour from king, or queen either, that sent you to us as a prisoner.'

'You are wrong!' Morgan flashed out. 'I come of royal blood by my mother's line.'

'Your mother has a son now, safe where you'll never find him. What should the Pendragon's queen want with Gorlois's daughter?'

That sealed the hatred between them.

But Morgan spoke true. Rathtyen did not beat her. Did she fear that if it came to a fight, she would not have had the strength to win? I did not meet the older nun's eyes. I dreaded that she would ask me to help her hold the girl down. I shrank from the thought of that physical encounter. My battle must be with her mind.

Instead, the breath hissed through Rathtyen's teeth.

'We'll see who is mistress here.'

She strode up the hillside out of sight, and we knew she had gone straight back to Bryvyth.

The child Morgan seated herself on a rock beside the door and waited. Very still, she was, with her hands locked in her lap. She smiled slightly, like a cat that has been at the cream.

I took an armful of hay.

'Watch me!' I said to salve my pride. 'This is how it is done.'

She did not turn her head.

I made up a bed for her alongside mine in hurried silence. The space between them was hardly wide enough to stand in. My mattress was thin and lightly-covered. I made hers deep and soft. I was almost as afraid of this bitter child as I was of Rathtyen. And Bryvyth had called me strong of will!

A younger nun came hurrying to call Morgan to Bryvyth. I thought she might refuse to go but she walked proudly up the path. I followed her. It was the first unwilling step after Morgan on the long and terrible road of the years to come.

We met Rathtyen on the threshold of Bryvyth's cell. She passed us, scowling. Bryvyth stopped me from entering with a curt word. Rathtyen and I moved away from the door, for decency. Yet we stood, not looking at each other, listening. The grey air was chill. The plumes of angry waves spurted towards us. Between the crash of the breakers I heard Morgan start to argue. But Bryvyth wasted no time on words. There was the crack of birch twigs on bare legs. From Morgan there was no more sound. At least her arguments were stopped. Bryvyth was stronger of heart than we were. Morgan came out in silence with her head held high. Tears flashed dangerously in her eyes, but she would not let them fall.

I moved uncertainly towards her. What did one say

to a child like that? What did one say to any child?

She walked straight past me. I thought she was going back to the cell. Then she started to run.

'Morgan! Come back!' I cried.

What use? From the moment I picked up the hay we both knew she was mistress.

Yet I had my orders. I had no choice but to run after her. I, Luned, before the stares of all the homecoming sisters. It was an affront to my dignity. Even as a child on my parents' farm I had soon outgrown the games that other children played. Here at Tintagel I was amazed to see nuns chasing each other in the meadow and playing ball on the beach. It astonished me that Bryvyth herself could lead our worship in chapel on feast days and then tuck up her skirts and run about the sands like any fisherman's brat. She would even paddle in the waves for the fun of it. I kept to myself, above their sport, with my legs decently covered.

But now I must run pelting over the fields after Morgan, with my gown snatched up in front of me for all to see. I could not guess what she might do.

She turned away from the causeway and made for the top of the island. She dashed across the pasture, startling the cows, straight for the furthest tip of the headland.

'Come back here!' I cried angrily into the wind.

But what could I do where Rathtyen had already failed?

She flung herself out on to the very last rock, sheer over the dizzying swing of the sea. I stopped at the foot of the outcrop. A black sickness took me. I could not trust myself out on to that height with only the singing air between me and the breakers below.

I sobbed a prayer, as much for my own sake as the child's.

'Lord, let her not throw herself over!'

Morgan turned slowly. Letting go of the rock, she raised herself upright, staggering a little with the force of the wind. One step backwards and she would have gone to her death. Never have I seen eyes more intense and yet as hard as polished stone. They filled me with dread. She smiled at me. If it had not been for those eyes you might have thought it was an invitation to a friend.

'You are afraid?'

'Of course . . . Get down.'

'Climb up here. Stand beside me.'

'I cannot. Get down at once.'

'Climb!'

I do not know why I should have obeyed her, when every nerve in my body protested against it, when I was the one appointed to keep her from danger, not aid her in it. Was this to be the end already of the fight Bryvyth had promised me? The two of us a foot away from death? I did not take that dangerous step because I had been ordered to stay always at her side. It was not because I cared whether the child herself lived or died. Not even the sting of pride to make me fall with her, because her death would be my failure. I went because that nine-year-old child *compelled* me to obey her.

I tried not to look beyond the grey stone, yellowed with lichen, under my fingers. As I reached up a small hand grabbed me and pulled me suddenly to the top. Too quickly. I felt myself totter and thought we should both have fallen over the edge. I screamed. But when I opened my eyes fearfully we were still swaying on the brink, buffeted by the wind. I clung to Morgan. Her fingers were twisted cold and tight among mine.

'It's dangerous here, isn't it? Do you like danger? Look down!'

I shut my eyes, but she dragged my head round. I caught a glimpse of hell's cauldron. I retched on a mouthful of bitter bile.

'Do you see those stones below? I wonder how long this rock beneath us will stand here. One day it will go crashing down through that space to join the others. Perhaps today, while we're standing on it. Doesn't that make your blood beat faster?'

Her eyes were burning again, too brightly green.

'Let me go,' I pleaded. 'Come home with me.'

She laughed, and tossed away my hand so that I gasped and clutched empty air. 'Bryvyth said you were to look after me. That you were to guard me from harm. You couldn't keep a crow from the corn.'

She jumped lightly on to the grass and watched scornfully as I clambered down beside her. The wind tugging at my gown could not disguise how my limbs shook.

That was the first time I followed Morgan into danger. And she had only been with us one hour.

# Chapter Nine

She tricked us from the very first day.

I marvelled that after the terrifying moments on the rock she came back with me to my cell obediently. As we neared our living quarters I saw Bryvyth at her own door, watching us anxiously. I turned to Morgan. She was walking a little way behind me, her eyes cast down demurely, her head inclined, her hands folded together. One would have thought her a picture of submission. I felt a thrill of triumph. The helpless instant of danger was behind me. I had passed the first test. I had brought her back safely.

Bryvyth smiled at me.

Oh, cunning Morgan! Even then she was scheming to hide the knowledge of my weakness from Bryvyth. She knew already she was stronger than I was, and that Bryvyth would have relieved me from the task if she had guessed. I, who was set to guard her, was already her tool. She knew I would never confess my failure to Bryvyth of my own accord.

I got another nun to help me carry a chest to my cell and stood it at the foot of Morgan's bed.

'Put your clothes away,' I ordered, pointing to the bag Gwennol had left.

She raised her eyes to me with a slow, insolent stare. She did not move from the bed where she sat. Should I go back to Bryvyth again and compel her? I knew I would not.

I unpacked her possessions and laid them neatly in the chest. There were not many, for the stepdaughter of a king. A few changes of clothes, not richly decorated. Girdles of wool rather than gold. Clasps of plain silver. A bone comb, but no mirror. My hands found something hard wrapped in cloth at the bottom of the bag. I hesitated. Morgan watched me without expression. I unfolded the cloth.

It was a knife, richer by far than anything else she had brought. The hilt was of polished bone, marvellously fashioned like a boar, with bristles of gold and garnet eyes. But this was no jeweller's toy. When I unsheathed it, the blade was long and wickedly sharp.

Do not mistake me. We all had knives. Even in a convent library it is necessary to sharpen pens. The littlest child carried one in his belt. But not a weapon like this. It was a hunting dagger. It could have slit a bear's throat or butchered a stag.

'What is this?' I asked Morgan, and my voice must have been sharp with worry.

To my surprise she recoiled at the sight of it.

'That! Merlyn gave it to me for a New Year's gift. I did not know it was there. Why did she pack it?'

'It was a handsome present. Richer than the one you wear in your girdle.'

'I do not want it. It is a man's weapon. I will not touch it.'

'You will have no need of it here.'

'Or afterwards. Gwennol taught me that. There are other ways. Which do you think is worse – the power to wound, or to have the power to heal and not to use it?'

She was on her feet. Her fingers were gripping my wrist. Then she seemed to realise what she was doing and sank down again.

'I do not want that,' she repeated.

I took the knife to Bryvyth. She raised her eyebrows.

'Why would that trickster Merlyn give the girl a gift like that? Did he want her to put Uther Pendragon out of the way with it and sign her own death-warrant, while he rears the brat Arthur to his own liking? Well, it seems she's too wise a child to play his game.'

She sent the knife back to Bossiney. It was almost nine years before I saw it again.

Supper was over, and it was time for evening prayers. Our oratory was small. In summer we sang our praises out of doors. When we were packed together against the winter cold it was hard to see past the tall nuns to the rows of children. Yet I found Morgan's face. Her eyes were blank. Her lips unmoving. I told myself it was not to be wondered at. Though she came from a Christian family, doubtless the words were strange to her. Then I saw her lips tight as a locked door. I knew she did not want to join her voice to ours. Our hymns were an alien language she would refuse to learn.

Suddenly I saw her eyes flicker sideways. Mine followed them. Bryvyth had turned to watch her. The child's rosy mouth parted on milk-white teeth. With a little smile she began to sing, lips shaping the Latin syllables exactly. Her voice rose pure and sweet among the rest. Bryvyth smiled back at her, warm and encouraging. She had duped us again.

So I closed the door on our first night together with a sense of foreboding. For three years I had slept here in my own cell. Narrow and bare, but a castle to me who had lived with a litter of squalling brothers and sisters crowding my days and nights. It was mine. The four-walled space. The silence. The view was grim from the doorway, the everlasting sea breaking upon the dark cliffs of Barras Nose, but it was a small price to pay for solitude. For the right to live with myself. Mistress of my own mind.

Morgan ended that.

It was already dark. A feeble rushlight made the shadows deeper. Morgan stood very still beside her bed. Clad, as she had come to us, in a dark blue tunic over a saffron gown. A tasselled girdle. Her black hair loosely braided. I sensed for the first time that she was uncertain what to do. I was shivering myself from the midwinter cold and my own unreadiness for this task. No one had explained to me the everyday duties of a fostermother. But one thing was obvious.

'Take off your gown and hurry into bed, before we both freeze,' I snapped.

Already I half-expected her to disobey me. Why should she heed me, who had now so little confidence in my power to rule her? But her head drooped. She touched the knot of her girdle and fingered the hem of her tunic. Then I understood. Nine years, and she had never been expected to undress herself or brush the tangles from her hair. At three years old my sisters had been learning to do that for themselves.

I waited for her to refuse. It was on the tip of my tongue to scold her. To pay back in scorn some of the hurt to my own dignity. But when I saw her begin to tug at her dress she seemed to shrivel in stature before me and become a tired little girl. Something stayed my bitterness. I am not gentle. I was never gentle with myself. I hate to touch others. My movements of caring are clumsy. Yet I argued with myself that it was too cold to stand and wait. Let me have her in bed and forget the darkness of my own altered future in sleep.

I took away her hands from her girdle. They were very cold. I undid the knot. I lifted the tunic over her head. She stood and let me. I think she counted it defeat and not victory to have me serve her this time. Perhaps her thoughts were not on me at all, but on the old nurse with twisted hands who had done this service for her every night of her life.

Her loosened gown fell to the floor. On her flat chest I saw what had been hidden. From a thong around her neck hung a small leather bag. A jarring memory struck me. I was a country girl. I had seen many such bags before Ruman came. Once my mother had hung one round my own neck. I was more frightened of it than of the evil it was meant to ward off. Neither of us spoke. I knew Gwennol had given it to her. I did not want to know what it contained.

We stood in our shifts, barefooted. Cold in body and heart.

'Raise your hands to heaven,' I ordered. She followed me without argument. It was hard to move in that narrow space without brushing each other.

'Pray: O angel guardian of my right hand, attend thou me this night. Drive thou from me the taint of pollution, encompass thou me till dawn from evil. O kindly angel of my right hand, deliver thou me from the wicked one this night. Deliver thou me this night. Amen.'

She had uttered no sound.

'Repeat the Amen.'

She lowered her hands without a word.

'Say it,' I insisted.

Morgan turned her head to me. Her eyes were lost in the shadowed hollows of her face. She said nothing. And the dread began to grow in me again as I knew she would not.

After that, I did not settle her into bed. I did not heap the covers over her shoulders and tuck her round as her nurse would have done. I got straight into my own bed and blew out the rushlight. Let her freeze if she wanted.

She was a quiet child. She slipped between the covers with hardly a sound. I heard a faint catch of breath from her bed. So close I could have reached out a hand and touched her. I do not know if it was a gasp of cold or a stifled sob.

I could not sleep. That was common with me. Wakefulness had been hateful to me at home, with the snores and grunts of so many bodies close to mine. At Tintagel I had learned to treasure these extra hours. I might not burn a light late at night, yet I could lie awake letting my mind go free, escaping at first the demands of dirty beasts and muddy earth and the chatter of nuns hoeing around me. Now there was more to fill my thoughts. Passages from the Bible to memorise daily. The wonders of science and mathematics from the East. The detailed accounts of our farms and quarries and the convent expenditure. I had dreamed a great future for Tintagel and myself.

Now I saw this liberty threatened by one small child so close beside me, silent but trespassing by her very presence upon the space and largeness of my thoughts. I turned to the wall and tried to close my eyes for sleep.

The sound seemed to come from the walls themselves. At first I took it for the hiss and smack of the waves, dragon-like rearing themselves against our cliffs. Then for the creeping winter wind between grass and stones, snatching at us even in the hollows where we sheltered. At last I knew it was inside the cell with me.

Of course, I thought it was the child. I turned over quickly. It was utterly dark. The whispering was all around us. From the walls, from the roof, from the door. Vicious, insistent. Loud enough for me to understand the words . . . and yet I did not understand them. Like no language I had ever known or heard. Terror gripped me. The gap between our beds was very narrow. It seemed an unbridgable chasm. I summoned all my courage and strength of will to cross it.

My hand reached out in the darkness. I confess that I was seeking reassurance, not giving it. I was terrified that the voice might not be Morgan's. And more afraid still that it was. I wanted to tell myself that this was a human, mortal child. That whatever assailed us, there were two of us to stand against it, to defend each other from its evil. Evil it was, I did not need to be convinced of that.

My hand met Morgan's wrist. Very slight, she felt. A skinny, nine-years girl. She was lying very still. There was no start of movement when I touched her. Yet I knew she was awake. I had listened for the deep slow breathing of the sleeper, desperate to keep my ears from that other whispering all around us. There was nothing. She was lying on her back. I sensed her face turned to the thatch over our heads. I knew, without seeing, that her eyes were open. She did not seem to feel my hand. There was no response, except that the whispering rose to a gibbering screech so that I clung to her, shutting my eyes, babbling prayers.

'O holy Son of God, blessed Christ, who stilled the storm, defend us . . .'

The voices fell a little, as waves die back after the breaker foams. The gloom lightened a little, or my eyes became accustomed to the night. It frightened me more. I did not know what there was to see, and I did not wish to see it. I shut my eyes, still gripping Morgan. Slowly I felt warmth return to her under my fingers. Felt the bone of her arm solid under my hand. A little sigh escaped her, and her breath fluttered on my face as she turned her head sideways.

Suddenly she flung my arm away.

'Gwennol! Gwennol!' she screamed as if in terror. And then, 'Stop her! Don't let her! Don't let her!'

Her arms thrashed wildly. I jumped out of bed. She threw herself upon me. Hands grasping my shoulders, head butting into my breast.

'Where is Arthur? When he is king, who will be queen? I will! I will, won't I?' she cried passionately.

I am the eldest child. I had many brothers and sisters.

I know what needs to be done to soothe their frets. The words, the movements. It is a skill. It is not necessary to feel love to quiet a crying child. So I spoke to her, and stroked her, and patted her into a hiccupping silence. I do not remember what I said, or what I may have promised her. It was effective. The whispering in the walls had died too. I put it behind me. I had no wish to question what it might have been. I feared to know the answer.

I took a small revenge. I made her stand with me again between the beds. And the night was colder now than it had been before.

'Father of all, guard our souls. Christ in high heaven, defend us this night. Spirit of comfort, bless our beds, And bring us safe to bright morning, here or in heaven. Amen.'

I heard her say the Amen after me. Quickly, almost desperately. She caught my hand.

'Luned, Luned? Will your God save us both? Can he?'

'Of course he can,' I said. 'If you pray, and fast, and are obedient to your teachers in every way.' And then, recalling Bryvyth, I added virtuously, 'And I will pray and fast with you, Morgan.'

She dropped my hand. 'You? You're more frightened than I am. Why didn't Bryvyth give me someone brave and laughing? And to think that Gwennol was afraid of you! That's silly, isn't it? She thinks their star is setting and the Church's is rising. Where is the power, Luned? What is the strongest thing? Is it Uther Pendragon's sword, or Merlyn's spells, or your Christ on his cross? What are you going fight them with, Luned?'

'Go back to bed, child. God will defend us.'

'Is your cross a weapon? Will it hurt them?'

'Hush. That is sinful talk. You must make confession for it.'

I tucked her round this time. Awkwardly I bent and smoothed her hair. I almost kissed her, but I did not. I do not know why. I cannot tell you what I meant by it. I did not love her then. I wanted to be rid of her forever. If that had been possible I might have lived my life in peace. The nuns of Tintagel might still be singing on those cliffs, and much evil averted.

It was not my fault. Bryvyth should not have called me to fight this battle as their champion. I had neither the strength nor the humility. I did not love Morgan enough until I was deep in her power.

I dreaded to hear the voices again. I hid my head under the covers and muttered prayers to shut them out. Morgan lay silent now, so that I thought at last she was asleep. My prayers slowed and stopped. There was no sound inside the cell but our own breathing.

Then I screamed aloud as her fingers snatched at my arm.

'I will be queen! I will!' she hissed.

# Chapter Ten

That day was the first of many beatings for Morgan, and there was worse to come.

At first it seemed that nothing I or Rathtyen or Bryvyth could do would change her. She was possessed by a blind anger and a stubborn pride. Over and over again she swore to us that she would be a queen. I did not blame her for that. If I had been born in her place, and suffered what she had suffered at the hands of King Uther, I might have nourished such a dream, to oppose his might.

Ygerne and Uther Pendragon were still in Bossiney, waiting for the spring to come and the roads to the cities to be fit for travel and war to begin again. They were planning the marriage-feasts of Elaine and Margawse at Easter. But no word came from them for Morgan.

I thought that first day that she would have no friends in Tintagel either. You had only to watch her sitting on the bench in the refectory. She had a still intensity that created a space around her, no matter how closely the children's bodies might be crowded. I never knew a child who could sit so still. I watched the other girls' eager questions slowing, dying away before her contemptuous answers. I saw the looks they exchanged. She truly believed that Morgan, daughter of Gorlois and Ygerne, was greater by far than they were, though in blood she was not. Many of them detested her.

But not all. I say she had no friends, and she did not.

Yet there were those who followed her. Even some older girls fell under her spell. That sort of pale and quiet girl that follows in the shadow of someone strong and vibrant, seemingly unable to live except through others – Morgan had several such, waiting upon her every whim, hanging on her words, flattering her. Poor as she was, she would give them gifts. A piece of amethyst found on the beach, a curious shell, a choice morsel of food saved from the table. She did not do this to curry their favour. It was not to win their love that she bestowed her largesse – they already worshipped her – but she was her father's daughter. Gorlois had given gold and jewels and horses to his warband, a generous duke, an open-handed leader of men. So would Morgan exercise royalty in this little court. Through gifts she asserted her superiority over them. It was hard to stop.

There were no gifts for Morgan. Unless you count what passed at Imbolc, the festival of the Lady of flocks and herds.

On the first of February I woke early. I had not yet lost the discipline that had driven me out in the winter's half-light to milk the cows and ewes before morning prayers. With Morgan's coming I could lie in bed a little longer, my body rested but my mind uneasy.

Today someone was afoot before me. Morgan was going out of the door, wrapped in her cloak.

'Morgan! Where are you going?'

She did not answer me, contemptuous as ever.

I roused on my elbow, watching her disappear. Why had I called out? Where does anyone go on waking from a night's sleep? She would be back in a moment.

I leaned back on my pillow and closed my eyes. A picture came to me, a fleeting glimpse of Morgan departing into the gloom. The whisk of her gown beneath the hem of her cloak. I knew then why I had been alarmed. Morgan was fully dressed.

74

I leaped up and threw my own cloak over my shift. Barefoot in the cold mud of the paths, I ran after her. There was not light enough yet to see far. I was too proud to cry out to her. She would not have answered. I must find her myself.

I headed for the causeway. If she thought of escaping it would be that way, while Padarn was asleep.

A sound alerted me. The startled mooing of a cow somewhere above. I spun round and climbed towards the plateau and the farm. Was that someone moving through the steaming byre where the shuffling herd waited for milking? As I hurried after, the cows' muzzles seemed monstrous, leaning out of the murk towards me. Their horns barred my way. Was that a flicker of light at the far end, or a trick of the eyes? A cock crowed piercingly and all the hens on their roosts seemed to come to noisy life in front of me.

On over the cold wet grass. It was growing lighter here, with the wide sea all around me. A grey shadow passed by the pens of sheep and they murmured as if in recognition of her.

She was on the summit now, walking swiftly through the meadow. I could see the tracks of her feet in the dew. She was making straight for the southern edge. The ground dipped and I lost her against the boulders. My heart began to hammer. There is a gap in the rocks there, where a path drops sharply down on to a grass-grown terrace. I feared to follow her that way, as I shun all precipitous places.

But Morgan had paused, staring round her at the paling pasture and the still grey sea. I sped across the meadow to catch her. Then she bent. I thought I would lose her down that cleft in the stones. But she had found something.

At the side of that stair in the rock there is a shelf of slate, overhung by rock, like a natural shrine. I had

never investigated it. The sides of Tintagel are riddled
with holes, great and small. I kept away from them. Now
as I saw Morgan bending over it, I noticed two things
that made the hair rise on my scalp.

There were cups cut in the rock. Little circular hollows. I had seen such things before. I was not green. I
knew what they were. And today was Imbolc. The cups
had been filled. With milk. With bread. With honey.
With egg. I saw Morgan's hands make passes over them.
Then she dipped her fingers and ate and drank.

If I had been chilled to find such things on Tintagel,
and still in use, that was nothing now. I experienced
horror. You who have lived in the sophistication of a
Christian court cannot imagine the depth of my dread. I
was a country girl. Long before I became a Christian and
a nun I knew the meaning of such sacrifices. We made
oblations for the coming year. They were not for
humans. We did not eat of them ourselves. *We did not
eat of them ourselves!*

But Morgan was eating them.

I was too frightened to run and tell Bryvyth at once. I
do not know what it was I dreaded to say. Even to this
day I am not sure what name to give my fears about
Morgan. I must live with her. I must see her, speak to
her, touch her daily. How could I bear this if I spoke my
fear?

So I kept silent, and that memory was blotted out by
what followed the next day.

It was the feast of candles. Our little oratory was
aflame with light that dark February day. The rest was
holiday. We nuns would have been glad to sit over the
fire in our little hall, sewing and listening to some story
of the saints or the prophets, but the children were restless. Even on a winter's day the little boys would rather
be out of doors, running or hurling a ball, and not a few
girls too. Morgan was with them.

That was the other side of her. She, who carried herself so queenly in front of the older girls, would suddenly switch and become a mad thing with the younger children. She would laugh and leap and race like an unbroken filly, calling to them to try and catch her.

They adored her. They saw a magic in her vitality that made them dash after her, crazy with mirth and admiration and reckless of any warning we nuns might shout.

She taxed me greatly. I had risen beyond the mere copying of figures in the library now. Nonna's mind was failing. When merchants came to bargain at the gatehouse, it was I who was called to deal with them. I must be in the storehouse, making lists of what was needed in the kitchens. The guesthouse was always busy with travellers. All our wealth, and the accounting of it, was in my hands.

But when the day's work was over, I could not find the peace and solitude I needed. While daylight lasted I must follow a restless, growing girl over the rocks of Tintagel. Worse still, she tempted the younger ones to follow her. The cliffs are steep, the ledges narrow. The wind comes in sudden gusts. I would have to scurry after them, calling to them to take care, always afraid that one of them would fall. Afraid I might slip myself. Knowing it would not be Morgan who fell. Wishing it might be.

That day she stood very still in a circle of children. The smaller ones watched her. She fascinated them. Then, without warning, her eyes flashed. She dashed away up the path, calling to the little boys and girls to chase her. They screamed with laughter and scrambled in pursuit.

My heart was in my mouth. Morgan cared nothing for her own safety or theirs either.

I panted after them, but she was swifter than I was. I saw her flying across the grass to that gap in the rock on the southern edge. The little ones swarmed after her.

'No! Come back!' I begged in vain in the teeth of the wind.

This time she hardly paused at the ledge. Her white hand slid over the slate, its cups empty now. Then she swung herself down, dropping lightly to the grass below.

She disappeared. The children went tumbling through the cleft after her.

'Where's she gone?'

Their shrill voices floated up to me.

There was a laughing call among the boulders. The boys and girls went pelting across the grassy terrace in search of her.

'Don't run! It's slippery!' I yelled.

They did not heed me. She had escaped them again. They searched around, behind rocks, under the cliff-hang, even peering over the edge.

A white hand between the stones betrayed her. A flying lock of black hair.

'Here she is! I've found her!'

Howel shouted with glee. A small round boy with curly brown hair. The son of an under-king from the lower reaches of the Severn. He had found their darling.

Bolder than all the rest, he leaped from a rock over her head to land beside her hiding-place. He bounced breathless on the grass slope below. His tiny leather boots skidded on the muddy turf. He started to slither, to roll. At first he chuckled. Then he shouted, screamed. I saw his body bouncing over the rocks out into the air. Falling. Disappearing.

I am not brave. I rushed back to the convent. Half a dozen nuns, the hardiest, went pelting down to the shore, Bryvyth in the lead. That ledge is on the sterner side of the island. There is no beach there. The water is deep, the rocks cruel. They clambered over the stones, searching, calling, weeping. They did not find him.

Days later fishermen sighted his body, wedged in a

cleft of rock under black seawrack. It was monstrously bloated and pale. Beginning to soften into disintegration at a touch.

I did not follow the other nuns. Morgan was white and fierce when I caught up with her. What does one say to one who has caused death, at a moment like that? How do you reproach her?

She did not wait to hear me. She flew at me as though her clawed hands would rake my face.

'Where is he?'

'He is dead,' I said.

'He is not! He is not! Show me his body. Let me touch him. Let me try!'

'The sea has taken him. They cannot find him.'

She wept in earnest then.

'It's your fault! All of you! Why did you build your convent in such a dangerous place? You shouldn't ask little children to come and live here. Uther Pendragon was a beast to send me. I would never have come here of my own free will. Is this a fit place for the daughter of Gorlois, the warlord, the hunter? There are no horses for me to ride. Can I not even run if I want to?'

I do not know if the tears were for herself or the dead boy. They had ceased before the beating began.

Bryvyth laid a greater ban on her then, walking round the convent with her crooked staff, beating the bounds of Morgan's close imprisonment. She must not go beyond this circle. Tintagel is narrow enough, for those who must be alone, but this ward was tighter yet. Cell, schoolroom, chapel, refectory, a little run of grass, well back from the cliff. Morgan watched her, eyes flaring in her white face. Lips silent. None of us knew if she would obey, or how we might compel her. It was a fragile fence and we all knew it. One moment's anger, a second's defiance, and the sea lay half a dozen strides away with all its evil temptation. One could never escape far from it.

Yet she kept within the circle. The word from Rathtyen was that she worked hard in the schoolroom. Stiff and silent, except when she must read aloud or make answers. But clever, beyond the common range of pupils, and diligent and seemingly obedient now.

So in chapel. She sang and prayed. It did not seem a mockery this time. Her lips framed the words eagerly, even passionately, calling upon the name of Christ, her saviour. Bryvyth met my eyes. Neither of us was sure. Could it be she was saved?

Bryvyth had imposed a great fast on me for my failure. Morgan chose to share it, though we would not have placed so heavy a burden on any child. She grew paler than ever, and gaunt with hunger or grief.

I found her one day alone in the oratory. Her hands were stretched out to the dark-eyed Christ Eira had painted on the wall above the altar.

'Teach me!' she was crying to him. 'I know how they hurt you. They whipped you, they imprisoned you, they crucified you. But you were the Healer. You were stronger than death. Show me!'

# Chapter Eleven

Death was no stranger to us. Howel was not the only child who would not return from Tintagel. At Easter we put away our mourning for him.

Great Lent ended in Holy Week. Bryvyth would lift my penance from me. We had all been fasting now. I longed for the coming festival as never before. I felt that when the light of Easter dawned I could present Morgan to Bryvyth as my triumph. A soul snatched from darkness. Evil vanquished. Satan defeated. Like Christ, I had harrowed hell.

The Pendragons had gone from Cornwall. Margawse was to be married to Lot of Lothian, Elaine to Nentres of Garlot. No one sent to invite Morgan to their weddings.

Watching her walking the little round Bryvyth had set her, standing gazing across the cove to the cliffs where she had been used to run with her nurse, seeing the rolling haze of the forest she had hunted with her father, even I was moved with a kind of pity for her. The more because she no longer raged and complained. She did what I told her, not quite meekly but as if it no longer mattered to her, as if her body was a shell and the fierce will had gone somewhere else. She spent more time in the chapel than was natural for so young a child.

There is a ban on me even now that I may not tell you what sins she brought to me as her soul-friend in confession. Yet I marvelled that she should accuse herself of a wickedness greater than we thought she had done.

Howel's death had been due to no more than her folly. He was no kin of hers. Why was the boy's loss such a torment to her?

But if she was humble with me, she was proud before the older girls. She watched them riding home for Easter with an escort of servants, or receiving letters and tokens before the feast. There was nothing for her. She bore their taunts with aloof silence.

I thought we were a little alike – the pen trembles now as I write this with the foolishness of it – I thought we were akin in our pride, our estimation of our own worth compared with others', our contempt for weaker souls, our need of solitude. And yet there was this difference between us. I had come to Tintagel willingly. It was here I found my freedom. But Morgan was among us as a prisoner.

I went to Bryvyth on Easter Eve.

'Might we relax her punishment a little?' I suggested. 'She is a different girl now. Grave, obedient. And the children will not follow her so readily, since Howel died.'

'Hm! So she's softened even your heart, has she? Be on your guard still, Luned. You hear her confession. Is she as contrite as she should be?'

'More,' I said.

She looked at me keenly. She would have liked to ask me more, but it was forbidden.

Nectan came to visit us that evening. We did not allow him to shrive the girls. Any man, even a bony saint in a white hermit's gown, sends a flurry of excitement through a convent schoolroom. Many and wild the sins they might have invented to spend a little longer alone with him. Enough pleasure for them to kneel with eyes downcast and take the sacrament from his sinewy hands.

As we prepared for the great midnight service,

Bryvyth and Nectan talked close together. They summoned Morgan to them. Nectan had known her mother many years. He had been confessor to her father, Gorlois. He served as Uther Pendragon's house-priest when the king was in Cornwall. I do not know what he asked her. Morgan must have charmed him, like her mother before her. Very sweet are the women of that family when they wish to be. In the end, I too fell in love with Morgan, and damned my soul. Bryvyth had a sharper mind than Nectan, but she consented to take his counsel.

On Easter Day Morgan would be released from her close confinement. The narrow island of Tintagel would be her garden outside the tomb, so long as she kept away from the youngest children and conducted herself wisely and responsibly.

That Easter Eve we kept the vigil. All day we had been busy, labouring to make ready a huge bonfire. The sorrow of Good Friday was over. Saturday was like a holiday. The children picked primroses for the chapel. They ran to gather driftwood from the beach and haul it up the difficult path with the nuns' help. We put on stout gloves to cut the prickly furze. We dragged dead branches from the woods at the head of the coombe. We stacked them on the highest part of the island. Morgan smiled a little as she watched.

In the dark of night we gathered the children and shepherded them into the shadowed chapel. There was excitement in our prayers. Anticipation.

Then at midnight the bell was struck joyously. Bryvyth seized Christ's candle and brandished it aloft. As she strode through the chapel, lights sprang from her single flame to all our tapers. We followed her, nuns holding the youngest children by the hand. The river of light flowed up the path to the crown of Tintagel and Bryvyth thrust her flame deep into the heart of the Easter fire.

Thus Patrick had blazed the faith through Ireland, and overcome the Druids. But this was a custom unknown to me till I came to Tintagel.

The red light leaped in the faces of women and girls. It caught the wonder in the eyes of children. It threw back the shadows and cast a fiery dawn over the sea. The cry went up from all our throats.

'Christ is risen!'

'He is risen indeed!'

The cliffs rang with the good news.

My eyes flew straight for Morgan. I watched her mouthing the words, without smiling, as though she longed to believe them. The flames leaped in her face, leaving her eyes dark hollows. She looked away from our fire and stared into the gloom beyond the light. On every side in the limitless night the cliffs and hills of Cornwall were dark. The Easter flame leaped to heaven in Tintagel alone. A solitary challenge to the dark. I thought she shuddered.

It was three weeks before our fire was challenged. Easter was followed by the feast of May Day. Of course, nuns though we were, we knew what happened on May Eve. Only a few of us were country-born, but even the nobility in the highest villas and duns of Dumnonia were no stranger to the drums and the May-pole and the dancing mare. They might keep the Roman ways and boast chapels and priests but there was something deep in the soil that had never been rooted out. They also went to the greenwood.

So we prayed the more earnestly in our chapel and went to bed that night determined to close our minds to such thoughts in pure sleep. Tintagel was a fortress beleaguered by more than the sea. In the morning of May we would rise and go to our prayers as usual, though in our hearts we would be remembering a different song.

May Eve was not a time of regret for me. I had always feared it. I was glad to escape from the drums when I came to Tintagel. For once I expected to sleep sounder than most.

But not this year. I woke with a start in the darkness. Morgan was standing in the doorway of my cell. There was a glimmer of moonlight catching her white shift and making black snakes of her hair.

'Come back to bed.'

I spoke sharply, confident by now of my authority. She did not move. I repeated the order. She might not have heard me. With a slow chill I knew that I had lost. That I had never really had authority over her. She had appeared to obey me only because it suited her to do so. I listened to the admission of impotence in my own voice.

Disturbed now, remembering what night this was, I rose shivering and came to stand beside her. There was a silver light over the sea, as though the whole world were reluctant to sleep. And as I turned inland, everywhere I looked pinpricks of light outshone the pale stars. On every hill and headland the fires of Beltaine were blazing. A necklace of gold and rubies beaded the throat of Cornwall.

Morgan's hand gripped mine, warm and small.

For the first time since I came to Tintagel I thought keenly of my home. Of my little brothers and sisters, of the drums and the dancing, of the pairs of animals driven for increase through the flames. Of young couples leaping high for new life. If I had stayed, it might have been the hand of a young man warm over mine instead of the small hard fingers of Morgan. I shivered strangely.

She began to tug at me.

'Come, Luned! Come now!'

'No! Come back to bed. May Eve is not for us. We leave all that behind us when we take our vows as virgins.'

I tried to pull her indoors. I should have been stronger

than she was. But her hand slipped through mine and she ran away from me. I had no choice but to follow her over the knife-cold grass to the edge of the cliff. Fire reddened the sky across the cove.

'Look! There is someone still in Bossiney after all! They have lit the fire. Do you see? They have lit it as a sign for me!'

Her hand held mine tighter than ever. I felt her whole body straining, yearning, as though at any moment her fierce spirit might snatch it up and soar into the air towards that beacon across the water like a gull.

'Do you hear it?' she cried passionately. 'The drums and the pipes?'

I listened. I could hear the shrill song of the wind and the endless thud of the waves.

'It is only the sea in the caves beneath us.'

'Listen! Listen!'

She was quiet for a while. Then we both heard a new sound, close at hand. Even Morgan drew back, startled, as though it was not what she was expecting. Holding each other's hand we strained to hear as we peered over our ledge.

There was a glimmer of white between the rocks far below us. A whisper of sound. Spectral laughter floated up. An irrational fear seized me that we had glimpsed what no human eye should see on this night. I tried to drag Morgan back to my cell but she pulled away from me and called out.

'Who is it? Who's there?'

There was a shocked silence. I was near to fainting. There was a sudden scrabbling. A stone tumbled and splashed into the water beneath. I could not move. Then there rose an unearthly wailing, chilling the blood. I clapped my hands over my ears. But Morgan cupped hers to her mouth. Her human voice threw back the same sound. She bent over and listened. When I took my hands away the cliffs were quiet. I could hear only the white wave-caps breaking and see the glimmer of a pool of foam round the rock in the cove.

I heard a strange sound beside me. Morgan was bent double, choking with suppressed laughter.

'Oh, Luned, Luned! Here, in Tintagel, of all places! What kind of holy nunnery is this they have sent me to?'

I could not bear it. I shut my heart and ears to her. I dropped her hand and ran back to the sanctuary of my cell, leaving her alone. Let the voices do with her what they would. I could not, must not, understand the truth of what she was saying.

# Chapter Twelve

'Wake up. Wake up.

'For summer is a-coming today . . .'

My eyes struggled open. It was barely light. Morgan was dancing beside my bed, singing the May Day song. Her feet were bare and her skirt swung above her knees as she whirled.

It was a double shock. That May Day should come in the old way, here in the chaste castle of Tintagel's convent. I almost feared to see the painted horse dancing outside my door. Blood hammered in my head like drums.

And then to see Morgan, who had been so sad and stately these last weeks, gay as a skylark. It had always troubled me beyond reason that women old enough to be my grandmother, and weighed down with cares for most of the year, should hitch up their skirts and skip and cackle songs because the calendar said it was a holiday.

As soon as Morgan saw I was awake she laughed and darted out of the door.

I groaned. For years I had stumbled out of bed before winter sunrise to milk the cows. I thought I had done with that. But now it seemed I could be piskie-led by this black elf at any time of the day or night. Besides this was May-morning, and still almost dark. The hour must be very early.

I dressed quickly and hurried outside. She was nowhere to be seen. A grey sea-mist hung over everything. There was no one about. Even the birds were not stirring yet. I caught my breath. I felt that time had slipped, that between night and day, between winter and summer, we had floated into another place and century. Or into no time at all, beyond this world. Then I saw the dark hump of the chapel on the ledge above. Even now there might be someone at prayer there. We had warrior-nuns who could choose to wrestle all night with the devil at such a time as this. I clung to that thought.

The mist walled me round. The silhouettes of rocks loomed darkly through it, with almost human shapes. I listened for the sound of Morgan singing. But there was nothing now. Even the sea was hushed.

My first thought was that she would have run to the beach, the place I most feared. Even in sunlight I avoided it unless my duties took me there. It was too open to the sea and the mainland. I remembered those whispering shapes in the moonlight and quickly turned my thoughts away. The path down to the beach was silent this morning. And that held its own dread. The sky overhead was clearing. But below, the fog hung in a thick gloom over the cove. I could not nerve myself to enter it alone.

I climbed the short path to the plateau, convincing myself that I could scan more widely from there. And that, to my surprise, was where I came upon her, wandering through the dew-wet pasture as though she searched for something. Nun though I was, I knew what she was looking for. She would not find it. There were no may-trees on Tintagel Head.

I stood and watched her, while the first pink flush of dawn crept over the hills to the east and found its reflection in the western sea. The grey turned to blue. At any moment the bell would ring us to chapel. And still the girl darted about the field, running to every bush and turning away.

I held my breath as she neared those hollows in the rock. But she came back from them also, disappointed.

A sharp pain pierced my heart. I did not put a name to it. I looked around me. The grass at my feet was starred with flowers. I would not otherwise have noticed them. I picked a handful, and sat down to wait for Morgan. My fingers had grown smooth and delicate now I worked with the pen. With my nails I pierced the furry stems of primroses and wove into them the slender threads of stitchwort and violet. The garland lengthened in my lap. Far below me the brightening sea washed with the gentle ease of the new-come summer. One tiny fishing-boat was pulling out of the mist from our cove towards Barras Nose. Two specks of people in it. A man rowing. Another hooded figure crouched in the bows. The only living beings beside ourselves. A thought disturbed me. What were fishermen doing out at work on this high festival, before the dance was over and the Horse had blessed the sea for its summer harvest?

A shadow fell across my lap. Morgan was standing beside me, frowning, with empty hands. Kneeling to greet her, I lifted the chain of flowers and laid it on her shining black hair.

'Welcome, Summer,' I said.

Two powerful words that linked me to my mother and grandmother, and to all those other women far back beyond. Passed on by me now to my own foster-daughter.

Her eyes looked straight into mine, brightly green as wet moss on thatch. Long they gazed until I thought they would devour me. Then she smiled, very, very sweetly, as only Morgan can.

'Thank you, Luned. You have crowned me your queen.'

She looked away to the sea beyond the cove, and started.

Then her face split in laughter and she dragged me running after her. In vain I protested. Down over the slippery path and tussocked grass. Past the doors of cells where the nuns might already be waking. Down, down to the very edge of the sea where the ripples curled in creaming foam along the shingle.

Dawn had not come to the deep cove yet. It would be hours before the sun breasted its cliffs. The air had a damp, chill feel. Down here in the mist I could not see the sunrise gilding the sea towards Ireland.

This cove held always a shadow of danger for me. Beyond its narrow cliffs the cold waves came rolling in unbroken from the west. Strange ships came sailing into it. Merchants from foreign lands. I could no longer avoid them. Swarthy men who sprang on to the wharf and bargained with me in broken Latin. I had risen too high now to hide in my cell.

A road led down the coombe to this beach, below the high guard of ditch and bank. Here was no dangerous bridge set between us and the world. Anyone might come and go, beyond reach of a shout from the porter's lodge so far above. I always longed to retreat within Tintagel's defences.

Worse than these were the caves, black mouths endlessly sucking in the sea. I had a horror of their slimy darkness. But the one cave that was light I dreaded more than all. Through it I glimpsed another, wilder sea. I always feared the tide would come flooding through this tunnel and take me unawares from behind. I knew the tides obeyed the moon. I was studying the science of the stars. Reading about it in the world of books I understood their movements. But here, on the shore, seeing the slither of seaweed in the foam, I could not reason and calculate. I dreaded the unguessed rising of the tide. I only knew that twice every day, moon after moon, year after year, the sea was eating its way under the roots of the convent.

Morgan picked up a flat slate and skimmed it through the water as I had seen the Cornish sisters do. It was a game I had never learned. I tried. My pebble dropped heavily into the first wave and disappeared. Morgan laughed gaily. Her wrist flashed and the little stones went dancing through the green May-Day sea like laughing porpoises.

But she was restless. She began to clamber over the wet slabs of rocks past the caves.

'Come back!' I pleaded. I was as much afraid for myself as for her.

I lacked the power to stop her, so I must follow. Clumsy and inexperienced where she was confident.

The mist eddied. I rubbed my eyes. There was a flame in the gloom. We had come to the convent wharf, though by a dangerous path. A little fire burned on the stone, with a clean steady heat. There was a basket beside it.

Morgan dropped to her knees with a glad cry and lifted the cloth. My mouth was too dry to speak. Who had left this?

There was not much inside the basket. Two pilchards, wrapped in dock leaves. A loaf of bread.

'Oh, blessings upon her! They have not forgotten me. Wait! There must be something more.'

Her hands began to rummage in the basket. I tried to pull her away.

'Leave it alone. How do we know where this has come from?'

She turned her eyes up to me.

'I know who it has come from. You know.'

The little boat, pulling away round Barras Nose. Where but from Bossiney? Well, she had had little enough from her people since she came to us. It was a poor present for a king's stepdaughter.

I was too innocent, for all my pride and learning. Nuns humbler by far than I would have read the signs.

Morgan turned the fish over. She was right. There, nestling in the bottom of the basket, was a handful of hawthorn blossom. I even smiled for her, fool that I was. She seized the white flowers and thrust them into her crown. The thorns caught in her dark hair. She laughed at me with a fierce joy.

'There! I *am* a queen! They shall all of them see it now and know my power.'

I curtsied mockingly.

Morgan picked up a fish by the tail and tried to hold it over the fire.

'What are you doing?' I cried, shocked. 'A gift must always be shared. We must take this up to the kitchen.'

Again that sweet smile. The brilliant eyes that seemed to swallow mine.

'Please, Luned! There is only enough for two.'

She laid her hands over mine on the basket. I cannot explain to you the power in Morgan's hands. When they touched you, the world changed. It still does.

From far away I heard a bell chime sweetly. I could not tell if it came from the sky above or from the depths of the sea. I did not heed it.

I do not expect you to understand why I searched the rocks for driftwood. Why I showed her how to spear the fish and set them to cook safely over the raked embers.

Only when the sweet taste of flesh and bread was finished did I come to my senses with a cry of guilt.

'What are we doing here? It must be time for prayers. Hurry! We must not be late!'

She did not scramble to her feet. She looked up at me solemnly, the crown a little crooked now on her tangled hair.

'It is already too late for you, Luned. Far too late.'

From far above the morning hymn broke chanting on the air. Beyond the mist. Above the sea. A song of thankfulness for safe deliverance from the dark night.

I started to run towards it, up the steep path from the wharf to the convent. I staggered into the chapel gasping for breath. It was in vain. The smell of grilling fish had reached Bryvyth before I did.

# Chapter Thirteen

The abbess gave me no chance to confess. This time, I was beaten as well as Morgan. It roused me to fury. No one had ever beaten me before. As a child I had scorned naughtiness. The sting of my mother's tongue was punishment enough for any careless fault.

Out of my pain and indignation I tried to argue.

'I would have confessed to you. I would have done penance. When have I ever not? You gave me no time.'

I, Luned, scribe and steward of the convent, heard the break in my weak woman's voice. I knew the humiliation of tears spurting on to my cheeks. Bryvyth should have seen her rebuke was a wound bitter enough.

But she would not listen. She had a strong arm and a high temper to which she could not often give full rein. She did not spare me, or herself. When the beating was over, she broke the twigs across her knee and flung the pieces from her. Tears stood on her own brown cheeks.

'If I cannot trust even you, who is there left?' she cried. 'Did I make a mistake? Was I wrong to believe the women of the west could live like angels, wielding a flaming sword to guard the gates of paradise? Is it too hard to be as pure as skylarks, soaring ever heavenwards? Must you all go down into sin and idleness and disobedience, even you? Didn't you know it is May Day, when we need to be hammering at the gates of heaven for our immortal salvation? I am thinking it would be better for all of us if I took the child away from you and sent you back to the cows and kale.'

I could have taken the chance she gave me then. I could have been free of Morgan forever. I could have saved my soul. But my pride would not accept the disgrace.

'Give me one more chance,' I pleaded. 'I will not fail you again. Morgan is not lost yet. There is a child's heart there still, that we may reach with patience. For the first time today there was something different in the way she smiled at me. Not wickedly, but as though she was beginning to love me. It was for that smile that I listened to her pleading. Not out of weakness, but in the hope that I might reach her soul. Do not throw the chance away when a door is beginning to open between us.'

'Have a care, Luned! She comes of a treacherous mother. The darkness is in her blood. Let it not be you that is beginning to change. Guard your own soul first if you would be tough enough to do battle with her.'

She understood Morgan's ways better than I who had lived with her day and night. I deceived myself, because I wanted the praise of victory. Morgan loves only one, and him she can never have. She uses the love of all others to their destruction. And with each fall her power increases.

At the door Bryvyth grasped my arm. In the urgency of her voice there was pleading now. Not for my actions alone, but for her own, just past. For my understanding, forgiveness even. That was not necessary. Did she not see that I dreamed of being an abbess myself one day? I should be hard, as she was hard. My Lord was the Christ of the desert who did battle with devils. I do not think I would have beaten my nuns. Physical contact is repellent to me. But my tongue would have been harsher than my mother's chiding. A whip and goad to drive the steep, rough road that leads to heaven.

My thoughts were winging to the future, rebuilding that dream out of the wreckage of my present humiliation. I hardly heeded Bryvyth's voice.

'Never again, eh, Luned? No more maidens washing in the dew. No more maying. No more fishing for pilchards. No more breakfasting on the beach when you should be in chapel praying. We are fishing for souls here, girl. Never forget that.'

She must have felt the tremor in my arm. Suddenly she swept me to her chest in a great bear-hug. Her own voice was not entirely steady.

'There, girl. Don't cry. It is over. I have forgiven you. Seventy times seven I'd forgive you, if only you'll promise to fight the battle alongside me and not run away.'

And all the time her strong hard hand was stroking my hair, my face was buried against the rough wool of her tunic and I was saying to myself incredulously, 'Then she doesn't know the half of it! She has beaten me till the skin split and the blood came, and she thinks that all I did was weave flowers and eat pilchards with Morgan on the beach. Can it really be that no one has told her what came to our cove? Was it only my eyes that could see those white spirits on the cliff and that fishing-boat pulling out of the mist? Does she still not know that Tintagel has had visitors?'

And, may the devil take me, I dared not tell her. I did not confess. Then, or ever. When the only human strength that could have stood between me and Morgan clasped me to her breast, I closed my lips.

I was afraid to speak. Knowing now that in spite of everything Bryvyth still loved me, still wished me reinstated in her trust, I dared not uncover this further, darker sin. She must not know that someone else had left those gifts for Morgan.

I was more afraid yet of those visitants, seemingly invisible except to me. Had they really only been humans from Bossiney? If not, I had eaten their food. I had put myself under their power. It would be more dangerous still to speak of them.

And most of all, that bright May-morning, I was afraid of Morgan. Not, then, of the harm she might do me. Afraid, rather, of what she might not do. Afraid that the sweet gay smile that for the first time had seemed truly to come out of her heart for me, might never dawn again. I believed I had had a taste of Morgan's love that morning. I wanted more. I live my life now in her service. I have seen her bend that smile on others to enchant them. Morgan has never smiled like that for me again. Yet I cannot forget. I go on serving her, though love has curdled.

So I did not even listen to Bryvyth's warning.

Morgan met me stony-faced. She had not cried after her own beating. She never cried, this child who was not yet ten. I could see she despised me for weeping.

As the world judges, Morgan must count among the losers in life. She had lost father, home, her mother's love, even her life itself was threatened by Uther's ban. But she had this which marked her out from all other victims. She would not believe that she had lost. Long before she had an earthly crown she carried herself like a queen. She would not allow those who had power over her the satisfaction of seeing her cry.

We kept our own holiday on Tintagel. Bryvyth had made a play for the children. Saint George and his white Horse battled with the Dragon, and the saint got the victory. The princesses of Cymru looked unhappy. They are Dragon people. But the Horse-women of Cornwall shouted for the white Mare till the gulls took off into the air, screaming. Rathtyen looked disapproving of both sides. I shared her view. It was too like the old ways for Christian children to dress up in the masks and skins of beasts, and for nuns to beat the drums and play the pipes and cheer the swordplay. Morgan laughed and clapped harder than anyone when the white Mare rode down the Dragon and the saint's sword went through his heart.

The long day ended and we came together in my cell.

That night I helped Morgan undress. There was no need for it. Morgan was accustomed now to care for herself. I had the charge of her soul but little thought for her body. I was not Gwennol.

Yet that night, I cannot say how it was, my hands reached for her clothes and drew them over her head. Her hair smelt of violets. Her flesh was warm from the day's sun. My hands lingered. Then I gasped as I touched the wounds on her back. They were as cruel as my own, and she was only a child. She did not speak, or pull away. It was not yet dark. Her face was still, without trace of movement, though her flesh had quivered at my touch.

I would not deceive you, seeming to mean more than I say. I wished to hold her, but I did not.

# Chapter Fourteen

Others stole Morgan from me.

We returned to our work, she to the school, I to the library. I missed her. I could not concentrate. The room that had been a haven of peace now imprisoned me. My desk did not allow me to see across the path. I listened for the sound of children's voices. The murmur of reading and the scratching of pens deafened me.

For months the bell that sounded the end of our labours had chilled me. I must put away the tasks I loved, the ordered world of books and figures, to attend to a violent, unpredictable child. This day it was different. I was like a dog pricking up its ears at its mistress's footsteps. At once I tidied away the abacus, the pens, the tablets. Eira was startled to see me move so quickly. I who was always so calm and dignified.

'What is the matter with you? Is it the flux? Too much fish for breakfast, perhaps?'

Her laughter was not malicious, but other sisters had enjoyed the knowledge that I was fallible, and had fallen from grace.

I did not answer her. I am never ready with repartee. I hardly understood myself the swiftness of my feet as I hurried from the library. I expected to see Morgan ahead of me on the path to our cell.

It was my rule that she should meet me there when the day's work was over. I would question her stiffly about the lessons she had learned. She would answer me easily, even scornfully. She was a clever girl. Already there were times when I learned from her some knowledge that my own late schooling had not yet opened to me. I tried to hide my ignorance from her. I did not wish her to think me less than her teachers. I do not think I deceived her.

Today she was nowhere to be seen ahead of me. I scanned the crowd of boys and girls running to play. Morgan with her raven's-wing hair was always noticeable. She was not with them.

A strange panic took me, such as they say a mother feels for her newborn baby. Had she been taken ill, and no one had told me? Eira was right. People had died after eating tainted food. Fool that I was to have trusted any gift that came from Bossiney!

Or was she well but in trouble, kept in the schoolroom by Rathtyen, to be summoned again to Bryvyth? But I saw Rathtyen climbing slowly away from the school. I noted that she moved stiffly as though walking pained her. Well, the damp cliffs of Cornwall are the cause of many aches.

Morgan would be indoors, out of sight. I rushed into my cell. She had not been there. The door had been latched and her bed was still neat from the morning. I could not give a name to my agitation. Two days ago I would have feared only that she might be making more trouble for me. Now my fears were for Morgan herself. I cared.

Deliberately, trying not to be seen to hurry, I traced the twisting paths of the convent. They zigzagged to and fro across the cliff, rising to little terraces with clusters of cells, levelling out to larger buildings like our refectory, dipping to the shore or climbing to the fields on the summit.

I found her at last. Sitting on the doorstep of Fyna's cell. They were talking earnestly. You might have thought it was another lesson.

Fyna was a nun younger than I. She had come to the convent scarcely two years before. She came from the moors of Cornwall, of a druid family. That was not surprising. There were still some in Cornwall guarding their secret scholarship when the Romans left. They watched the power of the Church growing: the learning, the healing, the priesthood. Some of the wise among them made common cause with us and were baptised. It was natural that such a family should send a daughter to Tintagel to get wisdom and to give it.

Already Fyna was a noted herbalist. It was a science that made me uneasy. I was sharp of eye and accurate in matters of detail. I could quickly learn to identify plants for my needs. Rose madder, sphagnum moss, woad, all the plants we used to concoct paints and inks. But I did not enjoy the blending of precisely the right tint, as Eira did. It was enough for me that my ink was smooth and serviceable and I could get directly to my task. Still less did I like to think of brewing medicines, tasting, administering the measured dose. I should have been scrupulous in identification and apportionment of weights, but I would have feared the practice. There is gain, but there is also risk. The heart not merely stimulated but racing to destruction. A sleep too deep ever to waken. The poison that kills not only the disease but the diseased. Morgan knows I dread such work and therefore delights to make me do it now.

Fyna showed no such dread. Her face was smooth as a child's. Pink cheeks and clear blue eyes. Those eyes smiled at me now. Round, innocent. Why should they not be? Where was the harm in what they were doing? If her work in the infirmary was not heavy it was common for Fyna to turn from curing the sick to nursing the youngest children, little ones just taken from their families, homesick and snivelling. She laughed with them and jogged them on her knee, and they played with the pretty hair that escaped from her veil. But Morgan was not a tearful infant, nor was she sick, unless you count the weals on her back. So I saw the two of them, heads bent together, with a start of anger. I did not recognise it then by the name of jealousy. I called her to me sharply. I did not notice that day if there were leaves and flowers on the step between them. There may have been. There may not.

Morgan came with me meekly. Fyna made no attempt to delay her. She only smiled at me, wider.

It was the first of many meetings. I could not prevent them. What could I have said? She talked with a nun who had taken the same vows as I had. She appeared earnest and attentive. She was not disobedient.

Next week it was Ughella, also recently come. She had taken my place with the cattle. Dark. Yellow-faced. But with a deep, bell-true voice. Already Bryvyth was planning to make her our cantor. She would lead us to glorify God with the beauty of her chanting. I found her singing to Morgan in the cow-byre. It was no hymn I knew, though they broke off before I came close enough to hear the words. Again they greeted me courteously, without resentment.

Another time, frantic with worry, I came upon her at last in the most unlikely place of all. The holy hermit Piala had made her cell in a hole in the rocks on the furthest point of Tintagel's cliffs, facing the wind. She came to the convent only to worship on Sundays. She ate almost nothing. Her body was angular, crippled by penances, her face deep-lined and gaunt, but luminous with the rigour of her rule and the intensity of her devotion. I did not admire her. Do not mistake me. I was punctilious in prayer, from the first thanksgiving when I awoke to the commending of my soul in sleep. I loved the order of the set forms of service, the common words sealing me into the great empire of the Church. But I felt no desire for contemplation. I was not one of those nuns who sat for hours perched on some distant rock, staring out at the sea and sky or stood waist-deep in cold water, praying.

Morgan was crouched outside Piala's cave, asking her questions, like the young Jesus at the feet of Gamaliel.

Once my first resentment was past, I began to understand this change in her. I could see the reason for her hunger for learning. She had no friend. Even her followers had dropped away from her after Howel's death. Tintagel was a close prison for a girl who had such a store of physical and mental energy. I even felt proud of my foster-daughter. I yearned for knowledge myself. No day was too heavy that I did not wish to fill my leisure hours with study. I despised play and gossip and idleness. I rejoiced to think that Morgan was becoming more like me, leaving the silly games of children for the serious company and wisdom of adults. It merely pained me to see her seek this help from others and not from me.

Yet I disguised my hurt humbly till the day I discovered she was going to Blatriad, our cook, and to others like her. Sisters of peasant stock who would never rise above the kitchen or the farm.

'Why?' I burst out. 'Why them? What in heaven's name can women like that teach you?'

Her face was sternly serious.

'Things that otherwise might be forgotten.'

I could not help myself. I had suffered the injury too long.

'Why always others? Why do you never want to learn from me?'

She seemed surprised, innocent, as only those who know how to wound can look.

'You? What could you teach me?'

It was like a slap in the face. Could even fat Blatriad

have more to offer than I? I pulled out the book I was studying and thrust it under her nose. The theorems of Euclid.

'There! Has even Rathtyen taught you this? The logical proofs of the geometry of the plane? Listen. I will tell you the first hypotheses. All else flows from them, like a mighty river from a few small springs.'

For a little while she listened, blankly. Then she pushed the book out of my hands and grasped them.

'Where is the power in that? Will it change the world? What is the knowledge you really treasure, Luned?'

'What do you mean? This is the wisdom of the Greeks. The greatest philosophers of the East.'

'Games. Toys for idle minds. *Power*, Luned. Where is power to be found?'

I felt my blood quicken, as it did when they summoned me to bargain with a merchant at the gate, as it would when I tallied the yield of the coming harvest from all our farms and calculated our profit or loss. But how could I tell the child that? I, a nun, vowed to poverty and simplicity.

'Power is in the Word made flesh, in Christ's crucifixion, in his rising from the dead.'

Did I live by that?

What had Piala answered? And what had Blatriad?

From that day I found myself looking into my sisters' faces. I am not one to observe others. When we met together my eyes had been for the cross and the holy altar, or for my book. Nevertheless I came out of the oratory one day after the liturgy. It had been a night of storm but it was now a bright morning. We left the chapel two by two, in the order of our seniority. After Bryvyth came old Blatriad from the kitchen with Rathtyen. Younger nuns like Ughella and Fyna walked behind me. Yet on the path beyond the door this pattern dissolved, changed, reformed into different groupings.

It was as if there were cracks running haphazardly through our community, separating some from others. I tried to make sense of it. Hens and eagles? Nobles and peasants? Foolish and wise? I could not determine the pattern.

Bryvyth was waiting for me with that broad, open grin of hers.

'Did you think you heard thunder in the night? They tell me there's another great slab of cliff fallen to the sea. One day we'll wake up and find we've lost the bridge that links us to the world. Do you want to come with me and inspect the damage?'

She knew I had never lost my terror of the heights.

It had been on the tip of my tongue to tell her what Morgan was asking. It was the abbess alone who held our community together, rejoicing in our differences, making them work for wholeness. How would Bryvyth have answered Morgan? But I would have to expose how little Morgan esteemed me, her soul-friend. I shook my head in confusion Bryvyth misunderstood.

She clapped me on the shoulder merrily.

'Why so green-faced, Luned? Are you afraid that next time the rock falls you'll be standing on the wrong side of the crack?'

# Chapter Fifteen

I expected it. I make no excuse of ignorance. I was brought up a country girl. A pagan. I had lived by the hinges of the seasons, though I tried to close my mind to those memories. I knew they would come again at harvest-time, that to them was Lughnasad. I held myself ready. Bryvyth had chosen me for this task. I was determined to fight this battle alone, and win.

I tried to hold them off by prayer. I kept vigil through the night, standing and prostrate. I knew Morgan was watching me.

That last night in July it scarcely grew dark. The sea seemed to hold the light, like a sheen of pearl. As I stared with heavy eyes and aching, lifted arms at the imperceptible paling of the sky, I knew that August had come. The blazing wheel would soon be on us.

There was a movement behind me. Quite slowly and deliberately, Morgan was pulling a tunic over her shift. This was the moment I had been armouring myself for.

'Go back to bed,' I ordered, my voice dry with praying.

She walked towards me. I barred the door with my body.

'I must go now.' Her voice was quiet, almost dutiful.

'I forbid it.'

I felt my blood beating faster. Power was rising in me. Her hand came up and caught my arm. She tried to twist me aside. I was heavier than she was. We struggled in silence, save for the panting of our breath. I felt degraded, outraged that she had driven me to physical violence. But I was winning. I flung her back on to her bed.

At once I was frightened of what I had done. I backed away. She knelt and stared at me, but when she spoke her voice was almost pleading.

'I cannot help it. She is calling me. I *have* to go to her.'

Morgan was coming at me again. Panic was rising in me. Why did she not scream and shout? If only she would not fix on me that silent intensity, like a sleep-walker.

We sprang at each other. She wrestled savagely. This time I thought I would lose. My body was stronger than hers, but there was a spirit within her driving her to a frenzy. When I hurled her to her knees, we were both scratched and bruised. There was a lock of her hair in my fist. I could not remember pulling at it.

I watched her rise for a third time, unsteadily, nursing her arm. In the faint light from the doorway I saw the red weals on her flesh, the mark of my fingers. My stomach twisted with sickness. This was not the fight I had planned.

She came closer. I could smell the sweet childish scent of her, and my own rank sweat. I fought for breath.

Her eyes looked up into mine. Shining, with a hint of tears.

'Go back to bed,' I panted.

'I cannot.'

There was a short step between us. She had not crossed it yet. She went on gazing at me as if she was waiting for something.

A great weariness came over me. How long must I go on fighting her? How much must I hurt her? I was not Bryvyth. I was not made to shout and spank and then hug her to my bosom.

Morgan still looked up at me. Tears started from the corners of her eyes and rolled down her cheeks. I do not know why.

She took my wrist, quite gently, and moved it from the door-frame. Still she stood waiting, as if I had disappointed her in some way. I felt humiliated.

'Let me come with you,' I muttered.

She gave a little sigh. 'You cannot help me.'

Yet she did not stop me. I followed her down the path in the grey silence before dawn. She went quite slowly. Once she stopped and looked up towards the furthest headland.

'I wonder if Piala is at prayer now.'

At the foot of the cliffs there is a natural ledge of rock. It is a good anchorage. Even when the gales sweep up the channel from the west, ships may lie safely there.

We stood without speaking on the wharf. That August morning the grey-green water of the cove was mirror-smooth. Beyond the rocks the waves were hardly moving. It had been a dry summer. There was hardly a wisp of vapour in the cove.

Morgan did not play games this time. She was not laughing.

Time passed slowly. It seemed to me that we had been hours abroad and still there was no colour in the sky. A fairy world. A fairy time.

I rubbed my eyes. The light was strengthening. I saw a single dot on the page of the ocean between the headlands. It might have been the head of a seal, but I knew it was not. I watched it, tense and troubled. With infinite slowness it became a coracle pulling into the cove.

There were two people in it. One of them rowing. A smaller hooded one hunched in the stern. I felt that all this had happened to me before.

'Help me, Luned,' said Morgan faintly.

But when I tugged at her arm I could not move her.

'Come away, quickly!' I urged. 'Let us run and tell Bryvyth.'

We had stayed too long. I had betrayed my trust.

The boat bumped softly against the wharf. An old woman's hand shot out of the fold of her cloak and clutched at the stone. Morgan shivered.

'What's the matter? It's only me, my lover. Come to Gwennol.'

Gwennol. The child's nurse from Bossiney, her arms clasped round Morgan as they parted in the guesthouse.

The woman was small and bent. She moved with difficulty. Why did I suddenly remember that day when the Pendragon's war-host had been ranged along the skyline? Why did I feel that Tintagel had been invaded?

'What have they done to you, my lamb? There's blood on her little face.'

Morgan's hand explored the scratches of our struggle. She stared at the stain on her fingers. But her other hand gripped mine. She had not stirred from where she stood.

I was never brave. But I call Heaven to witness that I used all my courage then. I cried out. 'This is a holy place. Go away and leave the child in peace.'

Throwing Morgan off, I heaved at the boat to push it out to sea.

The old woman caught my wrist, dragging me almost over the edge as the silent rower spun the boat back.

'Oh, yes! It's a holy place, and a holy day, and I'm a holy woman!'

I summoned all my piety and faith. I called on the threefold name of God to save us.

Gwennol heard me out. Then she raised her other hand towards me, her fingers spread and jabbing. I did not understand the words that poured from her, but in the depths of my being I recognised their purpose. They struck my hastily-constructed rampart of prayer a shuddering blow at its foundations. I was not always a Christian. I felt my faith collapsing into darkness.

She grinned and let me go. My wrist burned from the grip of her claws.

'Come here, my sweetheart.'

All this time Morgan had not moved. Then, as I reeled back, it seemed as if she could contain herself no longer. She dashed to the boat and grabbed at Gwennol.

'The baby, Gwennol? What news is there of Arthur?'

'Your little brother? He won't come back. His parents will never see him again, my lamb, don't you fret. Merlyn's got him safe and sound somewhere.'

'Not safe enough from me. Not safe enough from me forever. One day I shall find him. I will! I will!'

'There, there! Your time will come.'

The old crone murmured over her. The weeping stopped. Morgan was her small, proud self again.

'It'll soon be sun-up.'

The boatman's face was creased and brown as an oiled wood-craving. He settled to the oars and the coracle pulled out in widening rings of ripples. The first flush of pink was staining the eastern sky. When the boat had dwindled out of sight Morgan turned to me, mocking now.

'Let us run, Luned! We must not be late for prayers again, must we? It would never do for Bryvyth to catch us with this.'

Her hands were clasping a leather pouch.

# Chapter Sixteen

Morgan sat crosslegged in the bright morning sunshine outside our cell. As I came closer she put her hands over her lap. It was a ritual gesture. She did not prevent me seeing what was in her skirt. A heap of twigs, each one different from the rest. Grey, tawny, knotted, smooth, even the sere stem of a reed. Some I could name easily, others more doubtfully. I did not know then the wisdom they spelt.

Morgan looked me full in the face, challenging me.

'Will you tell Bryvyth?'

For a girl of ten she read the minds of adults all too clearly.

I should have answered firmly 'Yes' and not prevaricated.

I could not disguise my scratches from Bryvyth, or Morgan's either. She looked us all over. Her keen eyes seemed to miss nothing. I was sure that what we had done must be transparent. I even felt relief that my failure would be unclothed without my needing to speak a word.

'Hm! I think the oats in the west field may be ready for cutting. I'll see you there.'

I was about to protest that this was a feast day. A rest from the regulation of the convent farms. Between the hours of liturgy I had a pile of books I wished to study. But there was something in the set of her jaw that kept me silent.

The ripe oats rustled against our skirts. Bryvyth tested

the grains between her fingers absentmindedly. I knew that that was not why we were here.

'So Gorlois's kitten is not tamed yet. Is there something you should be telling me?'

As I climbed to the plateau my thoughts had been running around the walls of my mind, like a mouse looking for a hole through which to escape.

'An evil spirit visited her last night. I wrestled mightily against it.'

'And which of you won?'

'I never left her side. She cried to me for help. She held my hand. I called upon the name of the Trinity. At dawn the spirit left her.'

Could she not tell that I was begging her to see how I deceived her, speaking the truth, but not the whole of it? She was too open, too honest, too full of fight herself to understand the deviousness of others.

She threw her arms round me in one of her joyous hugs.

'Ah, Luned, girl! I did right, after all. Sometimes I've wondered if you're too pale and prissy for the fight I've given you. But I saw the mettle in you from the first. You came to us a peasant, but you had never a cowherd's mind. You were pagan-born, but you made a pilgrimage to the city of God. I knew you would not desert this battle until you had won.

'But I must see that hell-cat, Morgan. Gorlois's daughter she may be, rest his soul, but I will not have her wounding her foster-mother.'

We walked down the hill with the sun hot in our faces. Bryvyth was swinging along with her energetic stride. I think she relished the notion of combat.

Bryvyth failed me. She was my abbess. My mother in God. She had the care of my soul. She should have seen my inadequacy, my lying silence. She could have saved me.

Morgan did not betray me. She knew the victory was

hers. I was under her power. She bore the birching in silence.

Even then I made one last struggle. I took those sticks from under Morgan's pillow. I feared to touch them. There were marks scored through the bark, stained with sap. They were like no figures or letters I had seen before. I took the wood to the kitchen fire. I even moved a turf aside and the red flame leaped out at me. But at the last I did not have the courage to drop those holy rods into the glowing charcoal. I knew it was my own fingers that would burn. I crept back to our cell, shaking at the thought of my impiety. I wrapped them in the pouch and hid them where I had found them. The scent of their sap clung to my hands long afterwards.

The boat came again to the cove where no strangers should land. To the beach that should be holy, but was too open to the world. Yet it seemed to me that they were not strangers enough to that place. I would have feared them less if they had been truly more of the common world outside. In their own dark way they were holier than I dared to admit to myself.

They came not once but many times. All Hallows Eve. Candlemas. May Day. But to them it was Samain, Imbolc, Beltaine.

I could not bring myself to wrestle bodily with Morgan a second time. It could only have ended one way, and I would have had to explain my scars again to Bryvyth. There must be no evidence against me. I ceased to fight with Morgan. I heard her rise from her bed. I let her go. I tried to pretend to myself that I could not stop her, that I was powerless to move, that the girl had laid a spell of binding on me. Perhaps she had. So I closed my eyes and listened to my foster-daughter slipping away into the half-light.

I feared to follow her. I was not strong enough to battle with those others. I lay defeated, shamed by my cowardice, while the sky lightened towards dawn and her bed beside mine grew cold. She would come tiptoeing back in the grey of morning with her feet wet and her white shift muddied and stop by my bed with a mocking smile. Always her hands were clasping some gift.

After a while my prayers shrivelled into silence. Perhaps the words had never really held a meaning for me. While she was gone, I even slept a little. I wished to close my mind to the truth. I did not want to lie awake and wonder what was being done on the shore.

I came to dread those festivals.

Yet Morgan was outwardly more dutiful than ever in the schoolroom and the chapel. She was getting taller now. I would watch the ranks of the convent schoolgirls where she stood, black-haired, white-faced, growing more beautiful with every month. Singing the words, but staring often out to sea.

For two years I did not confess my failure, through outward pride and inward humiliation. I did not pass the burden back to Bryvyth, who believed in Christ's power to save with her whole heart.

It brought me no thanks from Morgan. She despised me.

Then, one October night, the voices began again. This time it was clearly at Morgan's will. She was sitting up in bed, her fingers plaiting and unplaiting three hairy cords, that Gwennol had given her. She stared not at me but towards me, opened her sweet small mouth and began to chant.

At first it was her voice. Clear and hard. Then as her eyes burned in her head and her fingers flew faster the voice deepened, altered. It was a man, a beast, a baby, then things terrible, shapeless, not of this world or time. I clapped my hands over my ears. I shut my eyes. I sobbed for terror. When the room fell quiet and I dared to look up, she was sitting there. White. Rigid. Eyes fixed ahead as before. But not staring. Blank. No life in them. I nerved myself to touch her hand. She was cold. I panicked then. I shook her, threw my arms round her, hugged her, called, screamed. Then instantly hushed myself, trembling lest anyone should discover her so. I thought she was dead. I feared more that she was not. At last I tore my arms away. I threw myself into my bed and crawled under the blankets. I lay huddled there, curled like an infant, terrified.

When the long night had passed and I rose again with a stale taste in my mouth, Morgan was in her bed sleeping. The colour was back in her cheeks, like a wild rose. The breath eased gently from her lips and the tendrils of her dark hair curled over her neck. She looked very lovely, very young. You would have thought her innocent. There was a sharp contraction deep in my body and I longed to gather her in my arms and hug her again, this time for joy. Instead I shook her by the shoulder.

'It is time for morning prayers.'

Fear drove me to tell Bryvyth now. It was not duty. Not love for Morgan, or for Christ. I feared to be left alone with Morgan on Samain Eve. I spun a tale for Bryvyth. I recalled my past struggle with Morgan, as if it was a thing long done with. I said she had babbled something in her trance to warn me she might try to leave the convent that night. Bryvyth believed me.

On the eve of Samain she came to my cell. She was a big woman, and she looked stronger still, standing in the doorway against the yellow evening sky. My heart yearned towards her, and what she represented. If only I could always lean on her. If only I could rest from struggle and let the strength of those shoulders carry all my burdens. But I could not. She loved me for the strength she believed we shared, not for my weakness. I dared not disillusion her.

Together we did an awful thing. We bound Morgan. It took the full strength of both of us to do it. Her screams must have appalled the convent. She had never once cried out through a hundred beatings. But she raged against those ropes as though her heart would break. I was sick with the sound of her bitterness, and Bryvyth scarcely less so.

Neither of us slept. In the hour before dawn Morgan lay rigid. When I spoke to her she gave no sign of hearing. I was afraid to touch her. I was frightened lest the soul had gone out of her body and waking might kill her. She has that dangerous druid power now, and uses it. I was not certain if she had it then.

Bryvyth made me follow her down to the shoreline.

There was a circle of water, like glass, reflecting the cliffs. Beyond, a haze of autumn mist walled us in. It was very still, very quiet. I watched the coracle coming slowly out of the fog. It was so like my memory of the first time, I thought I might be dreaming it. I looked around to see if it was happening in reality or only in my own mind.

I could not see the slopes of Tintagel above us. No one but ourselves would know what passed.

Bryvyth stood on the beach, arms folded across her chest, silent. Her face was grim. It gave no flutter of recognition.

The coracle came on. I watched Gwennol's face now, brown, lined, fixed on Bryvyth's. Morgan was in my cell, bound on her bed. She could not be here. And yet she was. I saw her. The small body of a girl in a white shift, floating in the shallow grey-green water over the shingle. Black hair spreading slowly just beneath the surface, eyes closed, face pale as death, between those two grim women. They did not seem to see her, and yet she lay between them. They faced each other over her gently rocking body and still, drowned face. I watched in horror.

Then Bryvyth spoke. She lifted her hand above her head and made the sign of the cross.

'In the name of the great and glorious Trinity. By the power of the Father who created the thunder. By the strength of Christ who harrowed Hell. By the flame of the Spirit that drives out evil. Be gone forever.'

The boat checked. The rower was straining at the oars, but it would not move across the intervening water. Gwennol was murmuring curses of her own, too low for me to hear her, with a sound like the growling of a cat.

The surface of the cove began to shake. I saw a horrible thing. Morgan's face and form began to splinter and disintegrate. I think I screamed.

'Set one foot on this holy shore again and I'll have Uther Pendragon hound you out of your hole in Bossiney, cut out your tongue so you can cast no more spells, string you up on a sycamore tree till you're half-hanged and burn your body on your own bonfire.'

The mist crawled about us, thickened across the cove, crept round the boat. I could only see Bryvyth now, massive as a boulder, white-gowned against the dark mouth of a cave beyond her. Her fists were clenched.

'By the might of St Michael, who cast down the devils from high Heaven. By the fire of Patrick, who confounded the druids at Tara. By the sword of St George, who slew the dragon. Go to him who begat you!'

The waves broke on the stones with a hiss of foam. We could see nothing now but fog. Oars creaked, bumped rock, were still. Bryvyth and I waited, and the sweat was clammy on my face. Ages passed. The sun bored a hole through the mist over our heads. Tintagel Haven was empty again, its water like satin. The two of us were alone on the beach. Bryvyth was trembling.

When I staggered back to my cell, sick and spent, Morgan was still there where I had left her, her eyes closed, her face turned to the wall. I should have been overjoyed, confident that Bryvyth had won the victory. But all I could see was the blood on her wrists and the clenched knuckles of her hands.

# Chapter Seventeen

I undid the ropes. Morgan lay so still while my fingers fumbled with the knots, she might have been a block of wood. Yet her skin was hot where I could not help but brush against it. I was afraid of her vengeance.

I thought too highly of myself. I was nothing to her. I was not even worth a furious word. She darted past me into the open air. I feared she would dash for that terrible beach or even fling herself over the cliff into the sea. But she went skimming like a dark swallow up to the summit and over the meadow.

I ran after her. Nuns gathering before prayers turned their heads to stare. I was humiliated again. I saw the wasted years crumbling to ashes. It was like that first day she came. Nothing had been gained.

But I was wrong. I had not guessed where she was going. Her flight ended at the very edge of the headland, the cave of Piala the hermit. When I came close Morgan was gasping out her story between sobs. Piala speaks rarely but she talked with Morgan then. I did not hear her words.

Bryvyth came striding up behind me, panting. We watched the two, girl and woman, prostrate themselves on the damp cliff-edge among the gorse.

'Leave them alone,' Bryvyth said, 'but watch her.'

All day I sat, a chill sentinel. When the chapel bell rang I mouthed the psalms. I was numb with cold. Bryvyth herself brought me food and drink. Morgan took nothing. She and Piala had not moved from their attitude of prayer.

Bryvyth muttered, 'It is not natural for a girl of twelve. It's either a saint or a sorceress we've got on our hands.'

Why did she give Morgan to me?

I was strict with myself. I rose before dawn. I kept the fasts. I was exact in every observance. But I did not lacerate my body as the hermit did. It disturbed me to think of Morgan's white flesh lying there in the wind, pierced by thorns of furze.

Thick cloud shortened the November day. Piala rose at last. I felt the pain as Morgan staggered to her feet.

I thought she would come home with me then. But she began to walk quite slowly along the cliffs. I followed her. For a while she stood, gazing over the bay towards Bossiney. Then she started to clamber down towards the shore, not by any path the feet of nuns had made, but climbing over boulders and slithering down the grass.

Fear was rising in my throat, physical dread of the steep drop beneath me, anxiety as to what she intended. The tide was high. Mounds of dark water heaved over the rocks. Morgan had hitched her skirt up round her hips. In the dying light she was searching frantically. I saw her disappear into the huge mouth of a cave. I heard her cry of triumph.

I met her on the treacherous wet rock outside. There was something in her hands. She did not try to hide it. I forced myself to look. A bundle of herbs and roots, tied with a scarlet thread. And I had thought we had won!

What I did next was rash. I am intelligent but my mind works slowly and with calculation. Any actions I make in haste are usually at fault. I tried to snatch the evil gift from her. She resisted me. We struggled on the slippery rocks. There could only be one end. She had spent her childhood running wild along the shore under the too-indulgent eye of her nurse. I grew dizzy over the smallest height. Stiff, awkward in my physical movements, I slipped, skidded, scraped my knees painfully over the rocks and plunged into deep, cold water.

Morgan did not rush to save me. I was not Gwennol staggering on the edge of the bridge between Tintagel's nuns and Uther's army. She let me fall, and did not stay to see whether I drowned.

I could not swim. Why should I ever have learned such a thing? I gasped and choked on salt water and terror. I clung to the rock, rasping my fingertips as I clawed for a hold. But it seemed the sea wanted me no more than Morgan did. Breakers tore me from my hold, washed me forward, engulfed my despairing head. Then they cast me up, scornfully, on the sloping shingle. I crawled to shore, all the wet weight of my woollen gown bearing me down, and the water running in rivers from my sodden hair.

Morgan had gone.

I staggered back to my cell, avoiding the paths. I hauled myself up grassy slopes hidden from view, with the sick knowledge of the drop growing beneath me. I was sobbing with shame and cold and shock.

Morgan was not in the cell. I was almost witless now, and shivering. Her presence would have terrified me yet her absence chilled me more than my wet clothes. So far was I under her influence, that waif of twelve years old, that I could do nothing but sit huddled on my bed, towelling myself as the twilight deepened and the owls began to call.

She came at last, with a puckish smile on her face. Her hands were cupped around a small clay pot which gave off a sickly steam.

She set it down on the floor and put her arms round me. I trembled at her touch. Her voice was like honey.

'Poor Luned. You're cold and shivering. Sip this. It will warm you.'

I retched at the smell of the brew she was carrying to my lips.

'Drink some. I must know what it does.'

I turned away and clenched my teeth. One does not take that sort of gift from Morgan.

She smiled, her teeth like white pearls in the twilight.

'Silly Luned! What are you frightened of? If you were to die and Uther heard of it, he would have me burned, wouldn't he? Well, never mind. There are two sick cows in the byre, poor things. Better to test its power on one of them.'

She was gone again. Without the ropes I had no power to hold her. The smell of that brew lingered in the room. I shuddered. Two of our best milch-cows were ailing. I had summoned Fyna to dose them. I had even turned to old Blatriad's memory for help. But the beasts still hung their heads in their stalls, nostrils dribbling, coughing mournfully. Cattle are valuable.

When she came back she threw her arms around me and kissed me gaily. I had longed for that for two cold years. But it gave me no pleasure now. It was as if a snake had coiled itself about me.

I woke next morning to find her shaking my shoulder.

'Quick, Luned! Wake up. Do you have a wax tablet? A scrap of parchment? I need to write.'

'Don't be silly. Those things are kept in the library or the schoolroom. I do not have a store of them in my cell.'

She slipped in bed with me. Her arms twined round my neck.

'Please, Luned. I must set it down before I forget.'

I wondered at her insistence. Was it a poem that had come to her suddenly, like the ones that Cigfa scribbled in the margins of her books? Or a dream that had visited her in the night which she must catch?

I felt my body quicken strangely at her urgency. I pushed her away from me with the horror of what I

could not name. She made a face and was off again in
the dawn light. I hurried after her to the door. Would she
steal what she wanted from the library now, as she had
the bowl last night from the kitchen? But she was coming
back already. Tintagel is rich in flat grey slates. She
carried one in her hand. Swiftly she scratched charac-
ters on it, a growing list.

I looked over her shoulder. She made no move to con-
ceal her work. It was a catalogue of those things she had
used last night. Their names, the quantities, her method
of preparation.

She smiled at me wickedly.

'What is the matter, Luned? Do you want to be wise?'

I should have destroyed it. Or taken it to Fyna, to see
what she knew of such things. Or told Bryvyth. I did none
of those things. I feared to touch that piece of slate, as
though the words themselves held the same dangerous
power as the things they recorded. Just so, we felt a
sense of the holy when we handled our Gospel books
reverently. I said nothing.

I feared Bryvyth's censure. Younger nuns were entering the convent. Rosslyn had come into the library after
me. Quickly she learned to mix the inks and paints, to
prepare the wax tablets. Now she was learning to write
a fair hand. In a few years she would be copying Latin
and Greek. She would be scraping vellum to cut the
pages of her first Psalter. Even the blessed Gospels
might be hers to beautify one day.

Not mine. I would never pen the Gospels now. I had
made myself too useful. I saw that sisters who could turn
a capital letter into a fancy of nature, who could trace
the convolutions of a spiral and embroider in silver, who
could talk easily of Aristotle and Augustine, could still
be daunted by rows of figures and the clicking of the
abacus.

I had a gift for such things. I went little to the library

now, even for the wordly tasks allotted to me. I must be often in the gatehouse bargaining with the men who came to buy and sell. I, who for shyness had once shunned the company even of women. Or walking about the farm and the drying-ovens and the kitchen, counting what stores we had. Or riding out in a chariot to collect the convent rents. Endlessly fingering the beads of my abacus. Tintagel had made me its Judas. The keeper of their purse. Strangely, I no longer minded or thought of the ambition I had lost. I had seen that this was another road by which to ascend. Wealth is power. No one in the convent understood that better than I. I must make no mistake.

Helpless, I observed the progress of the two sick cows. One of them recovered, but the other worsened, staggering now, and blind. One dark December day I watched it die, vomiting blood. I thought how Morgan had held that bowl to my lips.

I accused her.

'The dun cow is dead.'

She stared at me blankly. Her eyes widened with shock then grew brilliant with tears.

'It was not my fault. I had only enough of the herbs of power to heal one of them. And Uther will never allow me outside to gather more, will he?'

I stood staring at her foolishly, with my mouth hanging open, as I struggled to grasp the altered meaning of what I had seen in the byre.

# Chapter Eighteen

I thought that Bryvyth's defences held. The boat came no more to the cove in the grey time between night and morning. I slept more soundly than ever before. When I woke at daybreak, Morgan was in her bed.

I watched her grow in stature and in learning. Her mind was never idle. She piled up knowledge from anyone who could give it, with an insatiable hunger. Yet she had times of bodily stillness like no other child.

From the outside Tintagel looked a poor, plain place. Small huts. Low roofs. A standing stone marked with the sign of Christ. But inside, our little chapel glowed with beauty. Painted walls and ceiling, gold and silver sparkling on the altar in the candlelight, rich embroidered hangings for the sanctuary. In the school the girls learned fine sewing. Morgan herself was an expert embroideress. Our work was sent far and wide to deck churches and monasteries across the west. We nuns matched the work of monks, but they had little skill at ours.

There was plain sewing too in plenty. Making, mending. When the hardest labour of the day was over the nuns would often gather on summer afternoons, sitting on turf and boulders with their sewing in their laps, while one of them, Rathtyen perhaps, read to us some holy story. Though the younger children ran at liberty, the oldest pupils, those who were now young ladies in their own eyes, would come and sit around us with their own stitching. Morgan was one of those now, diligent, deft, almost silent in company. What did she think as she listened to the stories of prophets and apostles, virgins and martyrs, as her fingers embroidered the monogram of Christ?

When the telling was over there would be a sigh of satisfaction. We knew ourselves to be part of that story. The nuns would sew on in silence, with the breeze whispering in the drying grass and the waves washing against the rocks below us. But the girls would fall to chattering. Sometimes their voices would drop low, and there would be a sudden burst of laughter, quickly hushed. The nuns would frown at them for wantonness. We had all been girls ourselves. Well we knew of talk it is not fit for nuns to hear. We had not forgotten all of that.

Our pupils came from the noblest in the land. Tintagel had a high reputation for the fostering of girls. Morgan was not the only king's daughter. She always claimed the name of princess, for all she hated her stepfather Uther.

This pride did not go uncontested. The other girls would come back from the feasts of Christmas and Easter bursting with tales of great halls full of lords and ladies, of gifts exchanged, of mountains of rich food. Their eyes would turn to Morgan in her simple student's gown, sewing with her eyes downcast, within earshot. They would nudge each other as they looked across at her.

Giggling now, and growing red by turns, they would tell of wild young noblemen who raced each other after the boar, of wrestling and swordplay on the greens outside their fathers' forts, of compliments over the winecups and poems sung to the harp.

These girls were destined for marriage soon, perhaps for crowns. And Gorlois's daughter?

'Well, Morgan? Where did you go for the feast of Pentecost? They tell me Uther Pendragon wore his crown in Winchester?'

'Indeed he did, Talwyn, for I was there. Such a hosting of noblemen and women you never saw. I did not notice Morgan.'

'Ah, I was there too. And I saw her sisters. The Queen Elaine with King Nentres and Queen Margawse with King Lot.'

'Is it true that Margawse has four children already? Two boys and two girls?'

'Yes. And another coming by the look of it!'

'And you, Morgan. When will you get married? What handsome young king is Uther Pendragon keeping up his sleeve for you?'

And they burst out laughing.

What could she answer, Morgan, who never left Tintagel, who was not free to run along the beach or gallop on her pony after the stag, who was allowed no sight in all these years of her mother and sisters, who must be kept close, confined, guarded, living in a world of white virgins? Prayer, books, sewing, sleep, that was all her life. Plain convent food. Her parents never sent her gowns or gifts, jewelled girdles, trinkets for her hair. She went dressed sober as a nun, in things of Bryvyth's choosing. Uther had given rich gifts to the convent for keeping her safe. But for Morgan's own use, only the bare essentials. I knew, I kept the tally of the spending.

'Morgan's not going to get married, are you, Morgan? She's going to be a nun.'

'A hermit, like Piala!'

'Morgan, a nun! Holy Mother Morgan!'

The colour darkened in Morgan's face and went again. She made no movement. There was no sudden jerking of her needle. No spot of blood on the white linen to betray her.

'My father says that Uther Pendragon may not be high king much longer. The Saxons will overrun half Britain soon.'

'My father would strike dead a man who said that in his hall, however high his name.'

'Well then, why was the crown-wearing not in London this time?'

'The roads are too dangerous in the east.'

'You see? My father says Britain was not like that in Ambrosius's day.'

I watched Morgan's needle pause. The wicked, shiny point sticking up through the cloth. She would endure the insults to herself as unflinchingly as she did blows. But this taunt was to the honour of her family. It was a cruel catch. She hated Uther, and yet the glory of the Pendragon's crown reflected on her.

She said in the low fierce voice I always dreaded, 'Uther Pendragon will not allow the traitors to take one foot more of Britain.'

There was an astonished silence. Then a wave of laughter.

'What do you know about it?'

'When did you last see your royal stepfather?'

'Did a chough tell you that? Or a puffin?'

'No! The mackerel bring her messages down the coast!'

They all laughed so noisily that the nuns tried to hush them.

Then Whecca hissed very low, 'My father says that there are kings in the north who never wanted him for over-king.'

'Yes. His own sons-in-law. Morgan's sisters' lords, Lot and Nentres.'

'I've heard that at the next council they're going to challenge him to put off the crown of Britain.'

'What's left of it!'

'You know what's wrong? Why he keeps losing battles?'

'No. Why?'

'My mother says there's a curse on Uther Pendragon. He married into a family that was too wise. The witches have got him in their claws.'

The stares turned sideways again at Morgan, but not so mockingly. There was a little more fear in their looks now.

'How do you know?'

'Well, it's obvious, isn't it? A good-looking man like him. And what has the Queen Ygerne given him? Nothing. If he falls, there isn't a son to follow him.'

Morgan jumped to her feet then, throwing the linen cloth with the crosses on to the grass.

'There is! There is! How dare you say that? He has a son!'

'What do you mean?'

Their mouths fell open. Had they really not heard the story? Was it a secret to the rest of Britain what Morgan had done? Why she was here?

'He has a son! If Uther falls there will be another Pendragon. A better one. To rule over Britain and drive the Saxons from our shores. My brother . . .' and her breath caught on the name '. . . Arthur!'

A little silence. And then the laughter again, more uncertain now.

'That baby?'

'He died long ago.'

'They say the fairies took him.'

'There was a magician, wasn't there? Merlyn, he was called, or some such name.'

'That was ages ago.'

'He's in the Isles of the Blest now.'

'He isn't! He isn't!' Morgan raged at them. 'Don't say that. Don't you ever dare say that to me again! He's alive. Merlyn has hidden him somewhere. I know he has. You'll see! One day you'll see!'

And she raced away from us.

I followed her. She was not in my cell. I found her at last on the southern ledge where Howel had died. She had flung herself face downward on the earth. Sobbing, with her fists beating the grass.

The gulls swung in the sky. We could see nothing of the convent from here. Only the grave-mounds across the water where her father lay.

I sat beside her, saying nothing. I dared not touch her. I think I prayed then for her, with a rare sincerity. Not for myself, that I might rise higher through victory over her. Not in fear lest I should be brought down by her wickedness. But, simply, on that afternoon, for the girl herself, weeping into the earth as though her heart would break.

Such moments do not last.

She grew quiet, sat up and saw me. At once she was on her feet, tightening her girdle, brushing the evidence of tears from her cheeks. She walked ahead of me, back to the convent.

She stopped by the standing stone, with her eyes fixed on mine as though she swore an oath.

'They are right. Uther must die. He is no fit king. He cannot heal the land. I am his daughter now. They must make me queen of Britain.'

My question was cruel.

'And Arthur?'

Very steadily she answered me, as though this was something she had thought about many times.

'If he consents, we shall rule together, as equals. Sword and scabbard. The earth in balance. If he opposes me, I shall destroy him.'

# Chapter Nineteen

Bryvyth had set me to play the part of a mother to Morgan. I, that had never had warmth in my heart for children, that had chosen to come to Tintagel because more than any other place in the world it offered me the life of a man. I was ill-fitted for my task.

One night I stood as usual, arms raised in prayer. Outside, the autumn twilight was just beginning to thicken. Morgan was undressing beside me. The darkness in our cell should have been no hindrance to her. It was long since she had known the helping hands of her nurse. But now she dropped her nether garment to her feet and stood feeling awkwardly under her shift.

'Have you got fleas? Don't scratch yourself. You'll only make it worse.'

She stood examining her fingers.

'Say your prayers and get to bed,' I urged her. 'You looked pale at supper. I'll help you cut clean bracken for your mattress tomorrow and burn the old.'

I was not really tired, and I cared little if she was. It was the quiet hours ahead I valued, before that deep sleep claimed me. But as she stood gazing at me out of the dark hollows of her eyes, I felt compelled to break off my prayers and smile at her. She was sixteen now. She had left the wild mischief of her childhood behind her. I believed my patient forbearance had succeeded, where Bryvyth's beatings and Rathtyen's harsh words had not.

I say I did not love children. I never thought of Morgan

as a child, even from the first. She was always herself.

I cannot think now how I deluded myself. I knew what lay under the mattress of bracken I talked of lifting. Those secret gifts of Gwennol's, notes of spiritual counsel from Piala, philosophy from Rathtyen, country-women's lore from Blatriad. A hoard of knowledge, holy and unholy, all mixed together in a dangerous ferment.

I believed I had tamed her. And now I was in sight of my reward. Rathtyen had aged suddenly, as though she was being consumed by an inner sickness. We had all assumed that she would take Bryvyth's place when that deep-rooted oak fell at last. Rathtyen was a little the younger of the two, the grey only just beginning to invade her hair until just lately, when all of a sudden it turned white and sparse. She had been straight-backed, ferociously intelligent, naturally quick of movement, but holding herself in by a stern discipline. She was known to be holy, fasting more than our rule demanded, learned, yet always hungry for new books brought from afar, hard of hand and voice towards the schoolgirls, yet spending her days utterly in their service. Now she could hardly haul herself from cell to schoolroom, though she moved more eagerly to the chapel than any-where else. The keen light of her eye was dimming and the voice croaked as if the words came with effort.

I knew it weighed down Bryvyth, who had had such faith in her. The abbess's own hair was white now, and the wrinkles deepening in her wind-brown face.

Another successor must be found and trained. And who else was there in all Tintagel with a mind, a rule of life, a gravity to equal mine? Already I had all the affairs of the convent under my control. I had scholarship in plenty, though I did not often frequent the library nowa-days. I kept my body strictly disciplined. I was constant in prayer and confession of minor faults. I preached abroad now like Bryvyth herself. My public difficulties with Morgan were things of the past. My private struggles no one knew.

Bryvyth loved me.

I could dream now of esteem far higher than I might have had in the book-room with the mere delight of making beauty. What did Cigfa or Eira know of the world outside Tintagel? I could taste power. I had much to pray for that night, plans to make. The picture of myself for Bryvyth's eyes must be painted exactly right in every detail. I wished Morgan asleep.

Still the girl had not moved.

'Morgan?'

'I . . . I need clean linen.'

I must have been sleepier than I thought. Or more elated at the thought of Rathtyen's decline. I was slow to understand her meaning.

'You haven't taken the flux, have you? Two of the girls are in the infirmary with it. Let us pray it is not the blackwater sickness.'

'No. It isn't that.'

Her voice was subdued, unlike her usual tone of command.

I lowered my arms stiffly and bent to her in the narrow space between our beds. I could see only the glimmer of her shift in the dark now. But my hand found the linen at her feet. It was warm and wet. I sniffed at it reluctantly and the thick, sweet smell of blood told me the truth.

I felt a rush of heat and confusion cover my own body. Believe me, I had never prepared myself for this moment, still less her. I spoke rapidly, reining in my disgust.

'Oh,' I said. 'So you've started with *that* at last, have you? We shall have to find you a binder. I'll let you have one of my own for tonight, and in the morning we must ask Nessa to give you linen of your own. You'll need to wash them yourself, and privately. You're a grown woman now.'

Strange how close we could live to each other and still keep our secrets. Never once had I let her see the evidence of my own blood-time.

I busied myself in the chest at the foot of my bed and found my hands were trembling. This was no fitting task for a half-woman like me. I was chaste, virginal. I had chosen to put away from me all that side of life. I had not wanted it. It irked me even now that I could never free my body from womanhood as I had freed my spirit. I had heard it whispered that hermits who live on bread and water cease to bleed because of their holiness, but I could not bring myself to ask questions about such things.

How many years was it since I had first seen with fear the signs of blood on my own thighs? My mother had taken me into the orchard away from the younger children and told me what little she thought I needed to hear. I know now – oh, to my sorrow I know – how much more she could have told me.

But who was there to tell Morgan even that little? I could not nerve myself to do it. Not there, in Tintagel, in the holy women's stronghold. To speak of men and their bodies, and our secret places. Better to keep to the mathematics of the moons and the necessity of laundering linen.

When I had made her clean and comfortable again she lay down to sleep. But even in bed she was restless. The mattress rustled as she turned. Suddenly she sat up and her voice cried through my waking dreams.

'At last I am a woman in body as well as years! I am truly a woman! Merlyn said that when that happened the whole of Britain would fear me. They can't keep me here now, can they? Uther will have to give me my freedom. It isn't true what the others said, is it? He couldn't make me be a nun. He couldn't force me to be like you, could he, Luned?'

Her desperate words cut at my newly-swelling pride.

'Little a girl like you knows what she is despising. I am what I am here by my own choice. And I shall be greater yet. Go and be a queen like your sisters, if you like. Become the mother of drunken warriors. I have put all that behind me. Jewels and swords are not everything. I shall be more than you. I shall be abbess after Bryvyth. The high priest of my own tribe. I shall counsel kings.'

'Oh, Luned, Luned! What kind of power is that? Aping men. You only want this life because it's what men have. The real power is *over* men. My mother taught me that. Uther never took her from my father. She captured him. She used *this* to get what she wanted. Margawse told me.'

She grasped my hand and, dragging it across, thrust it down between her legs. I felt the moist, thickening ooze between my fingers and struggled to get free of it.

'Is this where power is, Luned? Is it? Is it?'

I pulled myself away from her grip, sickened and defiled by what I had touched.

'Stop it! I want no part of that. I am a holy virgin.'

In the darkness I could not see where my hands were spreading the blood.

'Holy virgins!' She laughed high and wild. 'Nuns! You can tell me that, here in Tintagel, of all places. Oh, poor, ignorant Luned!'

I tried to close my ears against her and clenched my soiled hands in prayer.

Then her voice dropped, fierce and low. 'No. You are right. They are holy. What is done here is holy. Above and below. It is not of the common world. It is not to be done carelessly, crudely, in a drunken stupor. That is not how I shall use my power.'

I would not answer her. It was terrible to me that a

maiden like that, who had lived seven years within the walls of a convent, should lie in the darkness plotting how she would join her body to a man's.

She went on whispering in the dark.

'I do not want to be like Margawse. I think I am too like you, after all. However I use this power, I shall always keep my true self to myself. No man shall ever enter that most secret place of all inside me. Except perhaps one.

'But I must tell Gwennol my gift has come. I promised I would. You needn't have blushed and stammered so, my poor tongue-tied Luned. Gwennol taught me all that before I ever came here. And much more besides. Things you wouldn't ever dream of.'

'You will have no more dealings with Bossiney. You know that boat never comes here now. Bryvyth has exorcised the evil from Tintagel.'

Morgan yelped with laughter.

'That's what you think! I should have gone mad in this place if Gwennol had really left me. She will show me what I must do next.'

'You cannot tell Gwennol. I forbid it. You must not communicate with her.'

Alarm was growing. For myself, not for Morgan. For the precarious castle of my ambition.

She rolled over so that her face came close to mine.

'Must not, Luned? Can't I tell her? You will see. Before long, all Britain shall know I have come to my womanhood.'

# Chapter Twenty

I went to Bryvyth in the morning.

'Morgan is a woman now,' I said.

'Is she indeed? And is that a reason to drag me out of doors before the sun is through the fog? Why shouldn't she be? Did you think it never happened to princesses? In law she's been an adult these two years past.'

Yet she folded her arms and hugged herself as if the autumn chill troubled her and walked away from her cell to the edge of the cliff. She stood gazing down, though we could see nothing, only the clouded air darker beneath us. Even the sea was noiseless, as it often was in the early morning.

'You'd think we were a thousand miles away from kings and wars. Not in the thick of the fight. A different king. A different battle. But the wounds cut just as deep. And now there is blood.'

'She says she cannot stay here. Will the king set her free and find her a husband now?'

Lips stiff and difficult, as though these were not my words.

'Uther will not do that, and well you know it, or we'd have been rid of her long ago. And do you know why?'

'Because she tried to kill her baby brother, Uther's son. But that was long years past. She was a little girl then.'

'Was that one ever a little girl? Oh, you don't deceive me as much as you think you do, Luned! She's not like

141

other girls, is she? How could she be, the way her father died, the way the boy Arthur was got?'

'You think Uther fears her still?'

I did not find that strange.

'Uther! At Tintagel we play for higher stakes than crowns and forts. Kings come and go. Morgan must fight an older enemy than him.'

I heard the waves begin to swish beneath me.

'Whom?' I said, my tongue dry.

'It was Uther sent her here, in a fit of rage. But tempers cool. I doubt that man would have had the wit to keep up his guard against her so many years, unadvised. She is kept here by the will of one stronger than the king of the Britons.'

'Who? The Pope? The Emperor in Constantinople? For Morgan?'

She had the sense to laugh.

'Oh, Luned, Luned! You walk about with your eyes downcast, but the eyes of your soul look too high. Do you think I'm afraid of armies of men or bishops' croziers? You're too holy to see the darkness under your nose here, in these very stones. It's Merlyn I'm thinking of.'

Merlyn. The fey magician of the tales. Soul-friend to Uther once, when Arthur was got. Now lost with that child.

'You believe he's still alive? And *he* fears Morgan would kill the boy yet?'

She took my hand and pointed where the mist was lightening in the cove. A shadow was growing out of it, a familiar darkness, upward-thrusting.

'Do you see the rock? It was there, Luned. On a night of storm, while we lay here in our beds or stretched in prayer, a little girl stood on that very rock with the waves dashing round her and her baby brother in her arms. How could she not have drowned both of them? But she did not. She held him safe. Think on that, Luned.

Think on it very well. Is this what Merlyn fears? Not that Morgan would kill Arthur if once she found him, but that she could not? It is in my mind that he may fear her love more than her hate. And so he works to keep them apart.'

The bell rang suddenly, summoning us to chapel. But Bryvyth, always the first to obey her master's call, did not turn yet.

'Why, Luned? Why did she bring him here to Tintagel Haven?'

'To drown him, I thought.'

'I have said she did not. Why? Why are they all drawn here? The unclean brood: Ygerne, Morgan, Gwennol, Merlyn. Yes! He was here that night when Arthur was begot. The shape-shifter, Merlyn, here, in our Tintagel itself!'

She was striding back to the chapel now, anger evident in every step.

'Are we never to be rid of them, then? Was I wrong? Is the place not clean yet?'

She stopped abruptly. Her eyes were on my face. I never found it easy to have Bryvyth look at me so boldly. I could not meet her gaze.

'Watch Morgan. As you love her and Christ, watch her. This is her dangerous time, when her dreams have power. There is something in these stones yet which is warring for her. We have come to the battle for her soul. But we shall win it, by the grace of Christ and his virgin Mother. We shall win it yet, you and I! Only tell me if you learn something strange, if there is anything you hear which I should know. Sometimes I think I've brought us to another world entirely here. A different time. Especially when the mist walls us round like this. I chose a dangerous place when I carved my cross here on the enemy's heart. Faith can be rash as love. There are nights when it is heavy on me that I may have endangered weaker souls. Is there anything at all you should have told me?'

She was offering me another chance. I should have told her then. I should have fallen on my knees and confessed everything. The gifts hidden on feast-days. The little pile of scratched slates under her mattress. The cow that sickened and the one that lived. The voices in the dark. I knew I needed Bryvyth's help. I needed her joyous strength. I needed the stronghold of her prayers.

But how could I tell her this now? How could I confess that all these years I had concealed the truth from her?

Rathtyen was dying.

'No,' I lied. 'I'm just afraid of what she may do if we have to keep her here.'

'Hm! I've been afraid of that ever since she crossed that ditch. But we're winning, aren't we? It was a bitter struggle at first, but it seems you're taming her. I've almost forgotten the feel of a birch in my hand.'

I bowed my face as we entered the chapel. The chance of help had passed. I had elected to fight this battle alone. But fight it I would, this time. And I must win. My abbess should not be ashamed of me.

Bryvyth did not dismiss Uther Pendragon entirely from her hopes. She wrote a letter. The two of us walked the short path to Bossiney. In all my years at Tintagel, in all my roaming the roads with a preaching staff in my hand, in all my rides round the farms gathering wealth for the convent, I had never ventured inside the walls of Uther's dun. I remembered how I had trudged past it as a green girl, on my way from Devon to Tintagel for the first time. It had been Gorlois's dun then, Morgan's home. I had thought its inhabitants had nothing to do with me.

I felt the high tower of the gate diminish me. I was conscious of how low I had been born and where I had come from. This was a royal dun now. But I followed the sweep of Bryvyth's stride into the yard and my pride rose again.

Uther had not been there for years, or Ygerne either. Cornwall held too many uncomfortable ghosts for the pair. The place had a rundown, slipshod air, the thatch ragged, dogs scavenging for scraps, slaves gossiping idlehanded, a few old warriors nodding over a chessboard.

Ulfin, Uther's close friend, had been made lord of Bossiney. The name leaped in my throat, a name from long ago. On the night that changed the course of Tintagel, and of Britain, he had been one of those three. An armed man, dangerous, unholy, in the heart of our convent. He had come in the guise of Jordan, Gorlois's bodyguard, the night that had tricked us and robbed Morgan of so much. Ulfin. Uther. Merlyn.

It was no wonder that Bryvyth's nuns kept their skirts away from Bossiney.

Seven years since, but I remembered him. He looked older now. Older than you would expect for a man who had been a laughing young warrior the morning after that shape-shifting. Had Uther aged so much? And Merlyn too? Was this the price of submitting their faces to magic?

Bryvyth gave him the letter.

'See that it reaches the high king within this moon. I stood security once for his stepdaughter, but not forever. She's a grown woman now. Let the Pendragons look to their own.'

A shadow haunted his face.

'Uther Pendragon has bitterer news than a woman to wrestle with.'

'Are the Saxons getting the upper hand in Britain? Man! Did he think that God would bless his banners after the way he fouled our holy house? Is he such a fool? He looked to other powers than Christ to aid him then.

Can they not drive the heathen longships back? Is Merlyn's craft too feeble to rescue Britain?'

'I'm a soldier. I spoke of Uther, not of Merlyn.'

'Pah! Uther? Merlyn? Are they two or one? Can Uther Pendragon ever break free of that soul-friend?'

'You know that Merlyn has not been seen these seven years.'

'Not seen? Or not recognised?'

He had the grace to blush at that.

The old men outside the hall raised their heads listlessly. Men that had won their fame in Ambrosius's time and lost it in Uther's.

An old woman hobbled out of one of the huts and stared at us. I started, and so did she. I saw her hand raised and the fingers spread towards us. She mouthed a string of words we could not hear. Bryvyth saw her too. She did not flinch, as I had. She drew the sign of the cross in front of us like a trusty shield.

'It's you, Gwennol Far-Sight, is it? Still alive to haunt us.'

'So Morgan's blood-time has come, you say?'

I think I gasped. I do not know what I had dimly feared, or how and when I thought Morgan might meet and tell her this. The truth was crueller. There was no need now. I had carried the news to her myself. Morgan had had her way. That thing that is most private to women, that should not be talked about, was no secret now to all Dumnonia. Morgan's womb had bled. The heat burned in my cheeks.

Gwennol nodded. Her bright robin's eyes searched our faces.

'So there's blood in our cup stronger than yours. You can't hold her. My little maid will never be the bride of your Christ.'

She turned and shuffled away.

'Do not blaspheme the Lord!' Bryvyth called after

Gwennol. 'If a silver coin is lost, God is the housewife who will sweep the floor until she finds it. She will show it to her friends with great rejoicing.'

The witch disappeared through a doorway as if she had not heard.

Bryvyth gripped my arm roughly. 'Be strong! Have faith.'

It was in my mind to say that Gwennol did not speak like one who had faith or hope, but as if she saw the future. I was too well-disciplined to voice my thought aloud.

# Chapter Twenty-One

Morgan was clean again. She knew of Bryvyth's letter.
The news was whispered among all the girls. There was
a bright excitement on her now, as though hope dawned
at last. Every morning she brushed her hair till it shone
glossy black as a chough's wing, and her green eyes
glittered like the sea. As the days of October darkened
around us, my own thoughts turned to chilblains and
mud and drenching winter gales. But Morgan flowered
like an opening rose.

As I watched her beauty blossom, panic clutched my
heart. If Uther relented, if Morgan left us, I should never
in all my life see her again. Hers would be the courts and
the dancing, the silks and jewels, the laughter and loving.
I would be left to the grey sea and the grey sky, the cold
chapel at dawn, the solitary cell. Seven years I had
wrestled for Morgan in my prayers. At last I saw what I
was praying for. If the answer were no, she would have
to make her life with us. My prayers strengthened
tenfold.

Yet even as I prayed for her to take the veil, I watched
her and admired.

Answers do not come quickly on long muddy roads. It
was full moon again. All day Morgan had been restless.
A brisk wind was driving white horses over the grey sea.
Gulls were flung sideways on sudden currents of air.
Since morning the students had been pent indoors over
their tasks. When they were freed the other girls

hurried to find shelter by the refectory fire. But Morgan flung a cloak about her and went skimming down the slope straight for the causeway.

I was late in finishing my day's work. I was still at the gatehouse with Padarn the porter. A consignment of flour had arrived from the mill. I must call for sledges to ferry it across to our island storehouse.

I saw her coming and my heart leaped with a warning of danger. I did not need to see the girl's face to know it was Morgan. No one else moved with that swift, decisive energy. No other girl had hair so black and wild and free. As she dashed on to the bridge I shouted out to her in fear to stay on the other side. The wind flung itself across the chasm with a prickle of salt in it. Her cloak billowed suddenly, tugging her sideways with it. She threw out her arms, spinning on the edge. Then she found her balance and came running on. I forgot the grave dignity of a nun and raced down the slope to meet her.

'What are you doing here? It is forbidden for you to cross the bridge. Another handsbreadth and the wind would have dashed you to the rocks! What is wrong?'

Fear, anger, concern were tumbling out of my lips. Another day she would have laughed at my incoherence. But today she needed something from me. Her eyes blazed urgently in her face. She grasped my arm.

'Who was it? Who was it came to the gatehouse just now? Is it a message for me? Uther's answer? How long, Luned, how long still before I am free?'

'Uther's messenger!' I looked over my shoulder at the speck of the cart still ambling up the head of the coombe. 'That was nothing but the man from Rawlyn's mill with our good corn ground into twenty sacks of flour.'

'Flour?' She seemed to check and steady herself. She stepped into the gatehouse. Padarn touched his head and bowed. To him she was still Gorlois's daughter. Her fist struck suddenly at the nearest sack and a puff of white dust fogged the air.

'Flour! I wait for freedom, and all that comes is dusty flour. Is there nothing from the Pendragon? Will there never be any hope for me? Will it go on like this forever?'

It was not like Morgan to despair. But winter was coming, the time of the darkness of the soul.

'You need not stay as a prisoner,' I reminded her. 'You could live here by your own free choice. Become a nun.'

'And if I did? Would Bryvyth let me cross this bridge, ever? Could I ride round the villages in my chariot, or walk the lanes preaching, as you do? Would I be free to talk with lords and peasants? Would I be trusted on the wharf when the ships come in?'

'Do you wish to go from us so much?' The words came harsh and painful from my lips.

Her eyes found my face with a sort of wonder.

'Seven years. Have I lived with you so close for seven years and you have to ask me that? If I would want to leave Tintagel, of all places!'

Fool that I was, I could not even tell if that was yes or no. I wanted to believe the holy place was precious to her. And, though the words are ashes on my tongue now, that I was dear to her too. Yet I had enough honesty of mind, even in my fondness, to doubt that what I longed to hear could be so.

I only realised I was clutching her wrist when she tore herself away from me and strode back over the bridge. Morgan was her own prisoner, as much as ours. We could never have held her, determined as she was, if she had truly wanted to run away. How often could she have been gone from my side in the night? How often could she have climbed down to the beach and a secret boat? She had friends outside. But she would not go from us only to hide in a peasant's hovel. She was too proud. That was to exchange one prison for another. We both knew that. She would leave Tintagel as a princess or not at all. Ulfin's men had orders to find her and kill her if her presence was rumoured outside our wall. So she must wait for Uther's mercy still. The loss of Arthur lay between them like an unsheathed sword.

I watched her climb the path, up to the plateau of the island, and set off swiftly along its edge. Tintagel Island is not large. Before I had finished my business in the gatehouse she was coming back again on the southern side. Round and round. A tall impatient figure testing the limits of her gaol.

The moon waned, and the leaves spun from the crooked trees.

We were together when the answer came. Three men in fur cloaks appeared on the opposite cliff. We caught our breath as we watched them halt their horses and stare across at our island. No merchants these. No panniered mules. Fine horses bright with display of bronze harness-trappings. The sheen of autumn sun on curried hides. Thick pelts cast carelessly back from strong tanned arms, showing rich-coloured tunics and wealth of warriors' weapons.

Suddenly I had a feeling that Tintagel was vulnerable. A band of women in white gowns, scholars and dairy-maids, unused to war. Our bridge, that had seemed an awful barrier, could yet be crossed. We knew that since the fatal night when Uther came. Nor was the sea a strong moat of defence. It had brought a nearer enemy to our island, as I had cause to know. Where was there for me to retreat now? Even the high fortress of Tintagel could not keep the evil world out.

I feared those men, but Morgan hoped. Beside me, her body was almost bursting out of her gown with a fierce excitement. Red lips open and panting, green eyes brilliant. So slender a human frame to contain so mighty a spirit. So small an island to confine such great ambition.

'At last! It is over! He has sent for me. I shall be free, I shall begin to be a queen.'

I watched them with despair.

Long the horsemen stared and seemed to talk together. It struck me that we were stranger to them than they to us. I began to suspect that they feared us too. By our nuns' simplicity and vulnerability we challenged all they stood for. My pride began to assert itself again.

They turned their horses' heads and trotted for the top of the coombe and the path to the gatehouse. It was then I knew the answer, as they filed past on the far lip of the haven. I had not spent so many years in calculation that I could not count horses. As certainty soared in my soul I glanced swiftly at Morgan to see if she had read the message too.

She was dancing. Laughing, with her head thrown back and her arms spread wide, circling on the short-cropped turf. Had she truly not seen?

They left their weapons, reluctantly, I have no doubt, at Padarn's lodge, and came on foot across our holy causeway. Swaggering more than was necessary, to keep up their pride. Glancing, for all that, at the plunging drop on either side. Laughing with each other to cover an unaccustomed shyness in the presence of nuns. Strange that I, who had ordinarily no interest in my fellow humans, could now read all that at a distance in their bearing. I had become wise on Morgan's behalf.

Bryvyth went to the guesthouse to talk to them. Heavy the load she had carried all these years. She must have wished to be rid of it that day. Her precious city of God, so painfully built here, balanced against the welfare of Gorlois's daughter. Two sacred trusts.

I know I prayed while they were closeted inside. Old habits of joyful praise reasserted themselves. I knew now that High God was on my side. Morgan too, her hands moving ceaselessly in strange patterns, her lips murmuring, moving away from me so that I should not hear what she asked. Morgan a beggar. At what throne? And my soul plunged suddenly to think what I would have to face from her soon.

The men came out of the guesthouse and cast curious looks around. They were not used to a convent. You could see what they would be thinking, and jesting about later. We are here. Here where Uther and Ulfin and Merlyn . . . and Ygerne!

The warriors walked back to the bridge, and Bryvyth stood at the door watching them. I turned to look at Morgan.

The gay dancer had turned to stone. The colour had left her lips. Even her hair seemed to hang on her cheeks like dark seaweed on rock, so heavy that the wind could not stir it.

And yet she lived. I could feel her thought screaming after the men. Bidding them turn.

Bryvyth sent for us both. I feared to rouse Morgan, to touch her. But she came, like a chill spirit beside my living flesh.

Bryvyth's face was dark with anger, though not towards Morgan. She relayed the message from Uther in a sharp, rattling voice.

There would be no freedom for Morgan. And no marriage either. As long as Uther Pendragon lived she would stay a prisoner on Tintagel. Arthur had not been heard of again. Morgan should think herself lucky to keep her life. Outside this island her penalty would be death. Only on this narrow rock could she claim sanctuary still.

The blood had not returned to Morgan's face. It was as if her whole being had frozen over. Only once had she started, when Bryvyth spoke of Arthur. Then no more. This was the depth of the bitterest winter, when not even a trickle of water can be heard underneath the ice.

Bryvyth, that strong abbess, was too ashamed to comfort her, and I too afraid.

Then, with a terrifying suddenness, she broke from us and ran. We caught up with her in the furthest sleeping-chamber of the guesthouse. She was leaning over the empty bed and beating her head against the wall.

'I must live out my life here! In Tintagel! Was that night so little to him? Does he not remember? It was *here*. Here in this very room, this bed. That . . . man lay with my mother, with his sword beside him still wet with my father's blood. Gorlois is not avenged, and every day I live, I must wake and be reminded of them both.'

'The Church bids us forgive those who wrong us. Do you think you are the only woman that loved Gorlois?' The words burst sharp from Bryvyth's tongue.

Morgan did not heed her. Where she had been cold before, a dragon breathed in her now.

'I am of age. I am a noblewoman. I am free. Free! He has no right to hold me here against my will. The law of Britain does not allow him so much power over a daughter.'

'The law of Britain lies in a sword now, by the look of it. He'll have a cold wait, if he means to sit there till you or the Pendragon dies.'

Our eyes followed Bryvyth's through the open door behind us. A young horseman was standing on the skyline like a sentinel where our track met the mainland road.

'Is it not enough that nuns are my gaolers? Does he mean to humiliate you too?'

'Uther's men have told me the freedom of Britain hangs trembling on that same sword. And with it, this abbey and every Christian monastery and church in the land.'

'And for your Church's safety, my right must be denied?'

'If freedom was all you wanted, girl, it might have been

yours. You could have swallowed your pride. You could have offered your love to the Pendragon, as your mother did. But you wanted power. A crown on your brow and your story honoured and your father revenged. The bards will not sing of you, here in Tintagel. Only we shall remember the wrong that was done here.'

I could not read Morgan's face. She wandered away, resentfully. I followed at a distance as she climbed up to the summit and the standing stone. Her fingers traced the initials of Christ's name cut in the rock. Her hands caressed the granite shaft, stone older than any carving. Her eyes swung round the scope of sea, the cave mouths gaping in the cliffs, the distant roofs of Bossiney. The horseman watching.

I left her. I had work to do. She did not come to supper.

When dusk fell I found her in the chapel. She was gazing about her as if she had never been here before. All around her the faces of saints and prophets stared down from the painted walls, large-eyed. Christ in Judgment watched her from the cove of the roof. She moved among them, studying their expressions, fingering the costly goldwork on the altar. She grasped the four-armed cross so tightly I feared she would break it. Long she looked up into the dusky face of the Virgin Mary.

Then she swung round, gazing past me over the sea. The chapel is not far from the edge of the cliff. The high tide boomed in the hollow caves. I did not dare to speak to her.

At last she broke silence.

'Well, I am a woman now, am I not? Even here I can take my fate in my own hands. She has asked me to make my first vows at the dark of the moon.'

My heart leaped with joy.

'Then make them! Put on the bridal veil and be welcome among us.'

But Morgan's eyes held mine without smiling. Wells of sadness I could not begin to measure.

'If I so choose, it is a high and fearful bridge I shall be crossing.'

'But there is power and glory on the other side!' I cried.

'Is there? Is this my only way?'

She was very pale. Still her eyes gazed at me steadfastly, with a look I had seen in them many times before. As though she meant me to understand more than she said. As though she pleaded for some other answer. I could not tell what she wanted from me.

# Chapter Twenty-Two

I blame Bryvyth for what happened. She should have seen how great a danger I was in.

It was All Hallows Eve and the dark of the moon. The night of Samain. It affected us all. It was not just from Christian charity that we doubled our prayers for the peace of the dead. Nuns we might be, but it was our own peace we, the living, prayed for secretly. That night was the threshold of the otherworld. By the old reckoning, the dying of one year before the next is born. A night of darkness when the doors of the hollow hills are open and the dead may return. We had not been Christians long enough in Dumnonia to break the bonds of that belief. No Roman calendar, no candles burning in the chapel, could wipe the darkness from our minds. Even Bryvyth was uneasy at suppertime.

I looked down the long table to where Morgan sat for the last time among her fellow scholars. Her face was white and she could scarcely eat. I did not wonder at that. In the new light of morning those lips would take the bread of the Eucharist from Nectan's hands and Bryvyth would lay the white veil on the tumbling freedom of her black hair. But before then she must keep the night's vigil alone in the chapel, like the new warrior of a mortal lord. This night of all nights. I could not have done it.

I glanced at Bryvyth, troubled. Why had she laid so terrifying a burden on the girl? The abbess met my eye, and I saw a strange sparkle there. Excitement and doubt, as though she knew even then the high stakes she gambled for. She was always a warrior-woman, Bryvyth. When Gorlois had staked his life on his wife's honour, she understood. I knew without saying that Bryvyth would keep this vigil too in her own cell, as I would in mine. But Morgan in the chapel must test her calling alone. It was required.

When the handbell called us to vespers we were more than usually reluctant to leave the bright fire of the refectory and venture the short dark path to the chapel.

That night only Tintagel flared with flame.

As the shadows deepened we filed up the path. Nuns, tall maidens near the end of fostering, the little boys and girls from the schoolroom. All around us the hills and headlands lay in muffled grey. Their lights were going out now, one by one, hearths raked and cooling, lamps extinguished, candles dead. Only in Tintagel the flame still burned. Even the nobles in Bossiney kept the custom, Morgan had told me, half in jest, for old times' sake, half in fear. Samain is not a night for jesting. When you gather in the dark around the unlit pile and the chanting begins, you dare not look over your shoulder. You dare not listen to the noises in the trees. You fear even the touch of your neighbour's hand.

On Tintagel we knew better than to jest about it. We fought to keep back the dark.

A whisper frightened me so that I staggered and lost my balance. Morgan was close behind me.

'Dark! Dark all the way to Bossiney. All the way across Cornwall. And the tide is rising with the dark. Everything dark. The lamps are out. The fires are cold on the hearth. All the light of the world goes out on Samain night. The powers of darkness are running free. The dead return.'

'Not here,' I said stoutly. 'Not in Tintagel. This is a

holy place. When every light in Cornwall goes out, the flame of faith will still burn brightly here.'

'Will it?' she said, with a little gasp. '*Will* it?'

We crowded into our sanctuary. Bryvyth stood, hooded, before the altar. One by one we lit our candles from her strong flame. Every one of us had a soul to remember. Morgan walked behind me. I looked round and with a sweet pang I saw that she carried her head higher than mine now.

Rathtyen could no longer leave her bed. Morgan would never leave Tintagel now. The thoughts went round and round my head.

Morgan's face was white as the taper in her hand, her dark hair covered, her look grave and melancholy. I felt an urge to put my arm around her.

I lit a candle for my brother Yestin and said a prayer.

Morgan moved to Bryvyth and lit her little flame.

'I commend into the hands of eternal God the soul of Gorlois, Duke of Cornwall. May he be resting in the peace of the angels this night and forever.'

'And God guard the soul of her who prays for Gorlois.'

The voices murmured on. The candles flowered. The little chapel was a field of blossoms. Out of the leaning shadows above us the dark face of the Virgin stared down. Mark and John. Elijah and Moses. The holy Marys. I followed Morgan's eyes, huge in the hollows of her face, as she turned to one and then another. I begged for their fortitude and sanctity. We sang fervently, as though we never wished our hymns to end. Even the sleepiest child and the weariest ageing nun would rather stay close-packed in the warm ranks of worshippers that night than scatter lonely to a dark dormitory or a solitary cell.

Yet we were women under discipline. Bryvyth blessed us. Before the bonfires blazed and the cruel games began along the headlands the nuns would be lying in

their chaste beds. Our candles would go out one by one.
But our chapel would never be wholly dark. One brave
oil lamp, Christ's holy fire, would still burn on,
unquenchable since Tintagel's abbess had lit it. On the
kitchen hearth, warm coals still glowed under a shield
of turf, waiting for sunrise. We did not need the druids'
new fire. We told ourselves that if an unhappy spirit
strayed on this island it would find peace and sanctuary. Here there was no gap between one year and the
next, this world and the other, no dark abyss into which
a benighted human might fall. Had not Christ harrowed
Hell for us?

Bryvyth and I were the last to go. We hugged Morgan
and left her prostrate on the cold floor before the altar.
I added my Amen to the firm armouring of Bryvyth's
benediction. What more could I have done?

We stepped into the night. It was fully dark. My
thoughts flew to Piala, alone in her cave on that desolate
headland, wrestling with devils on such a night as this. I
shuddered even to imagine it.

Now I stood sentinel in my cell to begin my own long
vigil of prayer through the hours of darkness. I did not
mean to sleep that night. Tonight, above all nights, I
must watch and pray and guard us both till dawn. I think
I knew this must be the last time I would fight for
Morgan's soul. Tonight I must suffer and struggle.
Tomorrow would see my victory.

The wind began to howl. Sea crashed against the
rocks. I had always hated it.

Hours passed. I let my tired arms fall to my side for a
moment and hugged my chilled body.

The whispering started in the stones. Words I had
thought I would never hear again.

Morgan!

I groped for her bed. She could not be here, tor-
menting me. She was in the chapel.

No flesh met my hands, but the stones were laughing all around me.

I plunged for the threshold. Darkness met me. Never, as girl or nun, had I gone out of doors alone on Samain night. Even Christians feed their fires, but bar the doors and windows. The old fear persists.

But the devil was loose, and Morgan was in danger. I could not stay alone. I must find her. I must save her. I must keep Tintagel safe.

With a moan of terror I stepped out into the rushing darkness. You may scorn me for a coward, but I used all my courage then. I was too frightened even to see the edge where the grassy cliff fell sheer to the sea. To my left and above me the chapel should be burning with light. I turned, and with a rush of thankfulness saw its windows lit with a golden glow. Our prayers lived still before Christ's lamp. Then, while I watched, the darkness overtook them.

# Chapter Twenty-Three

The blackness was horrible in its sudden finality.

I started to run up the path. I was too wise to misunderstand the meaning of what I had just seen. But my heart fought against accepting the truth. Morgan could not have done this to me! All these years I had struggled with her, taught her, loved her. In the eyes of my superiors she was redeemed. It was no longer a truce, the public price she allowed me, to shut my eyes in private. She had embraced the cross. She would take her vows tomorrow. She was my white lamb. The acceptable gift I would lay in triumph at the feet of the abbess. The purchase of my ambition. It must not be true. Morgan could not have done this to Tintagel.

Somehow I crossed the nightmare space. I staggered blindly up the ledges. In my panic I bumped the walls of cells where other nuns lay sleeping. I was the spectre let loose to trouble their peace.

At the door of the chapel I clutched the lintel to support myself. The smoke of extinguished wicks caught my nostrils.

I still prayed the worst would not be true. I prayed my eyes would clear and with all the blaze of candles out I would find the one small true eternal flame burning undefeated.

I hoped in vain. My daughter in God had committed the final blasphemy.

I must have light! I must rekindle the lamp. Never

165

mind the candles. Let the souls of the dead sleep. But Christ must live again. What death had he suffered at her hands, and mine? Quick! Before Bryvyth found out. Be sensible now. I must run to the one place where there would still be fire and warmth, to the heart of any home that I had so often despised but now I must cling on to for comfort. The kitchen.

I turned to go, and all the spirits of Samain came swooping across the plateau and whirled around me. I heard their laughter shrieking. Sobbing, I covered my face with my hands as I ran. I was afraid of dashing over the cliff. But I was more terrified still to open my eyes and see what might be round me.

Bruised by many falls I stumbled against the kitchen door. Inside, warmth welcomed me. I slammed the door and leaned against the wall, panting with relief. Close darkness stifled me like a blanket. The fire had been smothered well for the night. I groped for the hearth. Why couldn't I find it? Surely there should be one ember glowing through the turves? I tripped over a stool and fell. My hands plunged deep into something warm and soft. Ashes. I scrabbled wildly. It was all around me. The sodden ruin of fire. Trickles of water hissing on hot stones. Still I would not believe it. There must be one coal left with a spark of life I could coax back to flame.

'Oh, please! Please! Just one!'

Out of the corner something dark sprang on me like a huge cat. I screamed. But Morgan grasped me by the elbows and lifted me, dancing me round. She was shrieking with laughter.

'Oh, Luned, Luned! If only I could have left just light enough to see your face!'

'You wicked girl! You should be praying in the chapel. I must get Bryvyth.'

'Oh no, you won't. You wouldn't dare, would you? Think. What will you tell her? That she has lit Christ's fire on Tintagel and guarded it for twenty years, and you have let it go out?'

'It was not my fault. She must see that. You are possessed. Even Saint Anthony was beset by devils.'

'Why do you need to tell her? You never did before. Wait here and I will bring you back fire enough to roast a bull.'

'Where?' I whispered. 'Where could you get such a flame?'

If only I could put it right before Bryvyth saw. And never mind whose brand it was I borrowed.

She seized me by the wrist. Her hand was strangely hot and smelt of foul wet soot. She dragged me out into the gusting darkness. I tried to break free. I found I could not. For the first time I knew for certain that she was a grown woman and stronger than I, in spirit and in body. She pulled me to the edge of the cliff.

'Look!'

The headlands leaped with fire. The hills were chained with gold. Outside Bossiney the wind spiralled the flames up into the night. I could even see the figures dancing in front of the bonfire.

'Our time has come. My time has come. I must join my people.'

And still I did not fully understand.

'No!' I tried to hold her back. 'You must not cross the bridge. Uther's men will kill you, or you'll fall to your death in the dark. If Bryvyth finds out . . .'

I did not believe that anything I said would have force over her. I felt the power growing in her till I seemed nothing but a scrap of bone and flesh gripped by her fingers. I was dead beside her. I had nothing with which I could oppose her. The fount of my prayers had been failing for years. The words I uttered were now the rattling of dry stones in an old streambed. She knew it.

She threw me off, scorning my feebleness. She did not want me.

'Yes, be afraid! It is a more dangerous bridge than yours I am crossing to get this fire. And yet the flame is coming to me.'

She turned abruptly. Her feet started down the path, sliding on loose stones. I could have shouted out. Bryvyth's cell was only a little way beyond us. Even then I was too proud to summon help.

'Come back!'

'Let go. This is not for you.'

I grabbed her sleeve. I could not bear to be left alone.

She dragged me on. I began to realise where she was leading me. The terror of windy spaces was below me. The path was narrow even in daylight, jutting with rock.

'No!' I hissed. 'We can't go down there! Not in the dark!'

She pulled free of me suddenly. I was alone in the howling night, with the sea reaching up the cliff walls at me.

I groped blindly for her. I could not see or hear anyone. The path was steeply pitched. I could not tell what was in front of me.

'Fool!' Her voice came from lower down. 'You are on the threshold. Is this what you want? To be left alone on Samain night? What will you do? Run back to Bryvyth now and call her?'

I was lost. I could not tell which way to turn. Tonight of all nights I knew the spirits would blind my eyes and catch my feet. The convent was only just above me, but impossible to reach alone now. I had come to the edge of my abyss.

'Oh, no! Morgan, where are you? Wait for me, Morgan! Don't leave me!'

I stumbled upon her. My hand clutched hers again. I felt her warm breath coming quickly.

'Very well. I will bring you to the fire. The first fire of

the year, and the oldest in the world. This is the fire that I will kindle on the cold hearth of Tintagel. I will show Bryvyth which of us is the stronger! I will take the first vows!'

She was hurrying me down the path. I stumbled in panic, where she went swift and sure, almost running with eagerness. The path twisted again and I saw them coming into the cove.

Three wild eyes. Three separate lights soaring and swooping over the black waves. A hooded lantern held by a watcher with reddened hands in each prow. Boats, larger than the coracle. Light swaying uncertainly over a mass of shadowy passengers.

In a sudden release of hope I thought that these ships were coming to fetch her. Morgan would escape from us. I should be free of her at last. Ambition shattered. Love departed. But free. The devils would go away with her. I would wake in my bed tomorrow, alone. At that moment I truly longed for such humiliation.

But I deceived myself. When Morgan of Cornwall went from Tintagel it would be as a queen, not a hunted doe cowering from Uther's hounds. She must cross that bridge with a royal escort waiting. She was Ygerne's daughter.

She swung round to me. I could make out the white blur of her face.

'You see! They have come! I knew they would. They have come for me. Not to lay on a veil but to lift it off.'

What could she mean? And then I drew back from her with a frightened gasp. The fishing boats of Cornwall have other uses. They say that in the night they are constrained to ferry the dead. Trance takes the crew and they row out, following the path of the vanished sun, to blest islands in the west from which their passengers never return. It was what I had always feared. Morgan was going to drown herself and the ferrymen would bear her away. And I? Who had these boats come for? Where was Morgan leading me?

Keels ground on shingle.

She had not waited for me. I was alone to choose between the horror of these strangers in the cove or of the black spirit-filled path treacherous above me.

The lights vanished abruptly under the lee of the rocks. I heard muffled voices now, footsteps on the beach. In spite of my terrors they had a reassuring human sound. Women's voices. Then silence.

Somehow I tumbled out on to the shore. I could not see Morgan. The beach was sheltered from the wind. The sea came heaving towards me over ledges of rock, but the tide was not yet full. I drew my breath and looked around. The women from the boats had vanished. I could see the ships dimly now against the glimmer of the shingle. They were drawn high up above the tidemark. Three boats. Large, black, empty. Then I heard Morgan's voice from between them. She was laughing quietly.

'She has come. This is my night. They are getting ready for me. Do you still wish to follow where I am going?'

She could have forbidden me. I should not have been there. She knew what she was leading me into.

# Chapter Twenty-Four

I should have turned back. I should sooner have braved
the malignant spirits on the path. Better even to have
fallen to my death than to have gone forward into this
living hell. But that night I was too afraid to walk alone. I
needed some human close to me for comfort. I should not
have chosen Morgan.

For a while we stood silent. Then a drum beat three
times and was still. Morgan began to move.

Wet stones sliding treacherously underfoot in the
unequal starlight. The sudden shock of cold water seep-
ing through the shingle. Trembling, I followed as she
climbed over rocks that would still be dry at high tide.
Then I checked as though I had stumbled into some foulness. My groping hand had found something soft on the
cold stone. Cloth. Rough wool. Glimmering white as
Morgan's face. My heart lurched sickeningly. I knew
what this was. I drew one out. My fingers explored its
familiar shape and texture. A heap of habits like my
own. Oh, I had known. Ever since that night-time laughter on the cliff path years ago, I had known. But I had
denied the knowledge, even to myself.

In front of me Morgan too laughed harshly as she
dropped back on to the shingle.

'Now do you see? I have been well instructed here.
Go back, Luned. Run to Bryvyth. Beg her to put a
binder on this wound, stop up the hole, so that the
blood does not come out for the world of men and nuns

to see. This is no place for you, is it?'

She mocked me.

Go back? The lonely beach. The black boats. The towering cliffs in the howling darkness of Samain night. She knew I could not leave her. My tongue was dry. I knew where the drums were beating. I saw where she was bringing me. To the very mouth of what I feared most.

The Mother's Hole.

The words shaped themselves unwelcome in my mind. It was a name I had heard only rarely, and then smothered at once. It was never spoken aloud among the nuns of Tintagel. And yet I think that all of us knew its old name. We gave it no other. Indeed we never talked of it at all. Nuns playing on the beach or scrambling after shellfish would not enter it. I shuddered to think what had been under me all this time. The convent straddled it.

Tell Bryvyth? I think she must always have known. Why else had she chosen Tintagel but for the Mother's Hole? She wanted victory. Like me, she deceived herself. The past is always present with us. She should not have trusted her nuns to be as strong as she was.

All the black prohibitions of my life came leaping out of the cave upon me. That darkness into which I dare not set foot, even in bright sunshine. The unseen sea that I could already hear booming and sucking at the further end where the second mouth opened upon chaos. The thunderous weight of blank black rock towering up to the height of the convent. All poised over one narrow arch of dripping stone. How could I bear to put my fragile human skull under that load? I would have been terrified of that cave even if it had been empty.

But it was not.

A lantern opened suddenly in front of us, dazzling my eyes. I shrieked in fear, and heard my voice shudder away in horror. Something was sitting at the cave mouth. The watcher turned the light from us upon herself.

It was a naked woman. Old. White hair hanging waist-long around a grinning face. Pendulous dugs. Squatting with legs wide apart and her shrivelled hands holding the lips of her genitals gaping open. Her thighs and the mouth of her womb-way were black with blood.

She cackled with laughter as I fled from her. But Morgan, a girl new come to womanhood, stood her ground steadily. I could not bear to watch, and yet I had to. I tore my eyes with difficulty from that sentinel.

The watcher nodded. The girl fell on her knees on the stones. The lantern reddened her shift. Her face was in shadow. She called in a loud voice, shocking in its strength.

'I, Morgan, daughter of Ygerne, beg to be admitted.'

Another light flared, deep in the sounding passage between the two seas. It lit a roof streaked with rose and green. Dimly ruddied figures waited, faceless, shadowed heads turned towards us. A close-packed double file of strangers.

An old woman's voice answered hollowly. 'In the name of the gods your mother named ... Enter, Daughter!'

Another younger, lighter, followed it. 'In the name of the gods the women name ... enter, Mother!'

I started. If I had feared the ancient's voice, I had expected and recognised it. This second voice I had recognised, and not expected. Had the crack run as deep as that through the convent?

And then a strong man's voice, more shocking to me than all the others. 'By the name of the god in me ... Be entered, Wife!'

'No!' I cried out in fear. Not for Morgan, my foster-daughter, even then. Desperate fear for myself. Fear of that unquiet night outside the cave, and the darkness inside that was not dark enough, and the dark in myself that had followed too far after Morgan and was now too afraid either to go on or to turn back.

But Morgan had waited all her life for this. She walked in. White and tall. Maiden and woman now. And the shift seemed to fall from her shoulders of its own accord.

'No, Morgan!'

It was my last choking cry. I could not protect her. If I had truly loved her, unselfishly, I might have found the strength to throw my arms around her and drag us both away before it was too late. We might not have got beyond the beach, but we would have died together, whole. It did not come to that. I let her go without a struggle. I was not Bryvyth. I was not worth answering. We both knew that. In that one step into the cave she was as far removed from me as the width of oceans and the height of mountains. That last forsaken wail was only for myself.

It was lost in the full-throated greeting from the heart of the cave. No words distinguishable, but a long echoing roar that rolled towards us along the walls of rock. Morgan walked on, between the narrow ranks of waiting women, and men. A third light was lifted before her. She bowed gravely, took a torch and kindled it at this flame. She thrust it down, and another torch came to meet hers. Fire blazed between them. The light leaped on a naked man's body facing her. I covered my eyes.

So many years ago, in a coombe in Devon. I thought I had forgotten. And they called that holy.

The watcher squatted in front of me like an effigy in stone.

Outside the cave I felt utterly abandoned. The whole firm substance of my world had gone, lost in the gulf between one year and the next. This time and no time. The solid cliffs were shadows. The stones water. All around me the inlet was a shifting surface of silver and grey. The tidemark had vanished. There was no setting a limit to the sea. I felt it slide towards me, silent as a hunting lynx. Was it still far out, arching caressingly about the wharf? Or just beyond my feet, waiting, hungry? I am afraid of the sea. I never knew the patterns of high water in the haven. But I remembered Morgan's words.

'The tide is rising with the dark.'

A wave touched my foot. With a moan of terror I backed towards the cave, towards firelight and humans. I, that had always wished to be alone. I, that had embraced the coldness of chastity. I was not strong enough to stand the test.

I had forgotten that terrible sentinel. Suddenly I saw her. She had moved bewilderingly. Now she was perched on the rocks over my head, leering down at me. I checked, paralysed.

'Go on!' she hissed. 'You're late. What are you frightened of? This?'

She thrust her legs forward in front of my eyes.

'Nuns bleed like the rest of us, don't you? One week in every moon she strikes us. There's only two things dry that wound, and we all know what they are. There now, my lover! You didn't think it was my own blood, did you? With hair so white as mine? But a man that wasn't one of ours wouldn't think of that, would he? Or a book-learned nun! Lucky it's pig-sticking time!'

Her wrinkled body shook with delight.

Another wave washed over my ankles. I sobbed helplessly. I had no choice. The sea was driving me into the hole.

A hand clutched at my gown, tearing it from me. I clasped my arms around my shivering body.

The fire leaped up and robbed me of my last hope.

If only their bodies had not been naked and human.

Men among them. If only their faces had not been masked, and animal. I crouched in the shadows just inside the entrance, shuddering, hands over my eyes. I peeped through my half-open fingers, trying to see only the comfort of light I needed and shut out the rest.

I had retreated before the waves without reckoning. I, who had devoted my years to calculation. But all this while the tide was mounting higher and I saw that I had driven myself deeper into a trap of fear. I wanted to cry out to the reddened figures chanting round their fire to run before we were all submerged. But I could not speak or move. I looked back. Treacherous silver had flooded the beach behind me. I did not know how high it would rise in this cave. I had never stayed in daylight to see. With a whisper of fear I crept on ahead of it, towards the fire.

I heard a shriek, and fell to my knees on the stones. I could not tell if the thing that cried out had been human or animal. Then I saw through my fingers their priest holding in his hands something dark, darkly dripping into a vessel beneath. I saw the rosy flesh of Morgan beside him. I saw her lift the cup to her lips and then to his. I sobbed a little to myself, longing for the warmth of drink, the warmth of fire, the warmth of human company. I, that had been so proud that I needed no such vanities. All around me was cold stone, dripping with wet. I looked fearfully over my shoulder to find the cave-mouth corked with waves. I crawled still closer to the fire. I feared the devils outside and the sea more than I feared the living witches. I could not bear to drown alone.

I must close my mind to the vows Morgan was making.

At every lift and crash of the coming waves the ranks of male and female sighed and murmured an invocation. The passage bent now. At the far end of the tunnel I glimpsed past those terrible heads grey stars between

the waves. A black wall of water rose. I held my breath.
It smashed, and the sea came sliding towards us, washing the sides of the tunnel. I heard it suck and ebb away.
The distant stars glimmered once more. It had not
touched us yet. The worshippers round the fire held
their breath too, then sighed and moaned. As each wave
fell their ranks swayed a little closer to each other in the
narrow passage.

It was a powerful rhythm. The rise. The breathless
pause. The crashing fall. Then the long sobbing sigh.
The beating of the heart under the sleeping world. The
drums of darkness. Listening, watching, trembling for
the fall. I felt the same pulse begin to beat deep in the
unconsidered parts of my body. I did not know then what
it meant. I swear to you, Bryvyth, I did not know!

Fear was moving strongly in me now. Fear of the slow,
devouring approach of those waves. Fear of the creeping silver tide smothering the beach behind me. Terrible
fear of the unquiet dead outside. Fear of the urgent
shuddering of my body that was perilously close to pleasure. Fear of the more than human creatures in front of
me. The witch-fire hissed. I could smell the sweat of
bodies close to me.

A wave thundered down. Cold drops splashed my
arm. A woman screamed. My hands struck out, desperate to find some reassuring flesh. Then a last boom,
filling the cave. The walls shrieked and shrieked again
with women's cries. My voice shrill among the rest. A
wild groping together. Hands seizing, arms enfolding,
heat pressing down. My body in ice-cold water, bedded
on stones. Sea-water washing over. Warm flesh above.
Sharp pain. Devouring hunger. Gasping, crying. Release
of tears and uncontrollable shaking of my body.

Then stabbing cold. Separation. Light taken. A fea-
tureless, unaccompanied, anonymous stumbling from
the cave jostled by bodies I did not know and did not

want to know. Splashing through knee-deep water. Stumbling on a sodden roughness of cloth I knew to be my gown. People clambering into boats. Departing. Some of them shielding torches to kindle other fires. Some, white shadows from whom I turned my face away, climbing the path by which I myself had come. And I left on the beach, soaking, shivering with cold and deeply sore, sobbing my heart out. Not even sense enough to have salvaged one brand to light the kitchen fire.

Morgan had lost her shift, snatched by the undertow where she had dropped it. She did not seem to notice that she was naked. But even she cried a little now.

'There! I'll show them all! I *will* have power. There are ways Uther Pendragon does not think of. That fool knows nothing. But *he* understands. That trickster, Merlyn. He is afraid. That is why he keeps my brother from me. Well, one day he will have to bring him into the open. And I shall be ready for him. By then I shall have grown immensely strong. When Arthur stands in the sun, then Morgan will rise from the dark, and my darkness shall cover his light when we two meet together.'

She pulled me impatiently.

'What are you snivelling for? Do you think I care that you have lost your virginity?'

But I wept for the loss of far more than that.

Then she said, sniffing like a sad child, 'I do not know if I am still a virgin. The priest's thing was made of wood. He hurt me.'

# Chapter Twenty-Five

It is easier to maintain belief in the woes of the body than those of the spirit. Weariness. Disgust. Pain. I had no need to fear the Samain spirits now. Evil had done its worst. The wind still shrieked and the sea sucked, but they would not pluck me to my death. I had taken their service. The enemies of my soul would let me live and suffer.

In the first grey streak of dawn I knelt in the kitchen. My shaking hands tried to kindle a spark with stick and stone. If I had prostrated myself before the altar and begged as earnestly for light as I did then before the cold convent hearth, my life might have been different now.

Blatriad found me. Her fat hand flew to her mouth. She was always a fool. She thought she could keep the old ways under the cliff and the convent above remain untouched by them. The smell of simple, wholesome food. The pleasure of sisters trooping in to her supper. Nuns singing hymns while they cooked. Her bread lifted up in the Eucharist.

She had not thought what would happen when the two currents met.

Old dolt that she was, she had not even sense enough to see she must help me cover the traces of that night's work. It was her kitchen, her hearth, her heart that had been violated.

She went running away down the path, with her grey hair flying from beneath her veil.

I let my hands drop. The light was strengthening. It was

a still grey morning. The first of November. Grey sea, grey sky, grey chapel. And when I looked round, Bryvyth was standing behind me with a face like thunder.

'*She* has done this? So she has tricked us at the last. Seven years, and she has had her revenge. Wait till I find her!'

'She is asleep in bed.'

'In bed! And you did not run to tell me she had broken her vigil? This morning she should have been the bride of Christ! Did you think you could hide the news from me that we had failed?'

'I watched and prayed through the night. As God is my witness, I wrestled for hours to keep her intention pure.'

'And so did I. And still she has shamed us. Why? Michael fought with the archangels and cast Lucifer out of heaven. George slew the dragon. Christ conquered the grave. Are you telling me the devil is stronger than all these?'

'You do not know. You have not slept with her all these years. The voices in the stones. The spells spoken. It was Samain Eve. We should have bound her. I put my soul at risk to stop her. I ran after her to the chapel when I saw the light go out.'

'*What*?'

If she had a face like a stormcloud before, it was chalk now. She was off, running. I followed wretchedly.

The darkness had been merciful. Now cruel daylight showed the truth of Morgan's work. I stopped, appalled.

Bryvyth was standing in the wreckage of the chapel. The candles overturned. The paintings on the walls scored and scratched. The lamp beside the altar was out.

The abbess covered her face and wept.

'Christ and his holy mother! When the high king had set you . . . *I* set you . . . to watch her day and night. And you let her do *this* and still thought to hide it! Twenty years it is. Twenty years since I kindled this flame on Tintagel.

We've suffered poverty, drought, storms fit to wreck a lighthouse, pirates even. But always we kept the flame alive. Never till now has the darkness overcome it . . . Oh, Blatriad, what are you standing there crying for, you old fool? Give me that flint. Do you think my fingers have forgotten how to kindle a spark?'

With hands that trembled only slightly she lit the lamp and the life sprang again in the black and white eyes of the Virgin and the prophets, coloured their ravaged faces. Tears furrowed her own cheeks unchecked.

She prostrated herself on the stone-flagged floor, and Blatriad and I copied her. Her prayers called down Heaven's wrath on herself, implored Christ's mercy on the rest of us. It was a prayer Blatriad and I dared not echo. Here in the chapel we knew too well how we had merited wrath. We pleaded for mercy.

Bryvyth's mercy was for the soul, not for the body. She drove me before her to her cell and made me kneel.

'Oh, Luned, Luned. What was I doing when I set you to guard Morgan for us? I knew the Pendragon had set us a hard task, but I thought a nun could be wiser than a man of war. I planned a match for Morgan. I thought you two would understand each other. Mind matched with mind. Pride with pride. Ambition with ambition. Oh, yes, girl, we all know which way your heart has been set. Rathtyen is dying, and one day I shall wake up and find myself an old woman without an heir. And who shall I look to for help now? Who is there to rejoice my heart and take up the torch? Tell me that! I thought you were a sapling from my own root. I would have done better to have chosen a different guardian entirely. Someone like Eira, perhaps. Meek. Loving. Armoured with humility. How would Morgan have fought with that?'

Eira, painting these faces on the chapel walls that Morgan had ruined.

Eira. A fresh sweet voice thrilling down the tunnel.

'Enter, Mother!'

'You know little of the courage of loving, Luned. It is my fault. I saw coldness, and called it strength. I saw discipline, and took it for faith. I trusted you. I deceived myself. Your love for Christ has been a service of the will, not the heart. A matter of pride, that will not let you beg for help. Oh, I know. The blame is mine. I should not have so imperilled your soul, and all Tintagel. My softness and your hardness have lost us Morgan.'

And then she beat me. I doubt if she had ever given such a beating in her life. A lesser woman might have died under it.

Later, in private, she beat herself.

When it was finished, and I lay weeping on the floor, she knelt beside me and gathered me in her arms.

'What do you say, Luned? Shall we go away together? Leave all this behind us? I'll get rid of the hell-cat. I'll tell the Pendragon he must take her back. Gold and lands cannot buy our peace. When she has gone, then you and I will cleanse Tintagel. We'll do penance for this shame. We'll set out on the road of pilgrimage that has no end. Build a coracle. Cast ourselves adrift on the breast of God's ocean. Trust the breath of the Spirit to wash us up where he will. What do you say?'

I could only sob into my arms. She wept for a flame extinguished. I, for another lit. She did not know the half of what had been done. Nor would I tell her.

I dragged myself back to my cell, more dead than alive. Morgan was sitting on the doorstep. She looked more child than woman that morning after. Thin. Pale. Her head bent forward over something between her hands, not straight and proud.

I could have believed it had not happened. The devils of Samain had curdled my dreams. I had ridden the nightmare. But the cloth was chafing the wounds on my back. My thighs were bruised. There was pain with every step I took. My body told me it had been so. Morgan did not look up to meet my eyes.

She had a kitten in her lap I had never seen before. A skinny grey thing. Large pointed ears, small face. Ribs showing through mangy fur and crusted cuts. She was feeding it with the hollow quill of a white gull's feather. There was a bowl beside her.

I stopped, sickened. What fresh devilment was this? What had those night-creatures taught her? What familiar was this? But then she lifted her head and smiled at me without apparent malice.

'Look, Luned! Poor thing. I found him trapped on a ledge of the cliff, mewing as if his heart would break. He has a loud voice for such a little waif. I think a hawk must have dropped him. See the wounds of the claws on his sides, the poor wee soul! Lucky it is my hands he has fallen into. I think I can cure him.'

She held the cut feather to his lips and his pink mouth opened trustingly. She let the golden droplets roll on to his tongue.

I staggered against the doorpost. Black imps danced before my eyes. Morgan jumped up with a cry and held me from falling. Her arm was round my waist. I felt an agony of pain and the joy of her touch.

Then she saw the blood on the back of my habit.

'So that's the way of it. It will be my turn next, I suppose. What did they think, she and Uther? That they could throw down a challenge to Gorlois's child and she not answer it? Well, I have taken the vows of Tintagel, have I not? We have done well, Luned. They begin to fear us.'

She led me to my bed, more gently than I would have expected.

'No work for you today. Let me see your wounds. Ah! This makes it sweeter. I did not guess that Bryvyth loved you so much.'

'I do not understand you,' I groaned.

'To beat you like this. You must have wounded her very deeply. I see now how it was. You were her darling. She let you into her heart. She built no defences against you. And now you have hurt her in her inmost place.'

'It was not I! It was not I who put out the flame. It was not I who defiled the chapel.'

'Oh, Luned. You know it was you.'

Did she mock me then?

'Lie still. I will run to Fyna. I need more ointment for cuts deep as this. We have made a powerful salve. I should like to test its effect.'

Fyna. The round blue eyes of the druid's daughter. Two heads whispering together in a doorway.

A concoction of these two mingling with my open flesh and blood.

Morgan was swiftly back. Her hands were cool and gentle, lifting my clothes from me. The work they did was cruel. I cried out as the sting of the salve bit the bared flesh. But her palms stroked on. Rhythmically, surely. I began to relax my clenched muscles and let my head drop on the pillow. I felt the blessing of her touch flow through my veins. She sang as she worked. On and on. I will not tell you what.

I ceased to fight her. I was in Morgan's hands. She had wounded me sorely. She must make me whole.

Bryvyth sent for Morgan. She did not return to my cell.

I could not move for the rest of the day. They let me lie. The kitten mewed, and crawled on to my bed. We slept together. Next day our wounds were clean and healing.

Bryvyth did not beat Morgan. I think she feared to. Morgan was of age now and a full woman. The high king's stepdaughter. She had not taken the vow of obedience, as I had. Instead Bryvyth sent for Nectan. Morgan did not tell me how the priest chose to wrestle with her.

# Chapter Twenty-Six

Next day I rose almost without pain. My scars were crusted, but closing quickly. Whether it was the salve, or the touch of Morgan's hands and the chants she sang that worked most powerfully, I cannot say.

Other wounds were not healed so easily.

They told me there was a pedlar at the gatehouse wishing to do trade with us. That was my business.

It was a clear grey morning, the wind brisk but not cutting yet. I seemed to see each detail on the mainland with a clarity it did not ordinarily have. Trees, houses, cattle. A world I had ignored and shrunk from.

I walked slowly towards the causeway, carrying myself a little more stiffly than usual. I looked with the same unaccustomed sharpness into the faces of every nun I passed. I watched their eyes drop before mine, or their faces turn away. The blood mounted in my cheeks. How much did each one of them know? Whose gowns had I fingered on the rocks? I recalled again that laughter and scuffling on the cliff path one summer night long ago. But it had not been like that! It had not been a matter of giggling for me. It had not! It had not!

I had to cross the causeway. It was a daily penance. All my womanhood had been spent on lofty Tintagel, but I had never lost my fear of those heights and the sea. If I could I would have stayed secure on the island and left that chasm between me and the world. For Morgan the abbey was her prison. For me it was a fortress.

There were two asses standing outside the gatehouse, with a man holding their heads. He looked me up and down. I did not meet his eye. Inside, the pedlar was a big hairy fellow, dressed in leather and canvas against the rain and mud. But he carried no common wares. They should have called him a silversmith. He spread out the goods from his saddlebags on the counting-table to dazzle my eyes. Enamel-studded bowls, silver chains for hanging lamps, bright, embossed dishes. I did not wonder that his servant outside carried a large spiked cudgel.

They say all smiths are men of magic. Certainly his goods had put a spell on me. I thought of the five Books of the Law that Cigfa had almost finished. We should be needing a jewelled cover for such a treasure.

'How long will you be staying in these parts?'

He shot a look at the churl in the doorway behind him. I had not expected to hear them laugh.

'That depends how rich the pickings are. Feast times are often lucky for smiths. Even white nuns have been known to exchange their treasures for ours.'

I had reached out my hand to fondle the twining metal-work. I saw his eyes undress me. Shockingly, I knew what was in his mind. I felt the sweat break out on my neck and between my breasts. His face split into a wide yellow grin and the wave of his onion-stinking breath came towards me. I turned, choking, snatching my hand away from the closeness of his. I turned and heard his servant laughing coarsely. *Who else had been in that hole under the cliff?*

I cannot say what I bought from him that morning, or what I paid. Cigfa would have to wait for her book-cover. If only I could be free of him and his knowing eyes. All day I was like a woman struggling to work in a sweat of fever.

But at night it was worse.

186

Morgan had been taken from me. Bryvyth had banished her to a cave next to Piala's. It was a punishment, not a penance. Morgan showed no contrition for the scarred faces of the saints. She was sent bread and water, a little butter and milk once a week. No one but the hermit was allowed to speak with her. Bryvyth had written in anger again to Uther Pendragon. Morgan must go.

But I could never be free of her now. Morgan had done two ills that Samain night. She had extinguished a flame that would never be mine to light again. And she had kindled another. A terrible burning down in the nether hole where the waters come and go with the moon. I had known it was there. But I had hidden the knowledge of its purpose.

I dreamed of men. Bodies in the darkness. Thrusting hands. How long would they make me wait and suffer like this? How long before the cave was filled with worshippers and the fire kindled? How long before Morgan led me down again?

She came back to us after a month. Thinner now. Her hair dull. Her face set in defiance.

For the last time she shared my cell.

I lay in bed whimpering, moving my legs in the darkness.

Morgan said crossly, 'Stop it. Let me go to sleep.'

I could not sleep. My fingers fumbled under my shift, feeling for unnamed parts of my body. Rousing a hunger they could not satisfy.

Was Morgan asleep? I lay in the dark, listening to her quiet breathing. And it came to me that she might have the power to ease this hunger if she would. My hand reached out across the gulf between our beds. I touched her side. Gently I turned the blanket back till I could feel warm flesh through her shift. She did not stir. Long I let my hand rest there, aching for her to feel my need and turn to me. She did not answer. I did not dare to tempt her further.

Several times in the agony of that restless night I felt the urge to pass water. I rose and unlatched the door quietly, yet not so silently I did not hope my movements might wake Morgan. I squatted on the chill grass and the liquid burned me as it passed. It did not leave my body satisfied.

The new moon looked through the open door on Morgan's bed. She was like moonlight herself. Black hair. White face. Cold. Single. I felt again her hands caressing the weals on my back. I thought that I would gladly have been wounded every day to have her heal me so. I stood in the doorway till I was cold and weary, waiting for her to lift her head and murmur something so that I might go to her side.

At last, disappointed, I crept back to my own bed. Cold now, as it had never seemed before. I scratched myself and cried a little into my pillow.

I think she knew. Perhaps that was her only kindness to me. Not to give me the terrible joy she keeps for men.

# Chapter Twenty-Seven

Next day, on Advent Sunday, Rathtyen died. Her soul slipped quietly away in the late afternoon. It was a holy death. We gathered round her. She put her hand on Muriel's and commended to her the charge of the schoolroom. I watched the young woman's face glow with the rush of gratitude and surprise. She spoke with Cigfa and Eira about the books in the library. She commended earnestly those ones which to her were of greatest value. She listed those which would repay copying and offering to the libraries of other monasteries, what works still needed to be sought from them in return. It was a sorrow to her that we had as yet no complete Bible in the translation of Jerome. She looked to us to mend that in the future. So it went on. Thanking Fyna for easing her pain, Blatriad for the special broths she had prepared, even Senara, newly-released from slavery to be a nun, for the milk and eggs that all of us enjoyed. And me, Luned, for my wise care of the convent, my stewardship of our wealth, my circumspection as I dealt with the world of men and money. I listened dry-eyed, but my heart wept. Rathtyen, whose tongue had always been so sharp in the service of truth, flattering us all with her dying energy. So learned and yet so blind to the truth.

Bryvyth was less inhibited than I. She held Rathtyen's head between her hands as the words grew fainter, slower. The tears ran freely down her cheeks for grief and pride and joy.

189

Then the sun dropped clear of a bank of cloud, and over the western sea came a path of gold. All down this celestial pavement ranks of angels hastened towards us with outstretched arms. They entered the cell. The radiance of their being lit Rathtyen's face with a bright glory. Their wings clouded our sight. Then the cell was grey, as it had not been before, and they had taken her soul. We all saw this.

We bore her body to the chapel and set a vigil.

I waited then for Bryvyth to send for me, for the vowed nuns to be gathered in council in the long room facing the sea which served both as refectory and meeting-house.

Morgan had not returned to my cell. I saw her walking in the dusk with Bryvyth on the summit, both wrapped in their cloaks as dusk fell with the murk closing over the sea and the nearer headlands. Bryvyth's back was more stooped than I remembered, Morgan tall and swift-moving. Supper passed, a sad, quiet meal. There was no summons for me.

When Rosslyn and I went to the chapel to take our turn in the vigil we found Bryvyth alone in the candlelight. She ordered Rosslyn to leave us. When she turned her head, I saw that the abbess was weeping. She rounded on me without troubling to wipe her cheeks.

'Well? Have you come to confess at last? Down on your face!'

I did not understand her. I was serving the penance she had set me. In all my daily work I was meticulous in obedience. How could she know the impurity of my night-time thoughts? Yet she was clearly angry. I prostrated myself before her.

I acknowledged my little failings. Rathtyen's death had shamed me. I had not been as devoted to study as the dying nun. I had neglected my reading. I had allowed myself to become impatient with a widow-tenant who had not paid the rent she owed us since Samain. Tean and I had struggled so long getting a chariot-wheel out of the mud that we had forgotten to sing the midday psalm. The sight of Nectan's chapel near Bossiney had brought our omission back to us, some time after the sun had passed its wintry zenith.

She heard me out in a grey stillness like that whole sad day itself. It was a short recital. I prided myself on honesty, on clarity of self-examination. But my daily life was disciplined. In the exercise of my monastic duties I offered little occasion for criticism. What I felt at night, who I was at night, in the close cell with Morgan, under her spell, that seemed another life, another time, another person. I could not have found the language to speak of it to Bryvyth. I did not think it either prudent or possible.

When I had finished, I expected to hear her rumbustious scolding, like the slapping of reins on the backs of her chariot-team. I waited for some light penance to be pronounced. Not heavy, but strengthening, like the effort of climbing a hill to see the greater vision from the top. I listened for the words of forgiveness.

Nothing came. Bryvyth stood with arms folded, face impassive, waiting still.

I raised my head, and it seemed that this was a mighty effort, as though a mountain slope lay between myself lying prostrate on the chapel floor at her feet and the abbess towering over me. I would not ordinarily have dared to lift my eyes until I heard forgiveness offered.

She met my look, with grey-blue eyes like the sea she lived so close to and did not fear. Clear, cold without the warmth of friendship in them now. Again that sense of otherworldliness. Where was the Bryvyth I knew? Where was the love that always raised me up, embraced me, set me striding once more on the pilgrim road beside her, as pupil and friend?

At last she spoke. Very cold. Precise. As though Rathtyen, dying in holy poverty, had bequeathed Bryvyth her voice.

'So? Is there no more you wish to tell me?'

Oh, the treacherous delicacy of women's faces. The skin too shallow. The blood too quick. The lips unsteady. She read the confirmation of my guilt.

'What more can there be? What do you want me to say?' Let her think it was only the heat of indignation.

'You have deceived me, Luned. Cruelly. Deliberately. Over seven years. I trusted you with the most difficult and dangerous of all our tasks. I saw you fail often. I blamed the strength of the enemy, and the weakness of my own prayers. Night and day I strove to arm you with God's power. I honoured your courage, your tenacity, your unwillingness to admit defeat and hand the burden to another. When you said you were winning the battle, I believed you. You let me rejoice that we had dragged Gorlois's daughter back from the brink of hell. Till Samain night.'

'You beat me for that. I made my confession. I still do the penance you laid upon me then.'

'I punished you for weakness, negligence, cowardice. For sins of omission. For the foolish pride that would not let you call me to help. You did not tell me of sins fouler than that.'

She waited. I was too frightened to question or argue.

'Today I talked with Morgan. Of what her future with us must be if she will not be a nun. She is of age now, and too old for the schoolroom. Rathtyen is dead, and her cell beside mine is empty. I put it to Morgan that she might have a house of her own, under my eye. I asked if it would grieve her to leave you. She laughed and said it would not. You had been no true soul-friend to her, and no gaoler either. She told me the truth of what you two had done.'

'What?' I whispered.

'Yes! She told me how all these years you had allowed her meetings with Gwennol. She confessed the black arts she has learned from that hag. She showed me these!' From her sleeve Bryvyth drew the little store of Morgan's slates that I had feared to read. 'Seven years. And you have connived with her. Studied corruption with her. You were here in the chapel. You stood by while she committed sacrilege. She said you smiled on her blasphemy in the hope of winning her love. Fool! What she wanted from you was your rage. Your shouts. Your hand on her arse. Your hugs!'

I could not speak. Treachery and despair whirled through my brain. Morgan was being taken from me. Morgan despised me. Morgan had accused me falsely. Yet still not of everything. The greatest sin of all had been left unsaid.

'Well? What have you to say for yourself that is not beneath contempt?'

What could I do? I confessed to the lesser sins I had not committed, to hide the knowledge of the greater crime.

She raised me up. I knew her arms around me and I sobbed like a little girl.

'The sin is mine. I should not have trusted you like myself . . . The Father is creating us anew. The Son is crucified for us afresh. The Spirit is cleansing us with wind and fire. God absolves the penitent.'

Bryvyth wept for me and for her own lost hopes. I wept for myself.

Today Rathtyen had died. Today Morgan had stolen my inheritance from me.

Before all the community, gathered in prayer, I falsely acknowledged my fault. There was no beating this time. Even Bryvyth's ready arm had grown weary at last. I think I could have endured that with greater pride than that public recital. I was condemned to return to the

193

cows. It was the most visible humiliation of my penance, though there were many others.

I stumbled from the chapel alone, crying bitterly. Someone caught me in the dark. It was Morgan.

'Well?' she demanded. 'Are you satisfied yet? Do you still wish to keep me here?'

I could not speak. My stomach was heaving.

'What is the matter, Luned? Why are you shaking?'

'It is nothing,' I moaned through gritted teeth. 'Just the cold wind.' But I could not fight down the retching in my throat. I spun away from her to hide this further degradation.

'You're not being sick, are you?' she said impatiently. Suddenly she threw back her head and laughed outrageously, while I spewed up bread and milk upon the grass.

'Oh, you're not, are you? It couldn't be that! Not my holy Luned, of all people! Oh, that would be the funniest thing in the world. The sweetest revenge I could ever have on Tintagel!'

I did not know what she meant. I swear to you, I did not know.

# Chapter Twenty-Eight

Bryvyth and Morgan. Both I had loved. Both abandoned me.

Morgan, my foster-daughter, was taken from me. She moved into the empty hut beside Bryvyth's. She had no human guardian now to fail her. Her door was barred at night from the outside. Bryvyth battled with her for love, a different love from mine. She was a strong-armed warrior defending her tribe from evil. It was too late. I had already betrayed Tintagel. Morgan had taken her vows. She belonged to the Goddess. Doors could not hold her any more.

Even the kitten deserted me for Morgan.

I slept alone again. I, who had waited years, desperate at times to regain my solitude. And now I cried myself to sleep for loneliness.

I did not know what was happening in my own body. Too little my mother told me in the orchard. Too little I had gossiped with other girls. Such things were never spoken of in Tintagel among celibate nuns. Or not where Bryvyth might have heard it. I had not wished to listen. I had thought that only in a nunnery could women get knowledge. I did not know what every slave-girl knows.

I knew my body had altered. The moon no longer brought a tide of blood. I believed simply that my womanhood had been taken away. At one time that would have delighted me. That monthly aspect of my life had been a burden to me, a fouling weakness of a woman's nature, a reminder that I could never be truly like a man. I had clung to that once-heard scrap of conversation that lean, hard hermits fasting and praying beyond the norm were sometimes released from our common curse. It was another reason to aspire to holiness, discipline, abstinence. I had embraced them hopefully.

Now I had what I wanted. My body ceased to bleed. And the loss of it was a sharp grief to me. I knew better than anyone that it could not be a reward for Christian virtue. Therefore it must have come as a punishment for the sin I had committed. The clean male God of Sinai and the fasting Christ of the wilderness had rejected me. Now the Three fertile Mothers from whom the earth teems declared me unpleasing to them. I was unfit for any life, unwelcomed by any god. I would have followed Morgan blindly, greedily, after that first time, despising myself, yet exulting too in that uncleanness. But I saw that way was barred to me also now.

Once more I must be up in the cold winter dark, milking the stinking beasts. I must stagger under the weight of hard-filled buckets. I must muck out the freezing byre, when my body longed for rest and warmth. Often Bryvyth worked alongside me in the dark dawn, whistling hymns and scolding the cows heartily. She blamed herself as well as me. But the friendship between us had cooled. Her trust was lost. There was no talk of making that pilgrimage together now.

A week later, Cigfa was declared the abbess's heir.

When I heard the news, I looked at my rough, cracked hands, that I could not hold steady for the cold. I thought of Cigfa, nobly-born, delicately pricking with compasses the lacing patterns of a new title page.

Yet I was too valuable to be utterly cast aside. When I had finished with the cows, I must still turn to the trade and rents and provisioning of the convent. It gave me no joy now. I saw that there was no honour in it. To deal with foreigners in silver, that other nuns would wash their hands after touching, to take a portion of the crops from surly tenants, to scold the cooks when they were wasteful. I had lost my youthful dream of glory. Who would read what my stylus scratched on the wax tablets? They would never illuminate the monasteries of Europe.

And when at last the weary day was ended and I longed to throw myself on the hay to ease my misery in sleep, I could not. I must spend long hours on my feet in prayer. Bryvyth had commanded it. My body obeyed, but she could not compel my soul. Prayer was dry sawdust in my mouth. It meant nothing to me now. I was mocked by both God and Goddess. When Bryvyth stood in her own cell, as I knew she did, did she feel the unequal burden on her soul?

Many of the girls went home for Christmas. Some of the older ones would not be returning. Husbands awaited them. Ygerne's daughter stayed. A horseman came from Uther. There would be no mercy for Morgan until Arthur was found. Each week a party of warriors rode out from Bossiney to enforce his rule. Morgan must be presented before them, pale, furious. He punished Bryvyth too, making her inflict this indignity on her prisoner.

Once the abbess burst out in anger to me, 'If only she'd repent just once and make a full confession of her sins, I'd throw her out of Tintagel that very same hour and let Uther's swords make an end of it. I'd rejoice to see her die with a pure soul now and give us peace.'

But Morgan had made her choice. She showed no repentance. Uther was right to fear her.

Winter tightened its grip.

Still no blood came. I suffered under the burden of more than spiritual unworthiness. I had thought that this cessation might have brought lightness of body, a greater physical freedom, a freer step. It was not so. I was appalled by the growing heaviness of my body, the slowness of my mind. I could hardly bear that. I, whose sharp quick brain had been the match for any man. I, who could out-figure any trader at the gate, whose mind could grasp the tally before my fingers cast the beads. Why was I now so far removed from what Rathtyen had been, ailing in body but at the last reciting Plato as though the book lay open in her mind? Why was I growing so like fat Blatriad, waddling about her kitchen?

Even Blatriad was luckier than I was. I would have given anything that winter to have worked in the warm, yeast-smelling comfort of the kitchen, to have soothed my aching body before the oven. But it was a luxury beyond reach.

If I had been less strong, my body might have given way under the strain. Even that escape was denied to me. I did not know enough to seek release for myself. What was begun that night in the Mother's Hole must be endured to the end.

I accuse Morgan. She could have helped. I do not doubt she knew enough, even then. Her eyes met mine and mocked me. She knew what was coming, and I did not.

# Chapter Twenty-Nine

I dragged my heaviness of soul and body through the summer.

Clever, but ignorant, I woke in my cell one hot morning in August. Cramps gripped my belly. Believe me, I thought I had the flux. I stumbled to the latrine, clutching the pain. But no relief came. I crept back to my cell and lay there moaning, too ill to rise. Senara came to see why I had not milked the cows, and she went hurrying to fetch Blatriad from the kitchen. They roused Fyna from her bed. Wise though they were, they did not guess the reason. My belly was not as huge as Blatriad's.

They made me a potion. Hot, foul-smelling, strong. They went to morning prayers and left me in a quiet that held no peace. They nearly killed me. Time after time I crawled to the latrine. It was there at last that I dropped the baby.

I thought my body was bursting, that I who had aspired to the highest of honour and virtue was now a gigantic paunch of foulness. Now I would split and spill my guts into a stinking hole in the ground. My rottenness into the earth from which I had come. My blood to the Mothers. My skin once bloated then left empty as a shrivelled toad. No spirit left. No freed soul winging into the pale blue sky above me. No choirs of angels singing triumph as they had for Rathtyen. No Father opening heavenly arms to receive me. No radiant Christ to greet his bride. My soul had died long since. It only remained to empty this distorted body.

But before that, pain. Terror. How could my bowels have spawned anything so monstrous?

Nuns heard my screams, and then the child's, and came running.

I remember little of it, through that sobbing nightmare. Fyna pulled the baby from the filth of the hole where I had dropped it. I think some of the others, more shocked, would have let it drown. Even then, I hardly understood what had happened. That blackened, bloodied thing, bawling like a hungry calf. The mess that streaked Fyna's gown. The round eyes and open mouths of a ring of sisters. What had that to do with me, slumped on my knees on the earthen floor, spent and torn?

They took the baby from me. I never saw it again. I do not even know which kind it was. I could not ask.

'Take her to bed.'

I felt Bryvyth's presence, like the wrath that will end the world.

Some of them helped me to rise. Blood slid down my legs. I do not remember well. I think Blatriad was with me, and the slave-girl Senara. Not Cigfa. Oh, no. She stood, white-faced, at a distance. This was not work for her hands.

Back in my cell, they stripped my shift away and washed the blood and slime from me. They dressed me in clean linen and drew the covers over me. They spoke above my head, as though I was a baby myself, in anxious whispers. They let me lie.

I was not dead, though I wished I was. I knew now that I was horrifyingly alive. The blood that I thought had dried in my womb for ever had burst forth into doubled life. How could this be?

I groaned like those who would rip out the past and cannot.

I lay, exhausted, waiting for Bryvyth to come.

There were footsteps at the door. Through the black cloud of self-pity I looked up. Bryvyth must understand. She must see it had been none of my own doing. Not my choice. How could I ever have willed such a terrible thing? I did not know how it had happened to me. I would throw myself upon the generosity of her compassion.

It was not Bryvyth. The white moon of Morgan's face hung over me. Her hair, braided above the ears, and then falling free, brushed my face. It smelt of lavender.

She was a tall young woman now, no longer a schoolgirl. Her breasts standing proud above a slender waist. I smiled for the first time, weakly. I was not alone. Morgan had not deserted me. She had led me to this. I knew, without understanding how, it must spring from that night in the Mother's Hole. You must understand that I had sought in libraries for my knowledge. My parents' farm had never been my school. Yet I did not blame Morgan then. I was glad she had come.

A cold smile twisted her mouth.

'Poor Luned. Didn't you know anything? Could you not calculate the meaning of your own measurements? What was there ever in you to make you so proud? You should have asked me for help. I could have ended it long ago. I know enough for that. You could have done it yourself, even. The knowledge was there, on the slates under my bed.'

'How could I guess? Why didn't you tell me?'

'Because you did not ask. I am a queen. It was for you to be the suppliant at my feet. Well, you are mightily humbled now. You must go begging on your knees.'

'What have I left to beg for? Except death.'

'I will not give you that, though I could do it. Death is not alms to be distributed freely, like bread to the poor. I shall keep that knowledge close, like a sheathed weapon. Knowledge without the will to use it is not yet power. One day perhaps I may see the need and discover the will. But I shall not use it lightly. You are too small an object to deserve it. I have other powers I mean to use for greatness. Gwennol and her sisters have taught me. But I shall soon know more than they. The Mothers themselves are teaching me. My own eyes bring me knowledge. My fingertips speak to me. My nose is a scholar. In years to come the bards will sing of my skill.'

I believed her. I had to trust someone then. I would have believed anything Morgan told me.

'What will happen to me?'

'We must consider,' she said, studying my face as she smoothed my hair aside.

Her eyes were strangely bright. She was like a physician bending over her patient, seeing a new disease with interest, even excitement.

'You'll never be abbess now. That was over already, wasn't it? You can't stay here. You have been too shamed. And you're too proud to crawl back to your parents' farm. So what else is there for you? Would you go out of the gate and sell your body to the first man for the price of a meal? Do not turn your face to the wall, Luned.'

She wanted me to beg from her. She was a prisoner. Under a ban of death. Destitute, save for the meagre allowance to feed her with convent food and clothe her with the simplest gown. But in her own eyes she was already a queen. She had a court, a country, weapons, gifts to give.

I caught her hand. The smooth white hand that had healed my back.

'Help me! You can, can't you?'

'I can and will. Should not a daughter care for her foster-mother? Bryvyth trusted me to you for my salvation. Instead, I have made you mine. I have humbled

holy Tintagel. I have been revenged on the Church
that betrayed my father and imprisoned me. Uther
Pendragon is next. Let us move you closer to the king
himself. He killed my father and stole Bossiney from us.
It is a royal dun now, under that trickster Ulfin. Go there
when you can walk. Ask for Gwennol. Tell her I send you
to her for safekeeping, as the first of my women.'

'To Gwennol!'

The old witch from the sea. Bryvyth's mighty
exorcism on the shore. The spread fingers pointing. The
curse chanted.

'What is the matter? You're not afraid of her, are
you?' She snatched her hand from me, her eyes blazing.
'Gwennol loves me! Do you know that? Gwennol loves
me! When did you ever risk your life to save me ? When
did you ever hold me in your arms? If Bryvyth had been
my foster-mother, she might have done so. But you!
When have you ever loved me more than yourself?'

Her rage passed. We both knew I would not answer.

'Wait for me secretly in Bossiney. Gwennol will teach
you. This cannot endure. I shall need my own wise
women about me soon. One day I must be free, and then I
shall meet . . .'

She turned away from me and went to the door. For a
while she stood in silence, staring out over the sea. Suddenly laughter rippled from her, shockingly. She ran
back to me, merry as a mischievous girl.

'Oh, Luned! You were not clever enough by half. Do
you not know? Merlyn was the baby of a nun too! She
swore his father came to her in the night as an incubus
from hell. She was powerless to resist him. Many times
he covered her while she lay helpless. And they believed
her. The Church took her side. The world calls Merlyn a
holy child. Merlyn! Son of a nun and a devil. What will
your child be, Luned? What have they done with it? Did
they call it holy?'

She left me then. Alone with my loss. Everything gone. My pride. My future. My safe stronghold. Maidenhead. Baby. Even the cell that was my home. All lost to me forever. I did not need Bryvyth to stand over me and tell me that. It was too late to confess now and be forgiven. I had deceived her too many times to be believed. It was her fault. An abbess should be a judge of women. I never asked for such a task. I was not equal to it.

They cast me out from Tintagel, without my baby. They judged I was no fit mother for any child. With my belly empty and my breasts painful with unsucked milk, I took myself to Bossiney, the first of Morgan's people.

# Chapter Thirty

I could not pass Bossiney by this time, that place of men and wealth and war. I had not the strong presence of Bryvyth beside me to give me courage. I had not even the grip of my holy staff in my hand, a familiar friend. They had taken that from me, with my white nun's gown, and given me a dress of homespun brown. I was a woman like any other now. I had no protection.

Bryvyth had done her best.

'What will you do, child? I know a farmer, Govan, up Bodmin way. His wife died last Candlemas. He's a good spread of fields and a load of cattle and pigs. He needs a clever wife to help him manage it all. Will I tell him you're willing?'

I bowed my head and thanked her. I would make my own way. She would get no comfort from me.

There was pain in that last parting from her in the mists of morning. The ready tears ran down Bryvyth's cheeks, though not on mine.

Alone, she stood at the island end of the causeway, the fragile neck that held Tintagel to the land. Knowing my fear, she would have crossed the bridge with me that last time for friendship. I told her no. Briefly I saw her, square shoulders slightly stooped, watching me go. She raised her hand in an uncertain blessing. Too late for that. I did not look back again.

I had wanted to see someone else. My eyes had gone past Bryvyth, searching the ledges and the summit for a

tall, vital figure, the fall of raven hair, a fair face turned
to seek mine. There were a few others about their tasks
in the early hush of morning, glancing sideways to see
me depart, pretending in their innocence to ignore me.
There was no sight of Morgan. Then I remembered.
Bryvyth had set a bar on her door. She had divided us.

That was the only thing that sustained me as I walked
the short road from Tintagel towards Bossiney. That
this was Morgan's home. Had been Morgan's home, in
the days when her father Gorlois hunted this forest and
Uther Pendragon beat the Saxons and her mother
Ygerne prayed in Nectan's glade for a fourth child.
Before Arthur was born.

It was Gwennol's place too. Neither Uther nor Ulfin
had found the courage to turn her out. And with that
thought the solid walls of earth and wattle ahead began
to take on a fairy shimmer. If I was cast out from the city
of the angels, what had I come to now?

It was too quiet. A listless small boy switching at flies
with a spray of oak leaves. The cattle already lying
down in the shade after milking.

There was no lean young warrior on the gate with
excess of mocking courtesy to make a woman blush. The
guard was lame, with a facial scar making one eye peer
crookedly.

'I come from Tintagel. I have a message to give.' I had
fretted all the way over how to announce myself, how to
get past Uther's men to Gorlois's nurse and witch.

'You won't find Ulfin here, or any lord with four whole
limbs. It's my guess they won't be back for harvest
either. The Saxon dragon's eating up the best blood
we've got. But my lady Rozen should be up and about
soon, if you want to sit down in the shade and wait.'

Another jolt. I had nerved myself to deal with men.
After all, it had been my task for many years, though
never with warriors. My reckoning had not extended to

noble ladies. I had scorned the embroideresses'
workshop. I let them deal with their highborn customers
directly. I, plain and scholarly, found such noblewomen
oddly disturbing.

'There is no need to trouble my lady. My message is
for a woman by the name of Gwennol.'

Be wary. Do not use that name too familiarly. He must
not guess that I have been sent by Morgan.

'Gwennol Far-Sight? That's a rum do, now. What business do the nuns of Tintagel want with old Gwennol?'

'I am not a nun.'

'I can see that.' He looked me over shrewdly. 'But
you've had your hair shorn under that veil not so long
since. What was the trouble? Too cold a life without a
man in your bed?'

Was my sin so naked I might have worn the scene
embroidered on my dress? I could not hide the truth
from the first person I spoke to.

He laughed, not unkindly. 'Cheer up, mistress. I'm a
soldier. Or was, till Uther led us into a Saxon ambush.
He's had no luck since he killed Gorlois. Well, then. You
need keen eyes to stay alive in enemy territory, and
there's too much of that in Britain now. And shrewd
judgment too to tell friends from traitors. Don't you fret.
Hair grows again, at your age. And someone will put the
roses back in your cheeks . . . if any men come home this
time.'

I saw the reason for his kindness. His wounds had cast
him out from his own hope of glory. We were two of a
kind, driftwood on the beach, uprooted trees broken off
from life before our time.

'Well, you look harmless enough. There's only good
comes out of Tintagel. I say it's a pity the Pendragon
ever crossed them. He needs all the prayers he can get
now. Gwennol sleeps down there, this side of the bake-
house. A hut all to herself, she has, and no children to

mind now. Don't let on I said so, but I fancy Ulfin is
afraid to cross her. They've none of them been so sure of
themselves, since Merlyn went. Maybe she could help
you, if you asked, whatever the trouble is. She's good
with wounds. My sort, at least.'

So I was walking down the quiet path between the
houses towards the woman I feared most, after Morgan.

Gwennol Far-Sight was old now, but she was not abed.
There were many in that dun who had a drowsy, frowsty
look. After the convent it seemed an ill-disciplined place
to me. The best of its youth was gone, and many older
warriors had climbed into the saddle again to fill their
place. Those who were left without them spent too long
in bed and had too little work or reason to do it.

But not this one. The old woman sat on a bench in the
sun. She was carding wool. At close-quarters I saw her
hands were crooked, yet they moved in a steady rhythm
that made the finished work pile up beside her with the
ease of practice.

She picked me out before I had left the gate. Her eyes
were on me all the time, like a fisherwoman drawing in
her catch on a slowly tightening line. Yet I was not to be
caught. I had come of my own free will. I could have
accepted Bryvyth's offer of a husband.

When we were near enough for our eyes to meet she
gave me a slow, sure smile of satisfaction, dark eyes
intent as a robin on a worm. There was no surprise.
There was nothing I needed to explain.

'So she's sent you ahead of her.'

I dropped my eyes. I was not accustomed to stare
others in the face. But the silence made me look up
again. The smile had gone. She might have been that
bloodstained hag guarding the way to the cave, so grim
she looked.

'By rights we should kill you.'

A moth that had fluttered into a spider's web.

'You put your dainty foot in a place where strangers are not allowed. Only those the Old Ones recognise are safe in there. Lowenna's a fool. She shouldn't have let you pass her. She knows every sheep she has by name but she can't tell the difference between one nun and another. But you're clever. You must have known what you saw was only safe for the wise.'

'I did not wish to see it. Morgan brought me there.'

'And you were her keeper?' She spat with laughter. 'The Mothers will have blood for it, dearie.'

'There was blood. I have been punished.'

The soreness was still between my legs with walking. My breasts were hard and hot.

She looked me up and down, knowing everything.

'The Mothers have blessed you, I'd say.'

'It was no blessing. I did not want it. And they have taken my baby away.'

I almost cried then, being torn in two.

'But it was alive, wasn't it? Still is, though you can't see it. Life and death. That's what the Mothers give to those they love. Death for all of us. Birthing for the lucky ones. Maybe Morgan was wise after all to bring you down. I never had a baby. Hundreds of women I've helped fill their bellies. I've charmed the babies out of them too. I've nursed other people's children on my knees, even Ygerne herself, that's queen of Britain now. Morgan was my last. They took her away from me and gave her to you bloodless nuns instead. I never had one of my own.'

'We did not want Morgan.' Faithless Luned, to deny I loved her.

'Nobody ever wanted Morgan. Except Gwennol. But she's grown too big for me. And you want her, now.'

I bore that in silence, transparently red with anger.

'Well, what can you do? I take it you've come looking for work, and food in your belly.'

'I can write a fair hand. I can read Latin and Greek. I can figure and cast the reckoning on the abacus.'

'Can you sew?'

Indignation rose. Had I trained that hard, to be a woman like any other?

'That was not my work.'

She fingered my skirt and her hands moved meaningfully up the inside of my thighs.

'But you're not a white nun now, are you, dearie? You went into the shadow of death, without protection, and the Mothers blessed you. You're a full woman now.'

Then she let go of me and sat back, wincing. Just an aged serving-woman on a hard bench.

'My Lady Rozen will be tickled pink when she hears you've come from Tintagel. She's always had a fancy for fine embroidery, and there's no one can sew as pretty a stitch as the white nuns. But that abbess Bryvyth of yours has got a long memory. There isn't one thread she's let come to Bossiney since the day Gorlois died. Leastways, not by her knowledge. Though there's more than one thing been done at Tintagel that she doesn't know about, isn't there? You *can* sew, can't you?'

'Of course I can.'

We had all, even the highest of us, taken our share of mending, of sewing plain seams. I had shown Morgan how to take care of her own clothes. I did not deceive Gwennol.

'Well, you're clever enough to learn Latin. So you can figure out how to whip a silver thread. Do you want me to ask her for a place?'

A huge lump in my throat to swallow.

'Please.'

For a moment her head bent, muttering. Her nails snagged her skirt. Then she stretched out her claw for me to help her rise.

She hobbled away to the lady's bower beside the hall.

I was too ashamed to stand outside and be stared at. I crept into the darkness of Gwennol's hut and sat down on a stool. Dried herbs hung everywhere, scenting the air as I brushed beneath them. More than a normal woman's rafters would hold. I did not examine them too closely lest I should find that not all the bundles were what they seemed. As indeed they were not. When Gwennol came back she found me weeping from exhaustion and grief.

'My lady will see you. It's a funny thing, but she's torn her gown this very morning, just after you came. So there's your chance to show how clever you mean to be. Let's look at you.'

She wiped my face and then parted my clothes at the neck. Her hands reached in and gripped my breasts. I cried out in pain, as first golden liquid and then white spurted out. She mixed a powder with water and made me drink it.

'We'll have to take care you don't get the milk-fever. It's a pity it isn't a wet-nurse my lady needs, instead of a seamstress.'

She settled my clothes again and straightened my veil. I might have been a snivelling child, like so many others.

'There! You're one of us now. We're three of a kind, seemingly. I never had a baby of my own. You've borne yours, and lost it. And Morgan was robbed of her little brother Arthur. Well, the world's turning. Our time is coming round. Let's see if we can't bring one of those pairs together, eh?'

# Chapter Thirty-One

I was a good pupil. I do not mean the embroidery, though
I quickly became proficient in that too. Yet fine sewing
was a necessary burden laid upon me, the price of food
and shelter. There was another school I trained in that
excited my soul. I was Gwennol's pupil.

I feared the spirits of the otherworld and Gwennol's
powers. That fear was real and proper. It grows greater
with the years, not less. Those who do not respect the
realm of the Old Ones do not live long or keep their
sanity. Yet, like that night in the Hole under Tintagel, the
dark thing I feared also aroused me. I felt it first as a
tremor of danger in the mind. Soon it became manifest in
a kindling of the body. You may think from much that has
gone before that I was cold, hardly a woman, walled up
against the sensations of the flesh. Under Gwennol's
teaching I discovered truths about myself I had not
known. That coolness had been my defence against the
violence of my own physical being. Gwennol loosed it.
When the sacred drink was in me and the drums quick-
ened my blood and the darkness covered me, that other
Luned inside me was uncaged.

So some on Tintagel too approached the living God.
There were those like Piala who abandoned themselves
to Him, who allowed Him to invade and possess them. I
had never been one of them. Too late I caught a glimpse
of their ecstasy. Morgan had barred that way to me
forever.

213

I had not escaped her. Under the earth, between the waters, I met Morgan again. My mind told me it could not be so. Bryvyth had set a great bar on her door. But when the smoke eddied and the flame turned white flesh to rose and eyes sparkled under masks, she was there. The moon-glimpse of her face, the star-shaft of her body, the shadow of her hair. When we invoked the Maiden, Mother, Hag, she came. It could not have been anyone but Morgan. No one else was in the same perfect form both child and queen.

I am one of her people now. With a sharp clarity of memory I see myself prostrate on the floor of the chapel in Tintagel, repeat my final vows, hear Nectan raise me to my feet, feel Bryvyth place the veil on my shorn head. I felt that thrill of awe again. I crossed another threshold.

You cannot come. This time my dress is on the rocks. My new-given name is spoken at the mouth. The watcher's bloodstained hole beckons me but challenges you. Are you repelled? Or do you wish to come in, through the blood, to the cave where life is given? Our language is not so very far apart, you see, though we horrify you.

I told you what I saw that first time, in ignorance and misconception. Now I understand what is being done. And therefore I may not tell you what I see.

Gwennol saw to it that it was only enacted. There were no more babies to quicken my womb.

By day Lady Rozen exclaimed with delight over the work I did for her. The nuns had schooled me in delicacy and accuracy of stitching. Everything that was done in Tintagel was finely made, for the glory of God the Creator. And I had studied the patterns of the scriptorium under Cigfa. Most of the work I did there was plain scholar's copying, convent accounts. But I had learned early how to plot a lacing band of ornament, to mark a fine capital at the beginning of the chapter. It was not difficult for me to transfer the technique from the written page to a silk border. It needed a methodical mind, a knowledge of geometry, the patience to repeat the same motif time after time without deviation around the hem.

She boasted she had never had such a treasure. She displayed my handiwork for the envy of her friends. Luned's embroidery became a special gift she could bestow on those who pleased her.

It gave me a bleak kind of pleasure. I had fallen far in my own esteem. I was shut out forever from the scriptorium of the abbey, to spend my life working for women whose highest goal was to ornament themselves for the envy of others. Solace came at night. Yet I must endure my days somehow. It was a matter of pride to do the work I despised exactly well.

It was a strange dichotomy. Sober seamstress by daylight. Passionate worshipper at the dark of the moon and the four great festivals.

I needed Gwennol. She alone could show me how I might satisfy my soul now.

She did not like me. We sprang from the same farming stock, but our educations had differed. I spoke the high Latin of Cicero and Virgil, while she knew the coarse vocabulary of the market-place. It was natural to me to write down anything I learned, to list names and quantities and applications. She saw me doing this with rage and horror. She swept my careful records into the fire and stamped out the ashes. Such knowledge should be entrusted to the memories of the wise only, to be sung in a sing-song chant, to be recited in an endless chain. It was not impossible for me learn by rote. I had got the whole Psalter by heart and much of the theorems of Euclid. But I liked the order of the laced tablets of a codex, the sight of a growing store of knowledge, more valuable than gold, like Morgan's slates.

Gwennol needed me. I was an apt scholar, and she was old. She could not refuse to pass on what she knew

to one who would retain it so faithfully. I had little
natural skill in this field. I would never have the touch
of power in my hands like Morgan. My success came
from precise application of techniques studied, as I
had learned to embroider a hem without love but with
exactitude.

So, yoked unwillingly to each other, Gwennol and I
began to work for Morgan's freedom.

Gwennol excused herself. 'She was safer over in
Tintagel as long as she was a little maid. I knew Bryvyth
would never let those men harm her. But she's a grown
woman now. She must have her rights. And Uther
Pendragon's got his hands full with those pesky Saxons,
and his back turned on Cornwall. There'll be more than
a few will rally to her when she's free. There's her
sisters' husbands for a start.'

Such talk troubled me. I was a stranger to the world of
kings and armies. Ulfin came little to Bossiney with his
warriors now and in no good humour, his men few and
wounded, the news of Britain bleak. Lady Rozen tried
her best to cheer him but he wanted sleep, and brief
savage love-making, and then excess of wine.

Young men were needed elsewhere now. Yet week
after week a guard still rode to Tintagel to have Morgan
paraded before them. Old, lame men, almost too stiff to
climb into the saddle. But they were enough. She could
not have escaped without Uther's knowledge.

Still, when Ulfin's band came home the sight of an
armed warrior disturbed me. I have never known how to
speak to such men.

'The Pendragon violated a holy place,' I told Gwennol.
'It is not surprising the land is wounded and laid waste.'

Nun or witch, Tintagel was a sacred centre. The
women's navel. You must not be surprised that I still
hold Bryvyth and her kind holy. We do well to recognise
each other's power.

'Then we must find another ruler for Britain. One that knows how to heal the land,' said Gwennol, and set me to work.

Even now it quickens my blood. We two, and those we trusted, there in the far south-west corner of an island on the edge of the Roman Empire, working to shift the world on its axis. And so we did.

Long and secret were our preparations. Much there was new for me to learn. Much more that was old for Gwennol to remember, that she had never used before, perhaps had never heard before. I do not know. In places that I may not tell you of she sat cross-legged, her eyes closed but her face lifted as though she saw through red-veiled lids things it would sear the sight to look on naked. I fed the fire, dizzy with the scented smoke, put in her hands the things she commanded, sang what she taught me, not always understanding, knowing that to understand too much might rob the runes of power. My mind obedient, rational to begin with, saying that this, and this, and this, are what need to be done. The smoke taking over, the intellect melting, the body dissolving. Life running into water and blood and fire. I barely remained conscious to serve Gwennol.

When it was done, we were older, exhausted, and we had only gathered the means. Now we must make the great application. It must be done in the Hole, at night, at the dark of the moon, with the wisest of the wise. It was with a strange shock that I heard Gwennol summon me. I was not long in the mysteries. I had not known I had served the Old Ones so well.

The great rite of Unbinding began.

# Chapter Thirty-Two

The world shifted. That which had been bound began to be loosed. Things which had been hidden came into the light. Such power is not easily controlled. We did not suspect what we had woken.

I was alone. It was not my habit, and is not now, to sit with a flock of other women gossiping more than I work. I have a reputation for superiority. I cannot help that. I cannot disguise I am an educated woman. Better my own thoughts and the memories of my learning than filling my head with trivialities and driving out what I so hardly gained.

So I took my stool to some quiet place to do my sewing. I was not often interrupted. I think the men were afraid of me. I could have found greater peace outside the walls of Bossiney. The cliffs were wide and grassy. There were quiet coves. Gwennol still went to such places if the day was sunny and her rheumatism did not trouble her too much. But I went little out of the gate. We were too close to Tintagel still. I did not want to meet the white sisters on the road, going about their works of charity. It would have pained me too much.

I did not find it difficult to be so confined physically. My mind ranged far.

I had chosen a place on the rampart in the early afternoon. The dun was ill-guarded. The Saxons had drained it of its youth. But we did not expect the enemy to come this far. Those that were left in Dumnonia had little heart for raiding. War was no longer a sport, like hunting.

So I watched them come, and no one gave a shout of warning. I did not call out. It was not my place. But I stopped my sewing and lifted my head to follow their progress, as I thought, unobserved.

A man and a woman, riding finely-caparisoned horses. Behind them, two attendants on smaller ponies.

It was he who caught my eyes and filled my thoughts with wonder and disquiet. He was immensely tall. His robes were dazzling white and he wore a white turban, fastened with a ruby and a purple feather. His skirts spread loose and flowing over his coal-black mount. More startling still, his face and hands were black, gleaming faintly in the sun as though anointed with oil. I had seen such men aboard the ships that came to Tintagel. In later years I had traded with them, tuning the ear of my schoolhouse Latin to the strange jabber of theirs. But I had never seen one like this. A prince. With a great curved scimitar at his side.

I scarcely had eyes for the lady beside him. Except to note that she was as fine as he was, but of an opposite kind, as though his darkness had cast a bright shadow. Gold hair, tumbling in curls out of intricate braids. A fair face, shaded under the most delicate of veils. Clothes of as many colours as a meadow in May. A light green gown richly and colourfully embroidered. A rose-pink tunic, an underskirt all white and gold. Jewels on throat and arms and even on the fine blue leather of her boots. Where he was noble in his simplicity, she was a riot of extravagance.

The boy behind was fair and golden-curled. The girl was black and brilliant-eyed.

As they approached Bossiney the man leaned out his hand and caressed the woman's arm, saying something to her that made a smile flash in his dark face. She threw back her pretty head and laughed ringingly, then took his hand in her white one and played with his fingers as they rode side by side.

Reality dissolved. These were creatures out of fairyland. I sat bewitched. It did not occur to me to make any spells to ward against them. I did not think to warn Gwennol.

I lost sight of them as they circled to the gate. But I turned quickly, eager to see their entrance.

Bossiney had changed. The dusty paths, the mud-smeared walls, the ageing thatch had all taken on the bright shimmer of water. The strangers dismounted and walked in through the guard-post like brilliant fish swimming through their true domain.

Little Cador went running to warn my lady. A flock of women came hurrying out of the bower, my Lady Rozen among them. She advanced to greet the strangers, hastening for eagerness and uncertainty. I could see that she was both anxious and honoured to have such unexpected and noble guests.

I had not moved from the rampart. I could not hear the greetings that passed between them. But the name of Uther Pendragon floated up to me. For a moment confusion overtook my wits. This could not be the treacherous king come back to Cornwall, surely? This courtly Moor? They disappeared into the hall. I saw wine being brought, and cakes. The golden boy and the black-faced girl stood in the doorway, teasing each other with peacock feathers. I felt impelled towards the steps, but I resisted. A nameless fear kept me on my stool on the wall, as if the dun below were indeed a pool in which I did not know how to swim.

The guests emerged into the sunlight. The Moor's arm rested lightly around his lady's waist as she leaned on his shoulder. Beside the fresh gaiety of her robes, the stark white of his, Rozen looked shabby. Even the work of my needle on her gown seemed dull and lifeless. The black man walked across the open space in front of the hall. He carried his head nobly and his limbs had the grace of authority that needs no swagger. His eyes looked keenly on all sides. They found me. He moved towards me, slowly, still chatting courteously to his hostess, his finger-tips still laced in those of his lady. His brown eyes never left my face. I made no attempt to run or to protect myself, though my body screamed to me for help. I was a half-fledged bird trapped in its nest by a hawk.

He stopped beneath me, and I saw that his face was not truly black, but dark as old, oiled wood.

'Greetings, Luned,' he said, as though I had known and expected him. He extended his hand.

As I came down the steps, I knew. I did not have the name, but I recognised his power. I had felt that same lure, walking down the path towards Gwennol's hut, that morning of my expulsion. This was stronger yet.

'That is she, as you say.' Rozen answered, and I heard the puzzlement in her voice as I bowed. 'You are hon-oured, Luned. This is Saranhon Star-Gazer, from the court of Uther Pendragon. And this the Lady Nimue.'

But I knew from the way she tasted the names on her tongue that they were new to her.

'So this is the fair embroideress,' exclaimed the lady.

'She has a gifted hand, it is true.'

'And trained on Tintagel, you say!' Nimue laughed like rippling water.

Should I be afraid of her too? Could there be power in anyone so gay and pretty?

But Saranhon drew my eyes back to his and made my flesh tremble merely by smiling at me.

'So you were foster-mother to Morgan, Gorlois's daughter? How is she?'

Fear turned me faint. I had not spoken of that to anyone but Gwennol.

'I am no longer a nun. I have not seen Morgan these two years.'

His hand played with his companion's hair. His face did not change. He went on looking at me. He knew I lied. I knew I had angered him.

I was in the water now. Their element. It was cold about me and I was drowning. Words gasped from me, bubbles breaking on the surface, from desperation.

'She is still a prisoner. Against the law of God and Britain. She is of age to leave her parents' home. She has the right to live freely or to marry whom she chooses. Uther Pendragon denies that right by threat of murder.'

'Insolent!' Rozen cried. 'Do you want to be whipped, to speak so to the king's mage?'

'She speaks only the truth now,' said Saranhon. 'You know it. You and your husband are Morgan's gaolers, are you not? But for seven years this woman was the keeper of Morgan's heart. Her eyes say more than could be seen from Gwent or Winchester. It is well that the Pendragons know their danger. Morgan has not forgotten old grudges, has she?'

'How could she, there, where it happened?'

'Or forgiven?'

'Have the Pendragons ever asked for her forgiveness?'

'Or understood the necessity of that night?'

'Necessity?'

Nimue caught his arm. Someone was coming in through the gateway. A small, squat, humpbacked figure, walking lamely. Gwennol.

There was a flash in Saranhon's eyes. If he had not been black I think colour might have sprung to his cheeks. He watched her come in silence, as he had watched me.

She was not so frightened by him. She did not stop or hesitate or show surprise. It was as though, even out on the cliffs, she had known they had come, and who they were. I felt some of the sureness go out of Saranhon.

Then he stiffened. The muscles of his face became taut. I heard the breath hiss through his pinched nostrils. Even from where I stood I felt the heat of power radiating from him.

As she neared him Gwennol stumbled slightly. Her eyes glazed over and began to wander. She no longer seemed to know where she was going.

'Be off to your own hut,' scolded Rozen. 'We do not need you here.' She apologised to Saranhon. 'Gwennol Far-Sight. An old pensioner from Gorlois's court. We keep her for pity's sake.'

Nimue laughed. Her hand strayed along Saranhon's spine and fondled his neck. His eyes left Gwennol's. A shiver of delight ran through him and before us all he leaned towards his lady and kissed her rose-pink mouth. Very sure of herself and her lover was Nimue. As I saw his hand encircle her thighs I looked away for modesty.

My eyes fell on Gwennol. A change had come over her, as though a fog had lifted. The eyes bright and dark as never before in the two years I had known her, a brilliance of shock and triumph. Lame though she was she almost flew the last few steps to meet him. With an effort Saranhon tore himself from Nimue's hold. I felt him striving to regain mastery, too late.

Gwennol came so close that when she stopped at last and looked up at him, he had to bend his head to her. Her breath came quickly, as though she had been striding fast. Small dark eyes peering up into his large brown ones.

'Emrys Merlyn,' she said. 'Come back to us after nine years!'

There was a gasp from all of us, and a flash like lightning again across the Moor's face. It was a name known but not often or lightly spoken. A name out of song. A name bitter in the history of Bossiney. The Pendragon's magician. The trickster who had penetrated Tintagel's defences. The druid who had held Arthur in his arms that stormy night and stolen him away into silence. Lady Rozen backed away, doubt in her face. I saw that she was thinking of calling the guards. I do not believe they would have touched him. Nimue grasped at Saranhon's arm, alarm in her eyes.

The Moor laughed.

'Life is long. And the world's course is longer still for a multitude of livings. I have been known under many faces and many names. Still, I should have guessed Gwennol Far-Sight had not lost her power of seeing.'

She spat in the dust.

'I don't change. Not like some I could name.'

Yet for all that, he reached out a hand to her and she put up her own. They clasped each other almost like old friends.

'Leave us,' he ordered Rozen and her retainers. But Gwennol put out a hand and stayed me. Nimue remained too, holding the mage's sleeve and tracing her finger lightly on his arm, making him shudder.

'Gwennol Far-Sight,' he said, when we were alone. 'Since you have uncovered me so quickly let us speak plainly. It seems we cannot escape each other.'

'Hm! I thought you'd escaped us all for near nine years. And when did Emrys Merlyn ever say anything without a double tongue?'

'Be careful, old woman, or your own tongue will shrivel in your throat,' warned Nimue.

Merlyn patted her hand.

'Be easy, my love. Gwennol and I are old allies and old enemies. We understand each other.'

Gwennol looked Nimue up and down.

'Who's this pretty dragonfly you've taken up with? And what's brought the pair of you to Cornwall to trouble us again?'

'This is Nimue. She serves the Lady of the Lake. She is of the wise. And what brought me here you should know better than anyone. You and your sisters.' He looked sideways at me. 'You have shaken the land. You may have done a more dangerous thing than you guessed.'

'You still fear Morgan that much, do you? When she's shut up in a convent? And you've hidden Arthur from her for half her life?'

'And will do till he is a full man. That boy was hardly got. You and your kind shall not rob Britain of her king before his time.'

'You needed our kind nine years ago. You needed the magic of Tintagel to make such a child.'

He started then, though the dark of his cheeks hid the full force of his reaction.

'Life he has, however it was got. And life he shall have. Morgan is older than he is. She has come to her power before he is ready for his. The Saxon wars are bitter. Uther Pendragon may not live out his full time.'

'And what if he dies tomorrow? Do you think Gorlois's people are going to weep for him? Those few of us he left alive. You wouldn't weep yourself, would you, now that he's fathered the boy you wanted?'

'Britain would be left in danger without a high king.'

'Maybe better off without one, if that's how high kings use their power.'

'The forces of Britain must be led. Inspired! And shall be. I am breeding such a leader as will gladden your eyes as much as any woman's, you lecherous old harridan.'

'A sweet boy, and handy with a sword and spear,' smiled Nimue. 'I am teaching him well.'

I felt Gwennol tremble, standing beside me. I put out my arm to stop her falling. But she was firm again, giving them back thrust for thrust.

'A warrior already? Poor little mite!'

'We need time, Gwennol. He is not yet nine years old.'
Merlyn was pleading now.

'The same age Morgan was when he was got. And for
this boy's sake Morgan lost father, mother, freedom.
And now she must lose husband, children?'

'Morgan is dangerous. She will destroy even those she
loves.'

'Do you still fear the power you took from us? How
many Queens have there been in Britain since the
Romans came? How many women speak in the Great
Council now? Who still honours the Mothers?'

'This is no time for petty jealousy. Be practical,
woman. The Saxons! Are you so blind and backward
here in Cornwall, you don't know that half the country
has already fallen to the enemy?'

'Half of Britain is woman, by my reckoning. There's
more than Saxons have conquered and raped and had
their will of us. I should know.'

Merlyn gazed down at her, between cajoling and
despair.

'Is this your doing, then, Gwennol? Will you not let her
forgive? Have you taught her to destroy us all? Even
Arthur, and Britain?'

'Who said anything about destroying? I'm known
through all Cornwall for a great healer. Yes, I've taught
Morgan all I know.'

'But how will she use that power, Gwennol? Once
given, you cannot set a boundary on it. You know the
danger.'

'It wasn't us women that taught her to hate you. You
did that yourselves.'

'Then since I am too late to direct her power, I must
deny her its use. For the good of us all.'

'That's what men always say. And who is there to
curb your power, I'd like to know?'

'None but the gods.'

I do not know what made me turn to see Nimue's face. It shocked me. The lady was staring at Gwennol in wonder. Her eyes were huge and shining with a fierce desire. Then she smiled, gloriously. Her hand stopped its frivolous playing and closed round Merlyn's arm. Her white fingers imprisoned him.

They stayed the night. I thought we were done with them. But in the shadows of our hut Gwennol pressed something cold into my hand and whispered in my ear. Outside the door I looked at what she had given me. Nine years, but I still recognised it. A hunting knife, with a carved ivory handle. Morgan's, once.

Unwillingly I carried it to the gate. Merlyn and Nimue with their attendants were riding out. I held it up to Merlyn.

'Morgan returns your gift. She does not want it.'

He checked his mount. A shadow passed over his face, leaving it older.

'So the new moon has passed. The virgin huntress is a woman now. Well, new phases need new gifts. Then give her this.'

He reached into the saddle-bag of Nimue's mare and handed me a gleaming metal disc.

I gasped with the weight and then the richness of it. A mirror of polished bronze. The handle twined with serpents, the back incised with curling vines and inlaid with red enamel. I turned it over. My reflection met me. With a strange surprise I stared at my own face, as if in water. The stern contours softened, beguiling, almost beautiful.

'For a woman, a woman's weapon.' Merlyn smiled grimly. 'Let us see how Morgan will use it.'

# Chapter Thirty-Three

It was my hand that gathered what was needed from the forest, my feet that waded in the bogs as I searched with a net for the creatures who lived there. My tongue had joined with my sisters' in the spell. It is a strange feeling, the sudden leap of the heart when you know that what you have done in secret is all at once made manifest in the world. Stars fall from heaven, and it is by your hand.

Uther died.

They say the Saxons poisoned him. They spun some tale about his favourite spring of water, poisoned by enemy spies. Let them believe that. Better they do not understand our power too well. Better they think the Mother's daughters weak and worthless. If they thought we had power, they would take it from us. Only Merlyn knew. And he would not come into the open yet.

Mark came instead. His was a name we knew, but a face we had seldom seen. Little joy the nobles had in feasting each other in those days. Kings and chieftains did not tour the halls with their courts. War had the land squeezed in its fist. Even Dumnonia could not escape the shock. The dark tide was rising ever higher from the east, driving the Britons back into the cliffs and crags. Many the refugees who crowded west, destitute, scarred, bereaved.

We knew that Mark was strengthening his fortress at Caer Dore, that he was a grim warlord, that his warriors trusted, if they did not love, him.

He rode through the gates of Bossiney, a big, black-moustached man with a keen grey eye that saw too much. When Gwennol saw him swing down from his horse she gave a start and her hand flew to her throat.

'I don't need the bards to tell me where he got his blood from. Anyone can see he's kin to Gorlois.'

Rozen hurried out of the hall looking pale and anxious. She had been mistress in Bossiney these many months.

'We have food for your men, and beds in the hall, and songs it would not displease you to listen to. Be welcome here.'

It was a long time since such a warband had visited us. Our own men came seldom home. Harvests were smaller in these times. Young men were taken from the fields to follow their masters and did not return. Noblemen were too busy with war to oversee their farms. Kings small and great taxed us to feast and arm their warriors. But Rozen would not be shamed. Though it emptied our barns she would see Mark nobly entertained.

'Ulfin is still in the east? He has not come home?'

'Not since Uther died.'

'He is a fool. Britain has no high king now, and cannot find one. The petty kings quarrel amongst each other. Lot from beyond the Wall. Gwendoleu in Rheged. Nentres of Garlot. None of them is fit to raise the red dragon. I wouldn't follow any of them. Better to come west and set a guard along the Tamar. Let the Saxons take the soft-bellied lands of the south and the east. So long as they never try to pass into Cornwall.'

'You mean to stay at home and not fight, my lord?'

'I mean to stay, and to fight for what is mine. You have a poor place for a fort here in Bossiney.'

'It was not meant for war. Uther rebuilt it for Ygerne, as a marriage-gift.'

'It is mine now.'

Rozen blenched. 'How so, my lord?'

'Gorlois was killed, and Uther took it from him. Now the Pendragon is dead, and I am Gorlois's kin.'

She did not need his grip on his sword-hilt and the grins of the warriors behind him to finish his thought.

Yet she was a courteous lady. She led him to the noon-day meal and entertained him well.

Afterwards they rode out to see the estate. They had scarcely gone beyond the gate when Mark reined his horse.

'What is *that*?'

He stood looking, as though he had never seen it before, at the island of Tintagel. The curled body of a newborn baby, hanging from the womb of Cornwall by a single cord.

'Surely you have heard of it, my lord. They call it Tintagel, where the currents meet. It is a Christian convent.'

'It is a God-given fortress.'

'Alas, my lord. Many men have thought the same. But even you may not have it for war. Long before Uther came, Gorlois gave it to the nuns. They do not hold it by our grace and favour. It is theirs by right. They own farms as well, and get a good store of rents.'

'My kinsman Gorlois was a greater fool than I took him for. It is too good a fortress to be in the hands of women. I want that island. We must make them go.'

'I fear you will be disappointed. Those nuns are weak in body but obstinate in spirit. They will not be shifted. No man bearing weapons is ever allowed to cross their bridge.'

'Once I am king there, no weaponed men but mine will cross it either.'

'But how could you persuade the nuns to give it up to you? You would surely not force holy women?'

Gwennol came forward, leaning heavily on her stick, and caught at Mark's saddle-strap.

'Sir! There's other women besides nuns live on that island. Has my lady told you that your cousin Morgan has been a prisoner there going on ten years?'

Mark spun round on Rozen then with a face like thunder.

'Morgan? Gorlois's daughter? Is she still there? How is this? By whose orders was this done?'

'Uther Pendragon was her stepfather. She was a wild maid that needed schooling. He charged the nuns to guard her soul and body.'

'She's nineteen now,' said Gwennol. 'And still unwed. Neither a nun nor a free woman yet.'

'Bring her here,' Mark commanded Rozen.

So, after all these years, Morgan was led out of Tintagel and stood before us in the hall. It was the first time I had seen her by daylight since I left the convent. I found her presence had not lost its power to shock me. She had grown lovelier even than I remembered. But outwardly cold as ice. Her eyes passed over Gwennol and me with barely a flicker of recognition, ignoring our hunger for her gratitude. She stared levelly at Mark. She would beg no man for her freedom, though her heart was bursting.

'Well, my kinswoman. They tell me you once tried to kill your brother.'

'Do those who accuse me say why Arthur lived?'

'Merlyn prevented you!' Rozen exclaimed. 'When he was here this summer he warned us . . .'

'Merlyn was here!'

She did not know. Gwennol had not told her.

Mark looked at Rozen, startled, for confirmation.

'He came to us disguised. He bade us keep it secret.'

Morgan's voice was bitter.

'Merlyn! Always that man between me and the sun.'

Then she darted forward and caught Rozen by the sleeve. She could not help herself. It was like the first spurt of water from a breaking dam.

'Arthur! What did he say of Arthur? Where is he?'

Rozen shook her head. 'He would not speak to me of your brother.'

'That boy is dead,' Mark interrupted.

No one contradicted him.

Mark said slowly, staring at Morgan, 'Ten years. Why did Uther fear her so till he died? And Merlyn still?'

'It was foretold a child of Ygerne's would take the crown of Britain. When the Pendragon lost his son, there were only Gorlois's daughters.'

'Morgan! A woman? Third daughter of Gorlois of Cornwall! My kinsman was a mighty duke. A better war-leader than Uther. But he did not come of a line of kings. How could the Council acclaim his daughter?'

It was Gwennol who answered, startling me, from close beside where I stood.

'We have more than one parent. Her mother Ygerne carries the royal blood.'

I saw Mark grip the carved arms of the chair where he sat, two raven heads.

'So! Merlyn fears they might return to the old ways? A queen to lead the chariots. A queen who would kill any man who stood in her way. A queen, so you women would say, who can heal the wounded land. This is dangerous nonsense. Pendragon was no fool. I think it is better that my cousin stays with the nuns.'

He nodded to two of his warriors. 'Take her back and set a watch on the island. She gets no visitors. Have her shown to you every seventh day.'

I thought Morgan would have screamed out at that. I saw her heart in her face. Even then I pitied her.

But she said not a word to him. Instead she swung round and stared at Gwennol, white-faced.

'My mother. So it comes back to my mother, every time. She gave me life and she takes it away.'

233

# Chapter Thirty-Four

It was a dull November morning, with the air grey and lifeless. Gwennol sat wrapped in a shawl shivering, though the days were not yet cold. But the blood grows thin in old people. They feel a chill that others do not. She wore that shawl often. It was a fine piece of weaving, soft, silky wool, a shade of autumn red.

Gwennol did not settle the shawl about her shoulders and then forget it. She sat stroking the ends of it where they hung over her shrivelled breasts, as if it had been a living animal.

'Merlyn gave me this. The year that Arthur was born. The same year he gave that knife to Morgan.'

'The one she would not touch?'

'Morgan would never take anything from him.'

Suddenly she rocked herself as if a pain had gripped her. She snatched the shawl from her shoulders, screwed it into a ball and flung it on the floor. She stamped upon it, while I watched in amazement.

'A fire!' she snapped. 'Quick, you fool, light a fire.'

My hands shook with bewilderment as I set sticks on the hearthstone. I ran to borrow a hot coal from the kitchen. Soon the hut was filling with smoke. The flames leaped bright and hungry.

Gwennol could hardly wait for the wood to be well alight. She seized the shawl and rammed it into the fire. The good wool spat and shrivelled, turning black and throwing out clouds that choked us. My own eyes smarted, but tears were pouring down Gwennol's cheeks.

She watched the flames consume the last shreds of Merlyn's gift, pushing the stray edges of it into the heart of the fire. When it was reduced to a curled black ball she beat it with a poker until the embers fell apart. Then she poured water on them and rubbed them out, scattering them into nothingness and mumbling all the time.

At last it was over. She wiped her face and straightened herself into calmness. Resolute now, she walked to the door.

Mark was pacing the ramparts. He was a restless man. As many times before, his eyes turned to Tintagel. He was not one who took kindly to being thwarted.

I watched Gwennol cross the yard towards him and climb the steps. He stopped his prowling and waited for her. He even held out his hand to steady her up the last step. Already he looked to Gwennol to tell him what others would not. She had been Gorlois's servant long before she was Uther's.

She talked to him now and he bent his head to listen. Long and earnest was that conversation. I think Mark argued hotly. But ever his head kept turning in the direction of Tintagel. At last they both spat on their hands and clapped them together. A bargain had been struck.

That afternoon I was summoned to the hall with all Mark's household. We who had served in Bossiney many years; his warriors newly come from the wars.

Mark sat in the raven-armed chair again, his hand tapping restlessly on the bird's skull. We waited. Gwennol looked pale and faint. I led her to a stool against the wall. I had my face turned from the door bending over Gwennol when Bryvyth entered.

If it had been a shock of fear and joy to see Morgan appear before us in that hall, it was a blow of shame to me now to be in the same room as the abbess. I would rather have been anywhere than where her eye might fall on me. I never went to church in Bossiney, lest I should meet her there, though Nectan thundered at me for it. I did not know if Bryvyth had forgiven me. I had not forgiven myself. I still have not. Gwennol believed she was following the one true way. I knew the glory I had lost forever. Bryvyth's presence was a warning of hell.

She stood before him unbowed, with Cigfa and Muriel on either side. 'Bryvyth Crook-Staff?' said Mark. 'The abbess of Tintagel?'

'I am. It is ten years since I answered a summons to this hall. But I hear you are Gorlois's kin and no lackey of the Pendragon. Gorlois was always a good friend to Tintagel, until the day he asked too much of me.'

'He gave you Tintagel. You refused to give it back in his utmost need. You cost him his life.'

'The gift was made to God, not to me. I cannot give what is holy to men of war.'

'I will ask you Bryvyth Crook-Staff, once and once only, to give me Tintagel of your own free-will.'

'I may not do that. I am a nun. My will is not my own. And even if it were free, I would still not give the place to you. Tintagel is a holy island and shall remain so while I live.'

Mark stood then and beckoned in my direction. The blood flew to my cheeks. I could not think what he meant. But Gwennol rose unsteadily from the stool beside me and shuffled forward through the watching ranks.

'Well, Gwennol Far-Sight? And what have you to say concerning the nuns of Tintagel?'

Bryvyth started, and made the sign of the cross against evil.

Gwennol spat at her. 'I say that those nuns are not as white as they appear. There's blood in them like other women. And some are wiser. There's things done in secret on Tintagel Island that it would fright even men of war to hear about.'

A ripple ran through the throng that packed the great hall, alarm in women's faces, fear, excitement. We knew, all of us. The wise, the Christians, some who swam in and out with either tide. But we were all women. We knew Tintagel's reputation. Clearly or cloudily, we knew its past and its present. An island of awe. The men were only curious. They knew there was an edge of fear about the place, a name to be careful with. But only the wise among them understood why.

None of us could believe that Gwennol would uncover this.

Mark was a man of war. He had seen some opening in his enemy's defences, some weak place where he might breach and enter.

'Speak out, woman, as you promised. Say what you mean. If it is to my advantage, you shall have the price you asked.'

'I have a witness here who will say to that nun's face what has been done at Tintagel all these years under her cross of Christ.'

And she gripped my arm and hauled me forward into Mark's sight.

There was a gasp that was almost a scream from the wise. I saw hands signing, heard lips cursing.

I was terrified. I shrank from it. Believe me, Bryvyth, it was not done by my own choice. But what else could I say, with Gwennol's finger in my back and Mark's hard eyes on my face? What else could I stammer but the truth?

Under their cruel questions I told them about my baby. I told them I was but one, ignorant and unfortunate, among a host of sisters who worshipped at the Mother's Hole. I gave them names, times, the night paths down which the wise had led me, the gifts we brought back, the spells. Everything, except the mysteries themselves. Even Mark did not demand that of me.

I watched Bryvyth's face turn red as dawn on a morning of storm. I saw the shock in her eyes, the guilt, the grief. She stood bereft of words. Bryvyth, who had always been so ready of tongue. Her gaze fixed on me, wounds on her face deeper than she had ever scored on my back. She had truly not known. She had not so much as guessed, for all my sinning, that I was not alone. Strong-hearted, fired with high ideals, in love with God, she could not believe such double-serving possible. When I had done, she turned on me, dry-eyed, and found her voice at last.

'Curse you. Curse you, that you did not tell me this at the very first. Curse you, that you have spoken of it at all.'

Those were her only words, the last I ever had from Bryvyth.

Mark was a hard man but a fair one.

'You see you are disgraced. You cannot stay on Tintagel. Your nuns have fouled it. The Church would be mocked by everyone if you remained. Yield Tintagel to me. I will pay you compensation. You shall have a valley in the south of Cornwall where no one knows you. Where the wind blows softly, and the apple orchards are sweet. A more fitting place than Tintagel for women's bodies.'

Gwennol forced me to watch them leave Tintagel, a tiny remnant that had kept the faith, singing a litany of lamentation. The rest had gone, expelled as I had been, and many of the children had been taken away. I stood among the wise on the opposite cliff, casting stones and chanting scorn. Bryvyth followed her flock across the causeway last, her head bowed, carrying the cross from the altar on her back. We mocked and spat at her.

In the waters of the Haven, outside the Mother's Hole, foam gathered in an eddy, like spilled sperm.

They had scarcely gone when Mark and his troop of warriors came riding down the coombe and through the outer gate of Tintagel. They gave a great whoop of triumph and galloped their terrified horses across the bridge of rock. Tintagel was in the hands of the men.

I rounded on Gwennol then, and my cowardly anger broke out at last.

'Why? You have given Tintagel over to warriors! The sacred place of women. The convent. The Mother's Hole. You, of all the wise, who should have guarded it with your blood!'

Her face appalled me. It was contorted, staring. The breath rattled in her throat. Her eyes flew upward till they were white and sightless. She fell lifeless at my feet.

We women cried out. But there was another cry from the island. Mark's horsemen were circling the summit, shouting. They wheeled around the standing stone and halted. Someone was still waiting beside it. A lone woman in a green gown. Morgan.

She stood like a queen as the warriors reined in front of her. They raised their swords in a respectful salute. Mark helped her to mount a mare beside him. She had her way. She always wins, in the end. Morgan rode out of Tintagel with a royal escort.

Their horses trotted to where we stood, a frightened, close-packed crowd around Gwennol's body.

Mark called loudly, 'Well, Gwennol Far-Sight. Receive the price you set.'

We stood aside. Morgan sat tall and laughing on the mare. She held a thin grey cat before her on the saddle-bow. I recognised its scars.

The smile slowly left her fair face as we pointed where Gwennol lay, still breathing but the soul fled.

Morgan leaped to the ground and ran to kneel beside her nurse. I found my voice. It was then I understood my love for Morgan had curdled to hate.

'The Mothers have punished her. She betrayed them.

For you. As I betrayed the Church. For what good?'

Morgan touched Gwennol's face, and the breathing deepened. The eyelids flickered and closed, as if in natural sleep.

Then Morgan rose. She looked long at her old nurse lying on the turf, smitten by the elf-stroke. She turned her head to watch Bryvyth's bowed form dwindling away along the coombe. Lastly her eyes came back to me, glittering.

'She was the only one who ever truly loved me.'

To this day I do not know which of them she meant.

# Chapter Thirty-Five

Ruin. The king of Britain dead. The land overrun. The abbey broken.

Mark set a sterner guard on the Mother's Hole than Bryvyth had. Tintagel had expelled us from her womb into a cold world. We could not return.

Yet Morgan was free.

Gwennol recovered, in part at least. One arm and leg hung useless. One side of her face sagged, slack and dribbling. She would never see Morgan's face again. Not all our spells or Morgan's touch could restore her sight.

'It was Merlyn robbed my eyes of light ten years ago,' she mumbled. 'I've never seen clear since that night when Arthur was got.'

Then she smiled, craftily I thought, in the direction of Morgan. 'We gave him back your knife. He's left you something else, dearie. A gift for a grown woman, he said.'

I handed Morgan the bronze mirror.

She studied the beautiful workmanship of its back. Her fingers traced its patterns, caressed the enamelled bosses. Almost I thought she was turning it over to see herself in the polished face.

Then she laughed and let it drop. It clanged heavily on the floor, denting the perfection of its shape, disrupting the pattern.

'I am not Margawse. I do not choose that way, though they call me Morgan the Fair now. That woman who came with Merlyn? Nimue?'

'He said she was maiden to the Lady of the Lake, who-
ever she may be. One of the wise, seemingly, though not
our sort. And no more a maid than I am, if you ask me.'

'Nimue. A name like water. Shifting. Covering. And
she hides Arthur.'

'She'll keep him for Merlyn, and train him in her ways.
You won't find him, my lamb, until they're ready.'

'They do not understand. Nothing can keep us apart
forever. One day Arthur will find me.'

'He'll still have Merlyn to stand between you and him.'

'Will he? Will he, Gwennol Far-Sight? Even great
Merlyn has his weakness. A woman could be his
undoing. What if Merlyn were to drown in his Nimue's
embraces? Who would there be to keep me from Arthur
then?'

We did not remain at Bossiney long. Morgan's expression betrayed nothing when she told us she was to be
married in the spring.

'Mark has arranged it. Some kinglet nobody knows of
in the north. Urien his name. As far removed from
Cornwall as Mark could banish me.'

'So you'll have a crown of sorts at last, my pretty.'

'They tell me Urien is young and clever. There will be
time to shape him to my purpose. I shall need Luned's
help. I see you have taught her well.'

But the look of contempt she threw me belied her
words.

'It's me you'll want, my little maid, for work like that.'

'You will not be coming.'

'You wouldn't go without me! Don't talk so daft.
Blinded I may be, but I'm not so crippled I can't ride in a
cart. How do you think you could manage without old
Gwennol after all these years?'

Morgan gave her old nurse a gentle laugh that
wounded deeper than the bitter look she had turned on
me.

'You would not wish to die so far from Cornwall, to exchange these cliffs for the gloomy mountains near the Wall, the free-running sea for a land of still lakes. Your task is finished, Gwennol. I do not need you.'

'You can't leave me behind, my sweetheart. Not after what I've suffered for you. All the years I've worked for you. Yes, and wept for you. Keep me with you, my little maid!'

The tears were spurting from her sightless eyes.

'Did you not foresee this, Gwennol Far-Sight?'

Oh, cruel Morgan.

I do not want to remember the look on Gwennol's face.

But me she compelled to go with her against my will. She possesses me still. I hate her.

My pen trembles as I write these words, knowing that she will find them.

I sacrificed my soul for her. My hopes, my heart, my womb. I have had nothing in return.

Once I made myself too useful to the convent. That power corrupted me. Now I have made myself too useful to Morgan. I shall never be free of her.

All her life Morgan has planned to be revenged on Arthur.

Even as I pen this accusation I know with despair that you whom I write for will never read my words. Morgan will find these pages first. She will destroy them.

Morgan is the Devourer. She destroys everything she touches. Soon she will destroy me.

Yet Urien loves her. And the people here have another name for her. They call her Morgan the Wise, the Healer.

I cannot understand it.

Morgan must kill Arthur, must she not?

I look down with horror at my own hands, that have served her so long. I think I know how she plans to do it.

# A selection of bestsellers from Headline

**FICTION**

| | | |
|---|---|---|
| THE MASK | Dean R Koontz | £3.50 ☐ |
| ROWAN'S MILL | Elizabeth Walker | £3.99 ☐ |
| MONEY FOR NOTHING | John Harman | £3.99 ☐ |
| RICOCHET | Ovid Demaris | £3.50 ☐ |
| SHE GOES TO WAR | Edith Pargeter | £3.50 ☐ |
| CLOSE-UP ON DEATH | Maureen O'Brien | £2.99 ☐ |

**NON-FICTION**

| | | |
|---|---|---|
| GOOD HOUSEKEEPING EATING FOR A HEALTHY HEART | Coronary Prevention Group | £3.99 ☐ |
| THE ALIEN'S DICTIONARY | David Hallamshire | £2.99 ☐ |

**SCIENCE FICTION AND FANTASY**

| | | |
|---|---|---|
| THE FIRE SWORD | Adrienne Martine-Barnes | £3.99 ☐ |
| SHADOWS OF THE WHITE SUN | Raymond Harris | £2.99 ☐ |
| AN EXCESS OF ENCHANTMENTS | Craig Shaw Gardner | £2.99 ☐ |
| MOON DREAMS | Brad Strickland | £3.50 ☐ |

*All Headline books are available at your local bookshop or newsagent, or can be ordered direct from the publisher. Just tick the titles you want and fill in the form below. Prices and availability subject to change without notice.*

Headline Book Publishing PLC, Cash Sales Department, PO Box 11, Falmouth, Cornwall, TR10 9EN, England.

Please enclose a cheque or postal order to the value of the cover price and allow the following for postage and packing:
UK: 60p for the first book, 25p for the second book and 15p for each additional book ordered up to a maximum charge of £1.90
BFPO: 60p for the first book, 25p for the second book and 15p per copy for the next seven books, thereafter 9p per book
OVERSEAS & EIRE: £1.25 for the first book, 75p for the second book and 28p for each subsequent book.

Name .................................................................................

Address .............................................................................

...........................................................................................

...........................................................................................